15-
KCF

HOW **HAPPY** TO BE

KATRINA ONSTAD

HOW HAPPY TO BE

MCCLELLAND & STEWART

Library and Archives Canada Cataloguing in Publication

Onstad, Katrina
How happy to be / Katrina Onstad.
ISBN 0-7710-6897-2

I. Title.

PS8629.N77H69 2006   C813'.6   C2005-905497-2

We acknowledge the financial support of the Government of Canada
through the Book Publishing Industry Development Program and that
of the Government of Ontario through the Ontario Media Development
Corporation's Ontario Book Initiative. We further acknowledge the
support of the Canada Council for the Arts and the Ontario Arts Council
for our publishing program.

This novel is a work of fiction and the characters are fictional.
While some news reports in the novel may be based on actual events,
the timing of such events may be compressed for narrative reasons.

The pamphlet "Evaluate Your Drinking" referenced on page 98–102 is a
publication of the Centre for Addiction and Mental Health, Toronto.
© 2000 Centre for Addiction and Mental Health.
Text reproduced with permission.

Typeset in Garamond by M&S, Toronto
Printed and bound in Canada

This book is printed on acid-free paper that is 100% recycled,
ancient-forest friendly (100% post-consumer recycled).

McClelland & Stewart Ltd.
The Canadian Publishers
75 Sherbourne Street
Toronto, Ontario
M5A 2P9
www.mcclelland.com

1   2   3   4   5   10   09   08   07   06

To Julian

HOW HAPPY TO BE

Aᴼᴿᴇᴿ SHE DIED, EVERYTHING TASTED WORSE. UNLIKE my father, my mother had no contempt for the occasional dinner in a tinfoil tray, clean borders between tastes. I would imitate her walk down the frozen food aisle, breath frosting the air, hips sliding, shoulders back. A walk I only later recognized as sexy when I saw it worn by movie stars playing cocktail waitresses.

When she was gone, my father kept his eyes on the road and drove his truck straight past the glass spaceship super-market. He parked outside the health food store where walls and food were brown and moist. Pushing through the door was like stepping inside a redwood tree, all flesh and fibre. My dad wandered off by himself to finger the herbal teas and sugar cane, distracted and drifting, as if these foods were the source of all his sadness. He would look up, eyes running, unable to choose. So it was left to me, eight years old, to fill worn plastic containers with peanut butter and honey that lived in white tubs. But our old containers once held feta and butter and applesauce, and the system bred disappointment. Later, looking for the bumpy sweetness of jam, you ended up with yogurt, mean and tart. Longing for yogurt, you gagged on ropy tahini.

After my mother died, bread got crunchier and the house got messier and then we left Squamish, British Columbia, to see the country, driving east to Newfoundland until the edge and the water and then we turned around and went back west. We finally stopped at the Gambier Island compound, almost to the highway's end, a boat ride from Vancouver, where there wasn't a house at all but a monastery that resembled a roadside motel. A handful of soldiers had come back from the Second World War with Tibetan texts in hand, claiming a corner of the island. Unbothered by the farmers who lived there, they spent their mornings in walking meditation, barefoot up and down a beach so rocky their soles bled.

Two decades later, the hippies marched in, crossing water to escape the city. The soldier-monks packed boxes of burgundy robes and headed north, out of earshot of the rumble. To them, the Sixties must have sounded like a couple arguing down the street; the window's open and the noise gets closer and louder and closer and even though they swear it's just a friendly conversation, it sounds like yelling to you.

The new arrivals made a compound out of the empty buildings and called it a commune. Our dinnertime, once set for three, became a long Formica table occupied by other people's children. We slept in monks' barracks, kids above and kids below in bunk beds and hammocks, swinging in space.

My father faded out gradually, escaping to the woods for days at a time, though this was nothing new. He half-built a yurt, then gave up on pastimes and slept a lot. I was schooled in the gutted prayer hall and sulked in the classrooms, which weren't classrooms at all but circles of stained throw pillows on cement floors. Other people's mothers passing out finger-paints and encouragement.

People were everywhere, three or four in the bathroom at a time. Pull open a closet door and there would already be a kid or two crouched, piling rocks or chewing broken guitar strings, looking for some quiet.

On my eleventh birthday, during a walk through the woods, I peeled off from the group, cut across a sheep farmer's field and onto the island's main road. I walked in the muddy ridges of truck tracks. The path ended where the beach began. A round ball of an old man in a Mercury 9.9 outboard bobbed by the dock and let me on for free, a conspiratorial look on his face. A willing accomplice.

This was how you got around: foot and boat, boat and foot. The mainland pulled in, wet with rain and loud with cars slicing across the highway. Refrigerator-shaped station wagons driven by pretty middle-aged women escorting shiny children in polo shirts. Those cars suggested exotic phrases: *extracurricular activities*; *study hall*; *curfew*.

I'd seen the movie theatre before, around the corner from the sweaty windows of the general store, jewelled lights through the rain, a twenty-minute walk from the dock. I paid my two dollars and sank down in the vinyl seat, hardened by the dry indoor heat. That smell was chemical butter mixed with chocolate and I never knew you could miss something you were experiencing for the first time, but I missed it, my whole body ached with loss for those forbidden foods, right down to my soaked-through feet.

The cat with the tail of a rabbit; the big hamster eating the baby hamster; my mother balloon-faced from chemotherapy – all these natural freak shows had never impressed me much. My attention span was limited, my eye already on the next thing. My mother had said of me at seven, squirming during a Punch and Judy puppet show that held the other kids rapt: "You are one nonplussed kid." But that day in the movie theatre, I learned awe. I felt it in the quiet as the lights went down, in the expectation that plumped up the split second after the first click and whir of the projector when the screen was still dark and anything was possible, even if the story wasn't good, wasn't true.

I saw *Saturday Night Fever*. Three times, back to back. It could have been any movie; the joy was in staying in one place alone, silent and watching without being watched; the opposite of the compound's everywhere eyeballs, like a box of spilled blackberries.

My father arrived in outline first: ponytail silhouetted over John Travolta's platform shoes. Two policemen stood behind him, slightly bored. I found out later that my father, frantic and bed-headed, had led them all day; the cuffs on his corduroys soaked from running through the woods and combing the shoreline for my broken body, the police less anxious, lagging behind with obligation.

I rose and he put his arms around me to the boos of the small crowd. I felt him crying on the top of my head. I'd become used to it, thinking of my hair lately as a kind of organic matter, grass or sand, and my dad's endless tears feeding it, growing me.

I waited in that theatre for the perfect word, the dad moment. My father was a fish gasping, his lips moving in an O shape. He said nothing. I patted his shoulder.

All the way back to the compound, I wondered if one of us should say something, and what that thing would be. We sat in silence, the truck spraying mud on the windows, staining the view. I thought of all the people under the earth, their bones shifting as our truck plowed the mud. I thought of all the people who could not talk, and here we were, alive and saying nothing.

In that way, profound moments pass. Later, they become entertainment, banter, and one day you realize you are nothing but a daisy chain of stories, crowns for everyone else's pleasure. In that way I grew up.

So THE SECOND PROBLEM IS THERE ARE TWO CRUEL yellow Post-its stuck to my computer screen.

You left without waking me.

And: *P.S. All staff meeting at 11.*

I retired my watch a while ago, dropped it in a desk drawer with unopened pay slips and half-burnt birthday candles because, look around, clocks are everywhere. Right here, right now, clocks along the newsroom wall suggest with just two fingers jungle nights in Jakarta and crisp afternoons in London even though in the freezing pseudo-Gotham of Toronto it is 11:40, snow-clutched February 2001.

11:40. A brief flash of tardy-girl panic – latelatelatemycareerlate! – then I remember: I'm trying to get fired. Panic scatters and in its place nestles a warm, downy calm. Or maybe I'm still high. No matter. I'm forty minutes closer to losing my job, and that's the point.

The first problem is morning. My eyeballs were wearing tiny sweaters when I woke up, and I had to drag my recently shaking-it ass into an ice-coated cab and get to work. The newspaper, the place that funds this small life, has the gall to be situated, day after day, several miles from downtown in the grey industrial wasteland that is suburban northeast Toronto. Just left of the strip mall, right of the Tim Hortons doughnut shop, there it is: 80 per cent parking lot, 20 per cent tinted glass and steel, capped by a sign half the building's height that reads, *The Daily*. Often a man is roped up on that roof with a bucket, washing away the graffiti that turns the D into a swastika. That's how *The Daily* is viewed by most of the public: the paper so right that Hitler would have made the commute.

I charged the thirty-dollar hangover-justified cab ride to my expense account and then – nice – got a fistful of chewed gum from rifling the depths of my bag for my security pass, which was now a relief map of bumpy peppermint Trident tucked away last night in some bar or other so I could – what? Drink more? Smoke more? Reuse it later and get my money's worth? Whatever, the security pass proved useless, demagnetized, and I had to enter the building via revolving door by catching a ride with Knee-Socks Steve from Sports, which required plastering my dank self to the back of his doughy baseball-hatted self and shuffling forward, one inch at a time, as if his security pass was my security pass and we were one big lumpen secure body. This seemed to piss him off a little, but hey, let's face it, we're all looking for some semblance of closeness and dude (this is the kind of high-fivin' white guy who addresses his friends as "dude"; even his readers get called "buddy") just got the real deal. In daylight. He should have been grateful.

Upstairs in my cubicle the size of a detergent box, I dropped my bag and knocked over an empty Diet Coke can pyramid on my desk, which won me a snotty look from Hard-Working Debbie, she of the Life pages, who honest-to-God in my six years of employment has only ever said one thing to me: "Is that my pen?" And then I spot these Post-its welcoming me back to work and I Heart Fridays.

The wake-me note is from Ad Sales, recognizable from his measured grade-school handwriting. I remove the square from the computer and promote it to my Post-it wall, lining this one up carefully under row upon row of the Post-its I most love and cherish. Sure those poindexters over in Technology can fill up the paper's big blank pages with wordy wank-offs celebrating the age of the computer if they must, but nothing says "information superhighway" like a hostile yellow Post-it. At *The Daily*, they are a very popular form of passive-aggressive inter-office expression. *Where were you?? U MSSD DEADLINE!! Why so jealous of Julia Roberts?* (that one in deeply indented ballpoint, like the author was pressing very heavily in a very dark, very lonely room).

I hunker down in the chair, so low to the floor that my knees nearly hit my chin; an unfortunate necessity if one wants to make lengthy personal calls during the workday. E-mail check. Voice-mail check. Movie screening, a TV ad campaign I'm supposed to appear in, a publicist with a story that would be *perfect* for me, and on and on. A stammering message from the Ex: "I just . . . uh . . . I'm in a show in a couple of weeks and uh . . . I'll . . . uh . . . e-mail you the details." Pause. "I should probably get off the phone . . . Elizabeth wants me to . . . uh . . . I'm going to hang up now, but I'm on a cellphone and I don't know how it works. Hope you're, uh –" Dead air. That belt around my heart tightens a few notches.

Without returning any calls, I make new ones in order to purchase some weekend substances for ritual abuse. I go into the shared files to find the day's lineup for the paper: *Summit of the Americas protesters pepper-sprayed in Quebec City. Toronto homeless squat on toxic dump. Cellphone spontaneously combusts in Florida. Film festival will bring mega-bucks to mega-city.*

My head gets heavy. Log off. It's 11:50, naptime in daycares across the city and I feel a solidarity with those dropping toddlers. The rock-stuffed head requires an instant resting place, so down it goes, pulling the body with it onto a nest of newspapers under the desk. I arrange my jacket to create the imperative fourth wall so no one will disturb me and my skull and just then my one work friend and ally, Marvin, brutally tugs down the jacket. I blink in the fluorescent light, skinless as the *Eraserhead* baby.

"There you are! Didjya hear? Ohmygod!" Marvin snake-bellies under the desk.

Marvin covers TV, as evidenced by his pinwheel pupils and ability to laugh gut-deep at things that aren't remotely funny. Most days, Marvin sits in a small room in the bowels of *The Daily* with the blinds drawn and the television radiating, occasionally drifting upstairs to steal unopened party invitations from the mailboxes of fashion reporters. On his laptop, somewhere near the boiler room, he pecks out brief, ironic treatises on why we need more violence and fewer undergarments on television. In the inverted universe of our paper, he's interpreted as sincere and cheered as a truth-teller of the New Right. Marvin survives this killing life through a weekend scrim of clubbing and slippery-chested Latino boys.

"Our esteemed publisher is coming for drinks this afternoon. You have to be here! The Entertainment section is hosting and I'm serving my famous perogies."

"Marvin, you know I don't do Fridays any more."

Marvin gives me a gentle whap on the head. He thinks I'm kidding. It's a strange thing to try to leave your life. People say it so often that no one recognizes a sincere retreat. *I'm outta here. Really. Watch me. I'm quitting. I ain't gonna work for the man no more. Eat my dust – just give me a minute to pack up these things over here, seriously, then I'm gone. Does anyone feel like grabbing a coffee first, or a drink?*

Marvin pinkens a little when he gossips. "Oh please come! I can't promise anything, but he might wear an ascot. And don't you want to see the nasty sidekick?" Marvin pouts, and if there's anything more coercive than a thirty-seven-year-old underemployed balding television critic propping up a triple-chin pout with a cream-coloured cashmere turtleneck – well, call me a sucker for cute, but I'm won over.

"I'll go," I tell him, at which point I try to sit up but feel my cheek seared to the carpet with Diet Coke dribble from the fallen pyramid.

Even more so than the rest of our countrymen, we at *The Daily* are the property of the English. We're owned by Baby Baron, the youngest of several short, chinless sons born to a prominent London family headed by a liquor baron and his duchess wife. Baby Baron is the shortest, most chinless, and, reputedly, most disorderly of the progeny, an almost-thirty party boy often snapped by the U.K. tabloids outside a strip club at 4:00 a.m. looking like a lager-fuelled lad on a bender. Still, he is known for strangely octogenarian, sartorial flourishes: a bowler hat here, a seersucker suit there, offset by the occasional makeup-encrusted pimple where that chin should be.

As an unruly teen only a few years ago, Baby Baron was sent away to a prestigious boys private school in Canada. Those years paddling the lakes of Algonquin Park and playing lacrosse left an indelible impression, and he returned often as an adult for golf and fishing and drug-taking in a slightly more anonymous climate. But on one of his sojourns to Toronto, Baby Baron put down his drink, shoved the models from his bed, and, looking around, discovered that the country he had so romanticized was actually lazy and lefty. He who spent most of his year in Geneva was appalled at the Scandinavian tax rates and sniffly editorials praising the social safety net that took up the opinion pages of most papers. He knew several Canadians, and very well, who appreciated the fiscal restraint of his father's close friend, Margaret Thatcher. Why couldn't their dinner conversations in Geneva (ones he listened to from a low seat at the far end of the table, so as not to shame the family) find a forum in Canada? These thoughts, some of his first, coincided with a minor scandal involving a porn star and the unusual use of a very expensive bottle of port, and Daddy Baron gently suggested he take an extended holiday somewhere very, very remote. So Baby Baron bought a mansion in Toronto and an estate in cottage country, north of the city. He liked it there so much – "Loons," he said often in interviews, referring to the birds, one hoped – that he purchased the whole lake and, oh yes, a dying city broadsheet that he turned into *The Daily*.

And so, for a young man who will inherit distilleries and shipping lines, we are a hobby. If he were a middle-aged woman in a small town, we would be his knitting circle, something occasionally tended, a diversion. When he makes the trip up to see us in the suburbs, it is an event of sorts, a reminder that we are wanted, noted, like when the Queen visits Saskatchewan.

Marvin is obsessed with Baby Baron's personal assistant, a handsome, scowling reed of a man who towers over the junior mogul, accompanying him everywhere. There is much inter-office speculation that the assistant is the paper's real publisher, concocting story ideas and e-mailing editors late-night directives from Baby Baron's account. *What about bigger headlines? Shorter stories? Shorter headlines? More society gossip. More anti-union rants. Less use of the colour orange!* He has passwords and enters all data into his boss's BlackBerry himself because though Baby Baron is a man of strict views, he is not accustomed to interrupting his amusements to direct the help. Baby's only other job was a brief stint in the British military, another of his father's failed plans to drill some sense into him, and so he knows absolutely nothing about running a newspaper except that it is very expensive.

At parties, the assistant becomes a manservant, bitterly keeping his boss's glass filled, eyes rolling, wandering back and forth to the buffet at a cripple's hobbling pace to load Baby Baron's plate with angry, heaping helpings. The assistant shakes his head, lips envelope thin, when he feels his boss has imbibed enough, and Baby Baron shrugs and grins, never showing any embarrassment that his every move is reported back to daddy in London. He appears to enjoy the assistant's disapproval like a naughty schoolboy in love with his ruler-happy headmaster. Sometimes Marvin sends me his haunting, half-erotic dreams about Baby Baron and the mysterious manservant, and the e-mails are some of his most lovingly crafted writing.

Marvin has the courtesy to reconstruct my jacket-fort after he slithers out and I'm about to let that sweet sleep lubricate my dry corpse when I hear a fakey throat-clearing sound and there they are, pointy little high heels in the visible crack between my jacket and the polyester-blend beige carpet, right near my sticky face.

"Maxime?" quoth the heels.

"Yes?" I answer politely, if a little muffled by locale.

"Maxime? I'm Heather from marketing?" Heather is an up-talker. "I left you a message? In a few weeks, we're going to be filming the ad for the new television campaign? We really want you to be part of it? Can we count on your participation?"

"We can?" I ask back.

"We can?"

"We can?"

Heather's shoes are very still.

"Okay, then I'll send you the details?"

"Okay? Thanks?"

My paper is "at war" with the other national paper – *The Other Daily*. It's about two hundred years old and operates out of a twenty-storey art deco building in the heart of downtown that resembles a stack of birthday presents in descending sizes. The war is mostly polite and Canadian: sometimes *The Daily* gives out free copies at the subway and *The Other Daily* complains about inflated circulation numbers, and then *The Other Daily* starts popping up, un-requested, on people's doorsteps and *The Daily* complains about inflated circulation numbers. The ugliest moment is when a disgruntled employee at one rag e-mails the front page to the other, an hour before going to press, which happens rarely. In this war, bodies don't come home in coffins and *The Other Daily* appears to be taking the battle. Up here in suburbia, ads are down, sales are down, all numbers small and smaller. The anti-communist, anti-health-care readership just isn't what it used to be in Canada these days.

Most of the staff at *The Other Daily* are over sixty and write with quill pens, but compared to *The Daily*, it's a socialist newsletter over there. I wonder, as I complete my mocking of the up-talker, if such behaviour might earn a reprimand at a paper with affirmative action policies and an editorial page that doesn't refer to single moms as "greedy" and retroactively defend Pinochet on the grounds of sound tax policy. It's hard to get fired in a libertarian climate. Every screw-you rebellious gesture is interpreted as just another triumphant expression of the individual. This makes *The Daily* oddly similar to a commune – and I speak from experience here – where a child is praised for stabbing another child in the shin with a hoe because said stabber is merely acting on an honest urge of the unchained spirit. One person's pain is another person's liberation; that's how it was as a Marxist agrarian teen, that's how it is in a neo-conservative newsroom.

Under my desk, I sleep for what seems like a long time. Sleep is oceanic when you're watch-free. My body wakes my brain only because I need to be watered. Of course, the Editor sniffed out this possibility and is waiting for me by the water cooler, which here at *The Daily* isn't so much a metaphoric meeting place as a leghold trap for hungover writers like myself.

Procrastinating, rehydrating, ogling the sexy mullet-head who replaces the tank – whatever the reason, you will find me at the water cooler more than in the cubicle. I elbow aside a few red-eyed intern-types sucking at the tap and the Editor cries, "Theey-ah she is!" lips curled under her blue British teeth that come to a series of points like a package of leaking ballpoint pens. She has a hard-on for the third person, so I always think she's referring to someone else. I pat my body to see if her certainty regarding my presence is justified.

"There she is," I say.

"You are going to the film festival press conference Monday morning, you got that e-mail didn't you? I know you did because my computer tells me which epistles have been received."

I interpret this as a warning, a vague threat, which is the usual communication mode in an office full of embittered Brits less than happily removed from the really bloody newspaper wars and exiled to the peaceful colonies.

My Editor addresses her third-person edict to the space directly over her right shoulder, as if she has an assistant at her elbow jotting down her every thought. "So she'll cover the press conference for Tuesday, and we'll launch the festival with the Ethan Hawke interview for Friday, one day early to beat them." She almost spits with glee at the prospect of scooping *The Other Daily*. The Brits are much more fired up over the war than their privates. Our blank faces and mild suggestions at story meetings always seem to leave the Editor incensed, a high-school cheerleader standing in front of quarter-filled bleachers.

"Ahh-ight," I say in a kind of ghetto-speak that started out camp and has become habit.

The water isn't going down as smoothly as the crantinis of the night before, and suddenly I'm pushing past the Editor and the buzzing interns and it's not so pleasant in the bathroom cubicle, my hands holding up my hair, careful not to touch anything parasitic. Not so pleasant to be pushing up wave after wave of air, but with my eyes closed, I can almost imagine this as something honourable: I pretend there's a neo-Nazi combat boot kicking me in the gut.

The convulsions die down. I lean against the bathroom door and wipe my mouth with toilet paper, wait for the heart to stop boxing in my chest. Am I dying? I think, pulling a Southern belle, back of the hand on forehead.

No, this is bad, but this is not what dying is like – put the hand down – because I remember my mother dying, yes I do, I can still go back that far (a smell, a date on a calendar, oh, it's easy to go) and see her there, truly buckled and drained. That was illness of a different order. Serious. It occurs to me that seriousness must still be out there, free-floating around the universe, even sometimes touching down.

THE CAB IS CHARGING ONTO THE HIGHWAY TOWARD the city and the driver can't get the heat to work so the inside windows are frost-streaked and the radio is blaring a dispatcher who thinks he's a comedian: "So then the fare goes, 'Not *Bloor* Street, *Blur* Street!'"

The cab driver grips the wheel. "All day, every day, I must listen to these jokes on the radio. Not funny jokes," shouts Mohsen, smacking the radio with a fist. No matter what time of day, if I call 1-800-TAXI, I get Mohsen and his airless cab and his fury.

"Did you hear?" he asks, smoking and driving without his hands on the wheel. "Now you have to dial the area code. I live here eight years, just one area code for the city, one for the suburbs. Now when you're already in the city, you dial the city code. Is stupid. Why is this happening? I will tell you why."

"Yes, you will."

"World-class city," he says with scorn. "Mayor tell us we're world class. I tell you what makes a city world class. Not area codes."

The Toronto feeling is like living in a photocopy of a real city, or a photocopy of a photocopy, since Chicago is a version of New York and we're blurred Chicago. I'd like to know how to live in three dimensions as much as the next guy so I ask, "What's the secret?"

"Olympics. We must get Olympics. Good for business."

"Don't you think it could be bad for the uh" – I try to conjure up a contrarian compound momlike stance – "homeless people?" Also, I love the cabbie freak-out, and expressing sympathy for the poor usually gets one. Sure enough, Mohsen is off: He works hard, eighteen-hour shifts, supports a family, came from nothing, escaped in the dead of night eight years ago. Do I know what it's like to have my country invaded by Russians? Do I know what it's like to have to smuggle videotapes of American movies from house to house because some totalitarian regime says *Rambo* is bad for the comrades? Do I know what a bomb sounds like metres from a baby's nursery? Don't talk to Mohsen about homeless people who cash abundant welfare cheques and sleep in the comfort of palatial bank-machine foyers.

"Now, your paper. That's a paper. Truth! Not soft on communists!"

Grey skyline taking shape against a grey sky.

I'm a bit drunk because Baby Baron materialized, as promised. Post-purge, I had been feeling rested and was enjoying some hard-hitting research Googling Ethan Hawke ("Ethan is a vegetarian who enjoys skiing . . ."). A bit bleary, maybe, but goddamn it I was okay, running over the sober mantra as I wandered aimlessly around the corridors of my computer, opening window after window of the World Wide Web, its knowledge spanning the globe so we can all share cat pictures and Ethan Hawke: dear God, grant me the serenity to get it together, the ability to know that things aren't so bad ("Ethan is married to the talented and gorgeous Buddhist actress Uma Thurman . . ."), the wisdom to think that anything is possible, the ability to get up in the morning. That's not exactly right, but when you can name the designers of Julia Roberts's last three Oscar gowns, when you know the exact date of Frances Bean Cobain's birth (August 18, 1992), when the trivia gains mass and expands to fill the brain cavity, then who can remember exactly the details of those Cambodian bombings or how that AA prayer goes, and come to think of it, is that even a prayer at all, or some kind of Crosby Stills and Nash song?

The big question: How did I end up drunk in the afternoon when I came in drunk in the morning?

At 4:00 p.m., the e-mail ping went off, echoing across the newsroom, sparking a flame of human energy like when the DJ throws down everyone's favourite track and the whole club wriggles.

Marvin wrote the e-mail: "The Entertainment department wants you to live and love with the cool kids. Big w(h)ine and big cheese, outside the office of the Big Cheese."

The entire newsroom lifted itself, a sheet of thirsty butterflies migrating toward the alcohol. The Editor won't buy beer (too Canadian), so she stood slowly filling plastic cups with cheap red wine, barely hitting the halfway mark, while jonesing writers and editors hopped from foot to foot in a single-file line. Then Baby Baron appeared, the brass buttons on his suit gleaming, the assistant marching crossly behind. I felt obligated, as a semi-loyal entertainment writer and a more dedicated drinker, to help the Editor get this so-called party started. My help took the form of a jazzy, free-form riff of pouring one plentiful drink for you, drinking one plentiful drink for me, and even before the cluster of Style people were in front of me, all spine in their skinny jeans and stilettos, I was already a bit wonky on my feet.

This could be firing material at a place where people get fired. But no one with firing power noticed my slurred state because anyone with it was already off to one side, gravitationally pulled toward Baby Baron and his bitter shadow. The Editor went over to the power circle, and I hung with Marvin, making dead-celebrity jokes.

"Marvin, what was John Denver's last hit?"

"The Pacific Ocean," said Marvin, bored. "Everybody knows that."

In the middle of the group stood the reason I'm here, the Big Cheese himself, *The Daily's* editor-in-chief. The Big Cheese was wearing a windbreaker because it's Friday, casual day, the day he dresses like a big baby bundled up, hoping for a sailing trip, and Marvin was outdoing me on the dead-celebrity jokes front (Q: How is Bill Gates going to die? A: He'll fall out a Window), and suddenly I dropped into a rabbit hole remembering what it was like to get hired for this place, six years ago, before the paper existed and this floor was a mess of empty wires and unpacked computer boxes.

The Cheese had asked, "What's your dream job?" All the laziest, worst parts of me bobbed right up to the surface, the parts that had written fan letters to Jaclyn Smith at a tender age and gasped at the sight of Susan from *Eight Is Enough* – in the flesh – walking down Robson Street in Vancouver when I was thirteen years old. The parts that lied to my young compound acquaintances that no, I couldn't participate in the socialist board games (Panopoly) after school because I was taking a boat to *The Brady Bunch* set, where I had just been promoted to Jan. Really, I was making like a bloodhound toward any television on the island.

Dream job. I pressed down, down, deep inside those better years of literature and poetry and turtlenecks, compacted all that intellect into a little nut to be stored permanently away, right alongside my days at the downtown news bureau where I first met the Big Cheese and he'd lectured me about "off the record" and sent me to City Hall for my first scrum and I was high just to hit *Send* on the computer at 4:30 every day.

I blurted it out: "Entertainment" and now this is what it is, and in a matter of weeks, I will be thirty-five, a thirty-five-year-old woman who makes a living asking John Travolta how he finds his character's motivation when playing a plastic-eyebrowed alien invader named Terl.

I looked over at the Big Cheese, who has always been an elusive force. While clearly aligned with Baby Baron and his anti-welfare, anti-air policies, Cheese is also a movie buff looking for a viewing pal. He used to call me once in a while, from his Town Car in the parking lot around four o'clock, and his driver would take us downtown to a dirty rep cinema for a Marx Brothers matinee. On the drive back to my apartment, Cheese would dissect *Monkey Business* with the joyless precision of a film scholar, only occasionally asking my opinion before letting me out curbside with a nod. We never discussed this ritual with anyone. Most of the time, he is a workaholic of the first order, in the office before anyone arrives, would lock up with Jacob Marley's big brass key long after everyone left if they made big brass keys any more. He's many generations Toronto, though for a decade as the voice of the right at *The Other Daily*, he lived in Europe, and he wrote about the Berlin Wall coming down like he'd personally willed it. Meanwhile, his third wife was packing her bags and babies for a man who came home at 5:30 each night.

Suddenly, the Big Cheese swept his gaze my way, went too far, then backtracked, stopped, and locked me in place — just as my tongue was circling the plastic rim of my cup in search of the last drop of Chilean swill. He looked – swear to God – a little disappointed.

I turned and started trucking away before we were trapped inside some horrible moment, and I ran right into the formidably muscled chest of Ad Sales, who had somehow separated from the advertising flock – an unprecedented mutiny.

"You missed the meeting this morning," he said, looking over my shoulder. He once told me that refusing to focus on the person in front of him was a strategy he learned from a management book. It makes him seem busy and powerful, and far-sighted.

"I got in late. Nice note, by the way," I said, annoyed that I was annoyed. We'd been sleeping together, without the sleeping part, since the Halloween party, but I can't take any man seriously who has tassels on his shoes.

"We should talk," he said in his muffled office voice, the one designed to make people lean in and listen (this tactic from a seminar, not a book). It made me speak louder.

"WHAT ABOUT?"

Ad Sales scanned the crowd, probably wondering if he could escape me by ducking into the nimbus of food encircling Baby Baron as he scarfed down his cheese plate. Suddenly, something on my face distracted him.

"Maxime, Jesus," he peered closer. "What's that crusty thing on your face?"

"Diet Coke . . . ," I said, picking it free.

Ad Sales shook his head. "Wine and Diet Coke addictions are so 1990s, Maxime. We're in the 'Oughts' now. Have you thought of getting yourself a good antidepressant for your little disorder?"

You know when you're trying to think of some lacerating comeback, but you've had too much wine and there's that balled-up sock where your good timing used to be?

"I don't have as much of a disorder as" – I paused. I reached into the depths of my wit, which must be somewhere around here, just give me a second – and this is the retort I pulled out – "your *personality!*" Nearby, Marvin winced.

I wobbled away, past Baby Baron, past the Big Cheese, only lightly knocking the assistant, jostling ever so slightly the platter of snacks he was begrudgingly bringing to his boss.

The other big question is: If I hate it so much, why don't I just quit?

Because of some split second I caught on some high-number digital channel, lately I've been contemplating the Darlinghurst Gaol in Sydney. The prisoners built the prison themselves, marking the walls with thumbprints and small x's to show how much work they'd done, and some of them began to take a perverse pride in the cage they had constructed, so much so that they didn't really want to leave. The braver left their names on some of the bricks, and you can read them still. So there's a bit of that.

And then there's addiction, the dedication to feeding that singular desire. Celebrity addiction is uncomplicated, and when you're tired – did I mention how tired I am? – uncomplicated is good. It requires so much less effort than charting the differences between Liberia and Nigeria, or letting the mind swivel toward the Afghani women head to toe in their burkas getting their hands cut off for dashing out the door to get flour without their husband's consent – that's going on right now, right now, in daylight – and isn't the president of the United States not really the President of the United States? And did you know that baby boys born near Lake Ontario are born with smaller heads and genitals than the national norm because of toxins floating in the water and – exhausting, isn't it?

So you make the trade. You lay down the African dictator card and pick up Jennifer Lopez. Make no mistake, however, it's a trade: you can't have both. You think you can, for months and months and years and years you try to play smart and ironic as you feed your desire. But you're hooked. Cravings make your skin itch, your tongue puff and scratch. You indulge and linger over *Us* magazine while the letters on the front cover of *The Economist* (the same twenty-six letters) swim and separate, impenetrable to you, a dead language uncovered at the bottom of the sea. And though you know you should get out of it, and though sometimes you make feeble, girl-slappy gestures at the dangling meat of your daily life – you try to quit, you swear to God you are trying to quit – you are really just waiting, just watching, the one thing you know how to do.

And now I'm in this cab winding down the Don Valley Parkway toward downtown. The suburbs shrink behind me and Mohsen rages in front, grey hair twisting from his nostrils, and Sunera's name comes up on the cellphone to arrange drinks for later – she's bringing some guy she's considering – and I can barely make her out through the dispatcher's comic stylings so I ask Mohsen to turn down the radio. He pretends he doesn't hear me. I get off the phone and look out the window as the city comes into view, low brick and resigned, a meekness that somehow always surprises me in a skyline, even after all this time.

Dozens of *DAILIES* in their untouched plastic delivery bags form a perfect pitcher's mound on my front porch.

Mine is the ground-floor apartment of a divided west-end Victorian that's peeling and weeping from leaks on the outside and renovated to tragic blandness on the inside. The Italian landlords boarded up the fireplace and put linoleum over the floors for easy washing, stripped the cornices and pediments, and replaced the bay windows with brown vinyl frames. The Ex lifted the plastic and sanded the hardwood, opened the unworking fireplace so we could look at its green tiles, keep warm by its prettiness, but the apartment is still blank.

A cat might fill it up, but buying a cat is like lying down on a beach towel in a big Iraqi minefield and saying, Okay, universe, I do not care any more. Sometimes I think about it, about opening the door to my apartment and seeing a little brown fluffy face and that's cool for a moment, but then suddenly it's fifteen years down the road and the small brown face is as old and puckered as mine, peering up at me as I sit on my couch eating beans out of a can and watching *Entertainment Tonight*. Because I'm a little scared of him by now, the longest-running relationship of my life, I've taken the time to get Mr. Foofaraw his vewy own pewter cat plate so he's eating off the coffee table and that makes me the animal who people stopped taking for walks. They got busy with babies and gardens and no one wanted to eat out any more.

I know how that works because a year and a half ago, I lived there. I showered more then, and this apartment had more stuff in it because it had his stuff in it. Now it has endless white walls, which, luckily, seems to be the fashion. When I open the door, there's a lingering scent of expectation, some kind of sense memory of a life I once had here.

I need a drink to block the smell. The fridge is empty, except for a pitcher of water with a filter that's supposed to remove the cancer-causing microbes and a bottle with a teaspoon of vodka at the bottom.

Check my messages. Plans confirmed. Sunera: Tom and Nicole are breaking up! One from my dad, who's in Arizona living in a teepee with the Hopi Indians. One from a friend in New York: the market's still dropping, the jig is up, the dot.com shit has hit the fan, and she's worried for her fake corporate life that she hates anyway but the only thing worse than her fake life is not having it.

With today's *Daily* in my hand, I lie back on the one piece of furniture in the living room, a big white leather couch that seemed like a good idea at the time. But it doesn't have arms, so lying on it is as comfy as lying on a park bench and in the summer it speaks of sweaty thighs with an unfortunate farting sound.

Today's hed: "TENT CITY" EMERGES ON ARSENIC-LACED LAKESIDE. Today's deck: *80 residents set up home on industrial wasteland owned by big box hardware company.* Below the fold, also on the front page, in the corner of the paper known as "the basement" (lower right) is an article I wrote: MONKEY MAKES MOVIE, PLAYS HOCKEY. *Primate on skates rejuvenates children's cinema; our reporter interviews furry friend.* I throw the paper on the floor and pick up *Entertainment Weekly*.

Seems that Sunera is right. Tom and Nicole are breaking up – which may or may not have something to do with the dot.com meltdown, according to *Entertainment Weekly* – and there's this little part of me that's off doing its own thing altogether, which seems to be happening to me more and more lately. Know this? I'm half in the moment in that Be Here Now way my dad sometimes yammered about, eating my tuna sandwich or fucking Ad Sales or whatever activity I've chosen to help push me more quickly through the pneumatic tube of time, and then – bam – my mind just clicks over to some other image. It's like those monster suburban TVs where you have the big picture, and a little picture in the corner that shows a different channel. In that little picture is some other part of me I've been trying to avoid, and in the big one – here it is – Tom and Nicole dividing up their property and their children (India and Basquiat? I should look that up; I'm paid to know this stuff), but down in the corner of the TV, it's two years ago on a Friday night and I'm opening that door to the smell of paint, the Ex having spent the entire day covering a piece of canvas in two or three solid slabs of primary colour. Mustard dusk in the apartment and maybe I bought some vegetables at the market and I cooked something healthy and we sat in front of the TV and watched an old movie, or talked about what we were reading. We were doing an impression of something from a Woody Allen movie. We had been together most of our twenties, and our twenties were over.

He took the cookbooks.

I think I should get it together. I know I should get it together, but the problem isn't getting it, it's keeping it from taking off again. I mean, if you can't do it with three live-in nannies and a personal stylist and an eight-bazillion-dollar-a-year dual family income, how am I, a mere mortal, supposed to keep *gravitas* at bay?

I add my hat and jacket to the hulking pile of coats on the radiator that's migrating slowly toward the ground. As if reading my mind, Sunera – already stripped of her alpaca jacket and looking bad-ass angelic as ever in head-to-toe black – starts in with one of her weird facts: "If we were in Norway, we would have a place to put our coats and mittens. In Norway, there are cloakrooms in the bars, even little bars like this. The problem with Canada is that we're in denial of our Canadian-ness. We keep thinking we're in New York, but look out there, it's freezing. Now imagine the psychological state this induces. An entire country – a nation of imposters – perpetually longing for an identity that's already taken. Max, this is Stewey."

Sunera's not one for breathing between clauses. Thing is, she's still getting up early on Sunday and reading – she has to, she's an editor at a newsmagazine – so she has these crazy facts crowding her head and she needs to do some verbal trepanning and let them out. In an industry of mockers and haters, Sunera is universally adored, her big eyes and brown skin make men stammer, her clean kindness makes women feel safe. She takes care of everyone: parents, two sisters, me. I wouldn't be able to look this goodness in the eye except I know that 90 per cent of the time, Sunera is quietly and totally stoned.

"I think the coat-rack thing wasn't such an issue before the return of the puffy coat," I say. "Coats are too fat now. Unwieldy. Vodka and tonic, please."

"I wonder if there's a story in puffy coats," murmurs Sunera, always looking to fill the pages of the magazine. She writes *puffy* on a napkin.

Stewey is cute, in a tucked-in kind of way, and clearly he's already mentally signed the mortgage on the house he and

Sunera will raise their children in. The guy, a television producer who met Sunera at a party exactly one week ago, is full moony. He's got this grin that's aggressively twinkly, which is about all he's contributing, grinning bright and nodding.

Sunera is speculating about Tom and Nicole. "Gay, gay, gay," I offer, but I always think that. My dad sat me down at thirteen not only to have the birds and the bees talk but to tell me, nervously, that if I "chose to love women" he would stand by my decision. I was like: Man, I'm still in neutered boy-band fantasy mode. Check out this Ricky Schroeder foldout in *16 Magazine*. Don't rush me.

Sunera's clearly got a better view of the room than I do because suddenly she's all: "Don't look. AA is here." There are four million people in this city, but when I leave my house, it's always the same ten or fifteen who wander across the sets like some real-life *Truman Show*.

Allissa Allan is the decade-plus-younger, much-marketed city columnist at *The Other Daily*, and my physical opposite; I'm Lucy, she's the Little Red-Headed Girl. I get lower in my chair, taking the vodka with me, and then Allissa's next to Sunera, going, "So I just came from a panel on *Newsworld*. Check out this makeup! I look like a sex-trade worker!" Allissa Allan will not use the word *whore* any more, even though it's so often useful. She's gone "global action." I glance up and she's not wrong about the makeup thing; she's yellowy, like a Simpson.

Allissa Allan has something to say about everything. She's a pundit for rent, and that's a good thing to be in this city these days. Imagine: you're a TV producer and you have to fill your cable-TV roundtable with "opinion makers" day in, day out, year-round. I am only an expert in such things as celebrity shoe and hair trends, but still, these are the calls I get in a given week: *Swing music is back, could you take an anti-swing stance? What do you think of Gap greeters? Is sex the new virginity? Virginity the new modesty?* Allissa doesn't say no to any request. Last time I saw her she was drifting backwards down an escalator on the Women's Gynecological Channel weighing in on bunions.

"Hi, Maxime," she says, voice in the shape of a happy face. "How's the paper doing? I hear rumours of its demise."

I'm sucking an ice cube now to try to get the last drop of vodka so when I talk I'm all: "Fjklsos?"

AA doesn't require a response. She just keeps on talking. "Listen, do you guys know any women who are buying diamonds for themselves? I'm working on a piece about the new girl indulgence."

AA's column last week was on her vagina, which is logical since it's been a long time since the phrase *city hall* has come up in her columns. The city beat, it seems, does not preclude lengthy series about her ass, her boyfriend's crooked penis, her new loft, and the further travails of being a wealthy, overemployed twenty-something in a semi-thriving metropolis. The city outside her sixteen-block radius of lofts and lounges, the city with its racial-profiling police and ludicrous little mayor, proved too thorny for AA. She has now moved on to subjects that don't require her to get out of her chair, except perhaps to locate a pocket mirror.

As she scurries away, AA actually says, "Peace out."

"I hate her," says Sunera, which is a phrase we use a lot, surely betraying my radical feminist roots. I grew them in the mess hall pressing ferns into clay while the pottery mothers at the compound talked about false consciousness and the men who had abandoned them. All those Saturday mornings filled with well-meaning female bodies wrapped in scratchy natural fabrics rancid as wet dog from the West Coast rain. Too much kindness. Too many you-poor-orphan weepy eyes.

AA is tucked in a booth with a pair of married New Left ideologues – they have his and her talk shows on CBC – and the lead singer of a local band who's been waiting a decade for the big music labels to come up north for the rescue. I'm looking at AA's curly red hair and the way her mouth lacks those tiny paper-cut wrinkles I recently noticed above my lips and I'm imagining her suddenly choking on the toothpick in her olive, hands at her neck, skin turning from yellow to green.

It is not a sisterly moment, so I make a mental list of women I don't hate: Ms. Johannsen, my second-grade teacher back in Squamish who gave every person in the class a brand-new paperback at Christmas. My friend Elspeth, a once-aspiring reporter who said, "Fuck this noise" and moved to New Zealand to teach skiing. My mother. Elaine, dad's ex-girlfriend whose hands smelled like lychee nuts as she pulled the sheets up to my shoulders. I got a call from her just a couple of days ago, a coming-to-the-city message in an are-you-drifting? voice of concern.

But I couldn't face the prospect of sitting across from Elaine in a health food restaurant, those wide, unlifted eyes posing her kindly interrogations like she did when I was fourteen. I saw the West Coast area code and I turned off the ringer.

"Call display has fucked me royally," I tell Stewey and Sunera, diving into a fresh drink. "When's the last time you picked up your phone without knowing who was on the other end? If it says 'Private Call,' I physically cannot pick up. Too much mystery."

Stewey nods and says something at last, the first time I've heard his voice: "Information age."

New street signs recently christened the downtown area south of Queen Street "Entertainment District." If you find it entertaining to watch drunken college kids between club stops shivering around food-vendor carts, smoking and eating submarine sandwiches or puking off of curbs, then you believe this zone is well named.

Unfortunately, these dozen or so industrial blocks contain all the dancing possibilities in the city, and so, sometimes, regretfully and drunkenly, I have ended up down here. The clubs look the same: windowless boxes with one-word names like Liquid and Verve in silver sans-serif font guarded by bouncers in sunglasses and parkas. As soon as we're within the black walls of this one – Apothecary? Cadmium? – I have a Johnny Rotten thought: Ever get the feeling you've been cheated? I'm beginning to suspect that all this time Stewey and Sunera have had a little plan and he's right here at the bar in a T-shirt and dark jeans, that much taller than everyone else, head and shoulders hanging down a little, repentant, and he's waving at Stewey from a kind of half-profile position I can't fully check out until he turns and: "Hey, Max, remember me?"

This sentence makes me a tad nervous. I'm nervous enough as it is because in the cab on the way over Sunera pulled out her lipstick bong and we hot-boxed the car to the cabbie's dismay. Pot makes me buggy with curiosity, while Sunera gets chatty, and Stewey, it seems, already the silent type, develops lockjaw.

So here's the part where you're supposed to look at the guy and say, That's the one she ends up with, right, because when you see him from the back, he has that little patch of skin between the collar of his T-shirt and the uneven shag at the bottom of his hair that looks like it would fit your hand exactly if you pulled him closer, and in those fingers – long, squared – curled around a beer is all the possibility in the world. There's something endearing in messy hair and old-school runners at a time when most het guys are starting to overcoiff, like Stewey here in his bicep-enhancing pressed silk dress shirt and orange suede shoes. And then the body is turning and saying, as if I might not have heard him the first time, "So you don't remember me?"

"You two know each other?" Sunera looks surprised. Not part of the plan. He lights up this big smile, just plugs that sucker right in, and I still don't recognize it; was it directed my way once before?

"Theo McArdle," he says in this deep, sleepy voice. "From university."

Again with that smile and suddenly I'm all elastic in the chest, like he just leaned over and put a hand on my cheek and cleared away my hair and I fell over from the warmth of it – this is what memory is like for me these days, a full-body takedown. Why I'm avoiding memory are moments like these. I knew Theo McArdle a million years ago and then I didn't. He's broader all over, but thinner at the temples; no trace of the old chick-yellow buzzcut.

"I know Stewey from home," says Theo. I haven't said anything yet, and he's looking at me with both warmth and wariness, the way you look at someone who might be mentally unstable. "So I came out tonight." I'm drug-mute, so he goes off, not unpleasantly, on a little thing about how he just moved to the city from St. John, New Brunswick, and he wondered if he would run into me and he saw my columns and he can just keep on going and going because I'm back in time, feet on the ground in combat boots and ripped jeans back in the snowstorm, ice-block cold of our alma matter in another town. Theo McArdle did this thing with his eyes then, staring into yours like a doctor checking for vitals. I couldn't get out from under those eyes, even though we only hooked up maybe three times, and we never had sex even, but we stayed up talking and fell asleep on his futon. He was outdoorsy and into science and that made two strikes. But even though all signs said, No, no, no, this is impossible – those eyes and Theo McArdle's kiss. I went back a few times, and what I remember most is how well I slept those three nights next to Theo McArdle. Theo McArdle was a giant skateboarding sleeping pill for me.

It made my eyes hurt, all that gazing. So on the third morning I got up while he was sleeping. I pulled on my boots, and I left. I spent the next year of university hiding behind pillars and bushes, pretending not to know him. Over the months, his face changed. First he said hello, but I didn't say it back. Then he frowned. Then he glared. And then it was decided that we would pass each other like strangers.

It seems incredible to me now, fifteen years later, with Theo McArdle inches from me: those same hands have been on this same body. My hair in the curve of his armpit. Our mouths everywhere, and no record of it. What if every hand that laid itself on our bodies left a print? We could read each other better. The loneliest people would be flesh-coloured, and the most abused covered in black. I look at Theo's wrist, the spray of hair, a vein; no trace of me. Disappointing.

So I'm strolling from one stoned insight to the next when I hear him say, "I always felt bad about how things went with us –"

And then I stop him: "No, no, I always felt bad. I was really young." And stupid, I might add, though I don't.

He rescues me: "I've thought about you a lot since then. You were . . ." And this I want to hear – What was I? Really, what was I? My God, I'd like to know – but Theo McArdle lets the sentence trickle off. He averts his eyes, freeing me from his gaze. I take a big snort of breath, thinking I'll need it for later if he looks at me again.

He glances around the club, as if he's trying to locate the source of the snort.

Don't do this. They all start out looking good and then before you know it it's 3:00 a.m. two weeks later and they're confessing their sins and crying in your arms, telling you they're into motivational speaking or sports.

From a few feet away, Sunera delivers a royal wave – a signal that she'll come in for the rescue if need be – then turns her attention back to a rapt Stewey. Theo McArdle and I have descended into silence. Suddenly, he looks about five years old, staring out some picture window, waiting for his life to unfold.

I open my mouth to speak and this comes out: "I'm trying to get fired."

"Yeah?" He sounds curious.

I gesture to the pockets of pundits and writers and TV hosts and media chasers and former dot.comers clutching their pink slips. Only it's weird, because I look at Theo McArdle looking around and what he reflects back at me is totally different. It's like he doesn't see the things I see.

"Theo, let me ask you something. Are you in media?"

"No."

"Dot.com?" I ask.

"No." Then Theo McArdle says it, "I'm a physicist. I'm doing research at the university."

I pause. "What kind of research?"

"Theoretical research. On what makes up the universe."

If this were a teen sex comedy, I'd do a spit take. Instead, I laugh a squinty woodpecker laugh. Theo McArdle: physicist.

"Would it make you stop laughing if I told you that last year I was teaching in a village in Africa?" he asks. He's smiling.

"Oh God, that's even better," I say. "You're not safe in here. All these journalists and TV people – if they know there's a real person in their midst, they'll suck you dry. Don't tell them anything about your life. Seriously. You'll become a magazine feature."

"A feature?" says Sunera, suddenly by my shoulder, looking concerned. Have I been shouting?

"Theo's a real person," I tell her. "Can you imagine?"

At that point the DJ cranks it up to tooth-knocking levels and it's all too much so I take my high to the dance floor, leaving Sunera and Theo McArdle behind. I'm up and down and sweating from the nerves and goddamn it feels good, all slip away slippery, even this stupid bottled dance music that sounds like an upstairs neighbour moving a refrigerator – it's pretty good right now, like the next thing is coming up up up –

But then there's a visual noise, a blurry distraction at the edge of the dance floor that looks like a pair of giant pants sticking out of a speaker. I dance a little closer and realize they're not pants, they're a person, one of those crazy kids with his head jammed between the woofers and tweeters. Ecstasy. The E-kids get up my ass, and it's not just that these barely-not-teens are going to create the first spine-free wheel-chair-bound generation without a war but that they're going to be deaf as hell too.

The other Japanese anime characters are out in full force tonight: girls in pink fuzzy toques sucking on pacifiers and boys in goggles and no one is saving the guy in the speaker from certain deafness. This is the love drug? I dance over through the wet and steaming bodies, crunching water bottles under my feet, and tap him on the ass in the most non-lustful manner possible. Pants slowly emerges and he can't be more than nineteen, with this white puff of cottony hair. He looks like a sleepy koala bear, his small wet lips slack. He comes up to my chest. I'm staring now at this homunculus thinking how fast you get out of touch, how quickly you don't know what's beautiful any more, or even fun, but I can't do the thing I came over here to do, which is rescue him from a handicap because it's much too loud to warn him away from anything. So I mime his ears and how to plug them, my attempt at a *save-yourself* gesture, and he looks puzzled, then amused. He waggles a finger to get closer. I lean in, my ear practically in his mouth.

"Don't worry so much –" he giggles. But he's not finished: "MOM."

ON SATURDAY, THE TORONTO WINTER FILM FESTIVAL begins. I love this word *festival*. Get out your peasant skirts and clogs, tie ribbons round the trees in the town square, prepare the feast, sacrifice the children: the festival is coming! After weeks of teaser press releases (Big Names Will Soon Arrive in City), the festival executives have gathered the media in the gilded ballroom of a downtown hotel to announce which of the world's famous feel daring enough to fly directly from the Sundance Festival in chilly Utah to Toronto, earmuffs still frozen, mukluks still slushy.

Entertainment writers love a press conference. It makes them feel like they have real careers with meetings and nodding and catering; there's a lot of alone time in this job. The hacks are excited to be outside the cubicle, the older ones off in their corners staring down the eager young girl interns in their sleeveless sweaters. The free-food table lies a licked-clean mess of crumbs and wadded-up napkins. I spy a thimble of undrunk juice and aim for it, only to be cut off by a local TV entertainment correspondent, she of the bubble blond 'do, mouth liplined in perpetual grin. I remember some theory I once heard that what makes a person cute is the proportion of big head, little body, like a Muppet baby. The other way round is simply disturbing. So technically, she's cute.

Snagging my juice, she joins a circle of TV reporters, a far cleaner group than the print journalists. They stand next to their cameramen, tanned and glossy and waiting at attention to come to life, machines on pause. All that time laughing supportively at unfunny celebrity patter has distorted their interior judgment, and it would take only the slightest tweak of a plastic cheek or a stomp on the toe to uncork a giggle and a shout: "So true! So true! I loved you in that!"

Check cell. Nothing interesting.

The microphone bleats and there's the Film Festival Czar in his horn-rimmed glasses the exact size of his eyeballs. The Czar hasn't loosened his grip on this festival for years, and now that our fine city got a mention in *Vanity Fair*, and everyone's slobbering over each other in a big moist cloud of congratulations, he'll only go out in a pine box.

So off goes the Czar in his sensitive public radio voice, how this year's festival will be world class and a celebration of the best films from around the globe and he's on and on and on with how hard they've been looking for hidden greatness. Like what a tough job, machete-slashing through the jungles of Tanzania in search of some tribesman with a digital camera who's going to subvert Hollywood through his sixteen-hour epic on the plight of the fruit fly. We're world class, did he mention that?

But of course no one's writing this down, and no one's writing when the sponsoring cigarette companies and airlines send their representatives shaking into the spotlight to plug their products and contests (all the TV cameras shut down for the sponsors, cutting the light and sending the room into greyness), and the journalists are beginning to murmur and shift until the Czar regains the mic and finally gets on it: "And so, a few of the celebrities who will be attending next week –" He's off. Camera lights flare up, pens scratch. Funny, that Tanzanian fruit-fly guy doesn't quite get the attention of the Paltrows and Crowes and Cruises.

I'm not taking notes. I'm barely listening, in fact. It's the same list as last year and the year before: Americans, a few Euros, a handful of Asians, and Atom Egoyan. I can just tweak some titles and run the same piece I run every year. I can't remember the last time anyone spotted an error in the entertainment section of *The Daily*, or even read it at all. Mohsen may be our sole subscriber.

Instead of writing, I'm thinking about Theo McArdle's laundry soap smell when he leaned over to open the cab door for me, which leads me to think about the same thing I've been thinking about pretty much non-stop since I was eleven. Here's how it works with sex these days. There's the night sex, and the brunch sex. The night sex starts around ten or eleven when you meet the guy at the launch or the bar or the party and you zero in and he's zeroing in and if he's still around after you finish eviscerating whatever or whoever needs to be eviscerated that day, then you let him buy you the drink, then you move into the corner for some privacy, then one of you says, "Wanna get outta here?" It's the perfect line. I highly recommend it. If the answer is, No, I don't, you go: "Well I do. See you later!" and they end up feeling rejected. Chest-pass the pain whenever possible.

If the answer is yes, then you get the night sex.

The night sex is what it's like with Ad Sales. You always go back to his place so that you can leave early and avoid breakfast. Because rarely is the breakfast guy also the night sex guy (okay, once the night sex guy became the breakfast guy, and it lasted twelve years. But that's an anomaly).

Brunch sex starts sober. It's the guy who knows a friend who knows you and he calls and you say, Brunch? Because brunch means if it doesn't go well, you shake hands and have the rest of the day to analyze obsessively and tell everyone you know how bad it was.

If it goes well and he doesn't humiliate the waitress or order something weird ("Heated lemon, please. No, that's it."), then you can add the walk past the cafés and galleries of Queen Street, past the textile shops and the lofts bumping up against the mental institution that used to mark the edge of downtown. The walk could turn into a movie, which could turn into coffee at your place, which could mean sex just as the sun is setting and the light in the bedroom is that flattering mossy colour so you don't feel like backing out of the room in a lame attempt at hiding your ass, going, "I always walk like this. Better for the shins." And afternoon sex is imaginative, creative sex that ends with a nap and a goodbye hug (no kiss), then a long, solo bath with some good music. The difference between night sex and brunch sex is that with brunch sex, the next day, your skin is always better.

Theo McArdle looks like a man who could brunch.

I have a shadowy recollection that after my failed rescue of the kid from the speaker, Theo took my cellphone, and I took his cellphone, and we entered each other, so to speak. Then he stuck me in a cab and placed a folded ten-dollar bill for fare in my jacket pocket. So he has my number, but he hasn't called. I've checked a few dozen times in the last hour. Well, maybe I'll call him. We could meet next Sunday, see how he holds up sober. Then again, if we met up late enough in the day, we could have mimosas, or wine, or beer, or maybe a date. I'd be willing, I think, to risk nighttime with Theo McArdle, if he agreed to bring those hands.

The Czar finally gets his big round of applause, which snaps me awake and I move faster than I have in months to get the hell out, elbowing past the grabby publicists and Allissa Allan, who gives me a – could this be right? – black-power gesture with her fist.

The cab I'm targeting is blocked by the Flock of Critics. I know it sounds glamorous, I'm aware of the palpable envy around this job, but have you met any film critics? Would you really want to live among them? Film critics are mushroom people. They dwell indoors, light is not a friend, conversation not of the species. Spongy, white, male, between forty and sixty, a little socially stunted, incapable of eye contact, clad in depressed denim shirts and cords. This is not the eighteenth-century salon: exchange, analysis, debate – oh no. Just uncomfortable nods before and after screenings, the occasional suspicious "What did you think?" in the lobby (Proper answer: "What did *you* think?").

One pops out from the fold, stepping in between my beloved cab and me. "Hello, Maxime," says the critic from *The Examiner*, local tabloid with a propensity for the all-caps front page featuring the word *shame*, as in SHAME! SINGLE MOTHER CAUGHT WITH TORONTO RAPTOR! Or SHAME! GOVERNOR-GENERAL GETS PEDICURE, JET! *The Examiner* invented the hyperbolic six-star movie rating, and as the hobbity old critic scampers my way, he manifests those six stars in human form: "You look fabulous! It's going to be a great festival!" He delivers the two-cheek kiss, smelling like cigarettes and computer screens.

"World class," I tell him, trying to deke around his body and get to the cab.

He leans in: "I just interviewed Ethan Hawke. Super nice guy! Are you going to catch him while he's in town?"

Ah, a reconnaissance mission. My answer will determine when they run their piece. I should be like *The Examiner* guy: stealth and dog loyal to my newspaper, willing to kiss and hustle so *The Daily* will be first. But I'm too tired and hungover to protect my corporation. Instead, I give up all information.

"Yep. For Friday," I say, knowing that *The Examiner* will now run their piece on Thursday.

"Well, he's a super nice guy!" *The Examiner* steps to the side. I pull at the cab door, but it's stuck. I jiggle and *The Examiner* watches for a moment, then leans across me – oh, God, is he coming in for another kiss? – and grabs the handle, giving it a strong pull. A moment of kindness, or a declaration of triumph.

"Thanks," I murmur, off guard, swinging my legs into the backseat. *The Examiner* waves as we pull away.

No call from Theo McArdle. I can't call the Ex back, so I do something half-good and I call Elaine's hotel, waiting until the exact moment that the car is entering the ravine that divides the city in half so the message goes: "Hi! It's Max! Great to –" and then the gnarl of confused satellites. When we emerge, it's still bright and leafless February and I am guilty – I really do feel it, thinking about Elaine. After my mom died there was a lot of movement, and Elaine, who emerged at the end of our travels, brought welcome stillness.

The first months after the death had been quiet, a slow accumulation of squalor in the house that my father and I both silently consented to live with. The compost bin, a cutout milk carton on its side, overflowed with rot. I had to pick up my father's strewn clothing from the hallway and carry it downstairs. These things felt like an insult, more unfairness to add to the steaming pile of it I'd been walking around, trying to avoid. So I started lighting garbage cans on fire at school. Dad drove me home silently, and as he pulled into the driveway in his pickup, he said, "We're leaving, and that is what we're leaving in."

A rusted milk truck. He let me paint it, a gift I later recognized as one for himself; something more he didn't have to do.

I attempted a mural of Big Bird, which my dad would never have allowed anyway ("So commercial, Max!"), but my skills were lacking and the bird looked like a big yellow cloud, which was beautiful to him. (And these are all stories I have told so many times that I now just float away while they tell themselves. So beware, beware, beware of lazy embellishments to keep me awake, and out-and-out lies, the by-products of the very relativistic girlhood that's turning you on.)

We left Squamish for the year-long road trip, our bags sloshing in the empty space behind us where the milk bottles were before. Rainy nights we slept on foam and sleeping bags, the sour smell of gas and dairy on our bodies in the morning. In every province as we headed east, we crashed with people my father knew but I didn't, people we would never speak of or see again. Often these mysterious acquaintances lived in unfinished houses half-covered in orange tarps, pieces of land barely conquered by stacks of lumber, good intentions abandoned. Grown-ups who spent their lives at kid level, down on the floor, cross-legged or propped up on elbows and stomachs. The talk, the endless talk, came from lips moving somewhere under Brillo pads of facial hair. My dad hovered on the periphery, reading or staring into space. Perhaps if there had been dogma to go with the lifestyle, it would have made more sense to me, a vine climbing a strong trellis. But the ideals that others railed about late into the night (me lying on a piece of foam in the corner) were rarely parroted by my father. What I remember is that my mother was the political one, her fist pummelling the newspaper in outrage. Later, I could see that rhetoric was just a place for him to vanish; he was unnoticed, gazing skyward while the rest of them decided what mattered. Maybe they mistook his silence for consent, or maybe it was. But I always thought that he would live the same way in any time, which is to say, out of it.

Near Weyburn, Saskatchewan, we slept in a tent on an abandoned oil field beside the giant, stilled bird-machine, its beak frozen, poised to peck the unfruitful land. At the Winnipeg Folk Festival, I saw a woman make a wiry braid from three strands jutting out of a mole in her chin. We hit the stormy season in Newfoundland and turned a slick corner to find a car teetering over the edge of a hungry cliff, no one inside.

When we had used up all the road, we went west again, retracing our steps. We moved to the compound on Gambier, an island across the bay from Vancouver. The strangest, most unshakeable memory from those first weeks has nothing to do with my father: Taj Mahal is on the turntable in the dining hall, and I'm planting sea monkeys in a glass bong. They never grow but quickly start to stink like rotting shrimp.

There was rarely more than thirty people on the compound at any given time, though they changed so often that I never bothered to learn many of their names. They were city women, mostly, leaving behind husbands and jobs, screaming children tucked under their arms like briefcases. The few men who stayed, most of them single, spent their days in the rain building the boathouse and clearing the land for more gardens. In the most surprising ways, the great experiment bore tradition. The women ran things from the kitchen and raised the children; the handful of men stayed away until darkness and rose up with the sun to vanish again in the morning. Once in a long while, usually when a newcomer arrived, there were heated arguments and philosophical debates about the reason for all of this, but soon, the routine settled back to dull consensus and meeting after meeting to debate the quotidian. Voting for a new septic tank. Voting for selling eggs and milk to the mainlanders until we could become entirely self-sufficient. Arranging a boat schedule with the local farmers to get us on and off the island.

But there was never any real panic that it would fall apart because everyone knew that Elaine, my father's girlfriend, born to a wealthy family who owned department stores in Philadelphia, quietly funded the fantasy. She pulled out a black leather ledger and wrote cheques to the government for taxes, and to the grocer for staples, and to the plumbers who arrived in a speedboat to fix the overflowing toilets. It was not that different, then, from serfdom, except that Elaine worked the land as best she could too and got nothing in return but a reason to stay far away from Philadelphia.

On occasion a boatload of tourists would float by looking for whales, tossing plastic water bottles overboard, squealing and pushing one another with glee. Watching from the dock, someone at the compound would always declare bitterly, "Americans," without evidence. If Elaine minded, she never said anything. It was a given that the people we were hiding from were Americans. No one mentioned the department stores in Philadelphia that fed us. I could never figure out these contradictions, but the dining hall rage – "Look what they're doing now! Acid rain! Clearcuts!" – was such a force that I kept my mouth shut.

So to anyone who finds this girlhood among the unwashed romantic, I always say permissiveness comes with so many rules, so much disapproval. They're just less spoken, meaning you navigate them blindfolded. I wore fishbowl headphones to listen to ABBA or Blondie so as not to pollute the living space, but Bob Dylan never stopped moaning from the speaker.

If you really wanted out, it was simple to float away; the trick was to make it look purposeful. While the grown-ups did their thing, planting the vegetables (that never really grew – more trips to the co-op – because people with degrees in Marxist philosophy don't make good farmers) and talking talking talking, I would hitchhike across the water and spend hours in the drugstore reading *Tiger Beat*, tucking the good issues in the waistband of my pants and walking out slowly, smiling, because if you look happy like that, you can get away with anything. Then in the evening, I sat on the fence at the local drive-in staring at *The Wiz*, imagining lyrics to songs I couldn't hear without a speaker. Sometimes I would bully a smaller, snot-encrusted kid into acting as sidekick, but these kids were too hyper to sit still and too close to their parents to be good liars, so usually I went off alone.

I escaped house meetings to hide in the woods with my magazines and pin-ups, circling the addresses of fan clubs. I discovered that the farm down the road had a tidy blond family in it, and a girl in a skirt who was nearly my age. I watched TV there constantly, and began to skip out on the things I used to love: getting the shit-streaked eggs from the screaming chickens, milking the cows. I had fallen for Jaclyn Smith, the silkiest of Charlie's Angels, and also, in my estimation, the smartest. Her character was called Kelly, a name like mine, a name for a boy or a girl. We could be friends.

The back of the milk truck was littered with my dad's tools and thinning Mexican carpets. Without windows, I could go unseen in there. I got out my thesaurus and wrote, "Dear Ms. Smith," because I never knew Miss or Mrs. existed, "I find your show superlative. Your hair is very comely. How did you become an actress? Will you write me please?" On the envelope, I wrote the return address: Rural Route 1, Gambier Island, British Columbia, Canada.

I didn't notice the doors opening, my father a half-foot back, tentative. He stared at the envelope.

"Who are you writing?"

"Nobody." I shoved the letter in the pocket of my hemp flares, the ones the draft dodgers brought across the border like offerings to the families that protected them.

My dad nodded, but he looked sad. "I respect your privacy," he said slowly. Then he thought about this and revised it. "But we shouldn't have secrets." More thinking, a condition I could identify by the wrinkles curling out from the corners of his eyes. My dad is so biologically slow that any mental exertion registers across his face like a piece of paper crumpling. "You think about it." Uh-huh. "And tell me later." A direct order? Impossible! "If you want." That's better.

It was one of those cyclical moments of parenting at which my dad excelled. I nodded. Then he held out a fuzzy mass, seemingly offering me a dead cat.

"I made you something," he said, placing the object in my hand. It was rough and knit from yellow yarn with a pink explosion of ribbon on its head and two red buttons for eyes.

"Elaine showed me how to knit," he said very quickly, looking away.

"What is it?" I asked, instantly realizing I sounded cruel. I added, "It's nice."

"It's Holly Hobbie, you know. That girl with the bonnet and the skirt . . ."

I turned it over in my hand. The skirt was a square of dishtowel.

"You said you wanted one, remember?"

I nodded. "Thank you," I said. I'd asked for Holly Hobbie a year ago. Now she was over. I had developed an acute sense of fashionable timing that would have shocked my father.

My dad stood shuffling and made a quick gesture toward me with his hand, like he was reaching out for something, maybe trying to take back the present. Then he halted, shoving his fists in the pockets of his pants, the belt around his skinny hips puckered and sagging, a dad in a drawstring bag.

"Thank you," I said again.

I don't usually tell it like that. I just describe the grotesque felt-pen grin on Holly's face. Many laughs ensue. Lucky you. True version.

I T'S STILL A FEW DAYS BEFORE THE OFFICIAL OPENING, but the festival has already rolled into town. A few carnies barking into cellphones give off an L.A. scent, but the entourages have yet to arrive in full force. The newspapers are still covering other events soon to be shunted to the back pages (TENT CITY GROWING. *Homeless gather, light toxic barrels for warmth*).

On Bloor Street, next to designer clothing boutiques and stores selling thousand-dollar pens, a handful of teenaged girls fan out and cover the celebrity-spotting corners, pagers and BlackBerries at the ready: The Starbucks in the Chapters bookstore. Club Monaco at Avenue Road. The restaurant Prego. Within days, there will be more of them, underdressed for winter, jackets open to show their pudgy midsections, armies of Lana Turners looking for Schwab's.

Around the corner from Bloor at the Four Seasons, the crowds have yet to descend. There is only one man on a lawn chair staking out a square of sidewalk near the curb, drinking coffee with his mittens on, a camera around his neck. He looks proud, as if he did some investigating and discovered that this little patch legally qualifies for public space and he is going nowhere. The doorman has his eye on him.

The elevator and the hallway inside the hotel have been sprayed with a scent that's either florid or dental. Outside room 1215, the Ethan Hawke publicist paces. She sees me and freezes, extends a palm in a halt gesture.

"Are you with *The Daily*?" she asks suspiciously, as if all day she's been warding off civilians enacting their own personal Monkees episode, dressing up as chambermaids and waiters, smuggling each other past security by curling up on dessert carts, anything to get close to Mr. Hawke, who hasn't had a hit movie in ten years.

"Wait five minutes. He's finishing up," she tells me, and I lean against a wall next to an anxious, mouth-breathing young man from the *Halifax Bugle* or whatever. A few faux-Edwardian chairs might be meant for us to sit on, but they're covered with shiny stacks of slides, CD-ROMs, and press notes that outline the plot of the film, scene by scene, moment by moment. It's all designed to require as little of us as is possible.

Hence, *The Examiner* has been known to sleep through entire films and others don't even show up for screenings, writing their reviews from studio-penned plot summaries plumped up by the occasional "superbly observed" and "challengingly cast."

American publicists have an enviable don't-give-a-shit quality when they visit Canada. They must have done something really, really bad to get this gig, throwing bones to twenty-five Canadian journalists – "I'm sorry, did you just say RAGINA?" – ten minutes each with Mr. Once Was Famous, knowing we'll all write the same article about the first big star to hit town. American publicists in Canada carry with them the anger of a very recent breakup, of a really terrible morning, a missed-the-alarm, stepped-in-dog-shit, got-mugged, bled-all-over-myself morning that just ended five minutes ago. Your presence is only going to agitate that huge gaping wound that is her life. You're going to bother her with your pesky requests and refusal to wrap it up after she's given you the very clear finger-winding-it's-over signal. You're going to rub the star the wrong way with some mindless question about art or truth or, more likely, dating status, and then she'll have to spend the whole morning cleaning up your mess, calming him down, fulfilling requests for tranks or personal trainers or organic fruit, until she can finally stuff him onto an airplane and slam the door – her own personal, unique creative gifts overlooked one more long, unjust day.

The door opens and a beaming young reporter backs out, clutching her tape recorder to her chest. She's got the sticky coating of a chocolate-dipped ice-cream cone; this interaction has bettered her.

Ethan Hawke appears. He's just a little taller than the door handle. First thought upon seeing a celebrity in the flesh: if he's male, he looks like a wizened, less attractive, shorter version of the character he plays on screen, like the guy at Substop who serves you your daily six-inch Turkey Lurky about whom everyone back at the office goes: "He looks like Ethan Hawke, am I right?" If it's a woman, you think, I can't even find her under the Impressionist brush strokes of foundation. And also the shorter thing.

Wiping the (carefully placed) sleep from his eyes, tugging his (perfectly wrinkled) thrift-store old-man shirt (Paul Smith, U.S.$1,675) that rises above his prominent belly (what, no personal trainer? – you're right. He can't win), Ethan Hawke gives a little wave to the smitten journalist who's hovering in the hallway, unable to move. An intake of breath from *Halifax Bugle*.

Publicist #1, Curly, scampers over to the star on her tiny feet and is all: "What can I get you what do you need how did it go?"

I've got Ethan Hawke's number. He's a down-with-the-people celeb. He just wants a Diet Coke, no problem, man, whenever you can get to it. He gets the scene. He knows the deal. He's one of *those*.

"Who's next?" he smiles, and *Bugle* swoons a little, holding the wall to keep steady.

"She is," says the publicist, pointing at me with her chin.

Then Hawke does it, he turns and full stops at my eyes, lets loose a little, crinkly just-for-me smile. It works, I confess. I am not immune, and most of them have it, these actor types (except – and this is weird – Harrison Ford). That's the only difference between them and us. When I smile, I just smile. Two lips, a touch of tooth, a gum now and then on a really glorious day. It's a friendly but neutral act. With them, a smile is a declaration, a flag planted in your heart. Which is pretty nice, and it's been a while since someone bothered to send the troops my way, so I blush, remembering, out of nowhere, Theo McArdle's smile, and how young he looked laughing.

Hawke runs his hand through his bed-head, then offers a greasy handshake. We're ushered in, the publicist flutters, making an exaggerated NASA-worthy gesture with her fingers – ten minutes countdown! – then backs out of the room, turning the doorknob with nursery-room caution so as not to disturb the artist.

"Nice to meet you," says Ethan Hawke. "Can I get you anything?"

This question, this gesture to the stuffed food cart – fruit, bottled water, bowl of chocolate bars – gets me, I have to admit. I'm a call girl who's just encountered a charming trick, and I giggle: I'm fine, I'm fine, I have no needs, I'm *Canadian*.

Ethan Hawke's new movie is an arty little number about Swiss banks harbouring Nazi money, which means a lot of courtroom scenes and snow-capped candy mountains. He's okay in it too, especially when he takes a bullet and gets to do some testifying with a nasty head injury. Lolling his vowels and twitching and Nazis – I smell an Oscar!

Interview begins.

With this guy, the first, winningest question has to be the Serious Artist question. He has, after all, written a novel.

Me: You really pulled off a [decent crip impression]. Is there a responsibility in [appropriating the pain of others in the vainglorious attempt at grabbing an Oscar]? Tell me about your [self-serving research process].

Him: Thank you. My producers gave me a [list of crips because I have long since forgotten how to investigate the world on my own], I went over to the East Village on the subway [because that's the type of detail journalists love], and we hung out in the company of these people [with many nurses and orderlies close at hand in case of unexpected wigging on the crips' part].

Me: Is the final version what you hoped it would be? [Why does your movie suck so bad?]

Him: I'm really, really happy with this movie [because the handicap thing could pay off big-time from Oscar].

Me: Surprisingly, the film barely mentions reparations. [What up with the Swiss and the Nazis – seriously?]

Him: [First uncomfortable pause.] I'm not overtly political. It's more about art . . .

As Ethan Hawke is yammering, there's suddenly a cellphone ring in the room with us. Not a small, understated cellphone ring, mind you, but a robust one with a Wagnerian thrust. I look at Ethan Hawke. He stops talking.

"Is that you?" I ask.

A new, cooler Ethan Hawke emerges: "I don't believe in cellphones."

I'm diving into my bag, full body like a *Gong Show* contestant into a glass of water – Sunera's idea of a joke to program my ring like this – I locate the phone and it glows at me: MCARDLE. It's Wednesday. Four days after entering each other. I'm a touch irritated, really, wondering if I should pick up.

There's Ethan Hawke, one eyebrow raised, sipping his Diet Coke through a straw, and I think, Here's a man who probably hasn't had to wait for anyone in years, a man for whom the regular laws of daily life – the lineups, the wait-here-I'll-be-back-in-a-second, the moments of forced reflection in an idling car – have been bent so drastically and for so long, replaced with "Can I get you something?" And "May I take that, sir?" How odd it must be for him to be here with me, a lowly journalist, demanding of him something like understanding.

So fuck Ethan Hawke, I lust this guy.

"I'll just be one second," I offer in a shrill voice that I hope contains a note of normalizing reassurance, as if this happens all the time, and he has no reason to object, a voice that pretends we are equals. Then I swivel my hips, knocking the coffee table and the tape recorder, and hiss-whisper into the phone, "Hello?"

"Max? Hi, it's Theo McArdle."

"Mmm?"

"Is this a bad time?"

"Mmmm-hmmm."

"I'll be quick, then. You didn't enter your number right. I kept calling Moviephone."

Oh no. I do that sometimes, with less desirables. I can't really explain with Ethan Hawke eyeballing me above his straw. "Really? How weird."

"Unless that's a rather obvious way to tell me not to call you," says Theo. Then, with a little nervousness: "Was that the point?"

To give Ethan Hawke an impression that I am having an incredibly professional conversation with a superior, I thunder, "*Absolutely not.*"

Theo says, "Uh, okay."

"And the reason for your call?" I say.

"Oh. Well, do you want to do something tomorrow night?"

Something, something, what could that be? And I'm lit up then just because he called. That's enough for me, that's a touch of joy right there. I want to skip the movie or the dinner or the drinks and get right to those hands.

"*Absolutely.*" I spit out my address and press *End*, and swivel back to Ethan Hawke, who suddenly looks small, all by himself on the big brocade couch.

"So —" I say brightly. "Fatherhood!"

"Is everything okay?" asks Ethan Hawke. That's the weirdest thing about these ten minutes in a hotel room; it's so much like therapy, so quiet and intimate and meaningless. What comfort would he offer me if I started to cry right here, right now?

"I'm fine, thanks."

I have to get the Uma crap, which is what the Editor wants, so I give him a little spiel about how hard it must be to have kids in the city, and my deliberately gender-neutral "partner" and I (he strikes me as someone who might open up to a lesbian) don't know how to do it in this corporate Nintendo McDonald's universe and how do he and Uma and baby Maya keep it real?

Oh, he likes this, it's kind of great. He's over the cell-phone thing. Ethan Hawke is springing up out of his chair, talking about the dangers of globalization, pacing around the hotel room, on and on with some great tidbit about Uma's parents out in the garden planting flowers and how people abuse Buddhist philosophy to justify their passive existences and his fear that his kid will end up in a Batman T-shirt and this will symbolize some great loss of character.

I start to kind of like the guy and I feel a bit bad for lying to him about my imaginary lesbian lover's desire for an uncorrupted unborn child. There's an innocence celebrities possess, like they've been raised in wire cages by agents and studio daddies and when they're out there in the world, face to face with something resembling real people, they blink like albino squirrels in sunlight and you feel you could just crush them with a truthful comment. Ethan Hawke is almost worse because he genuinely thinks he can function normally in the world, ride the subway, make digital movies of his friends (who are all stars), and as he rambles I picture his and Uma's beautiful baby with her wooden, non-toxic blocks and I feel a little twinge of sadness. It will be difficult for her to reconcile the safety of her flowered Connecticut farm with the flashbulbs at the airport and the one-way windows on the limousines.

So I feel like confessing to Ethan Hawke, and maybe having a real conversation with him, but I don't want to interrupt his moment (this is great shit; the Editor will be pleased), and just as he's going on about the razor's edge of Buddhism, attached and detached, there's a knock at the door. Ethan Hawke sits down and shouts, "Sorry, no one's home." Curly Hair peeks in anyway.

"Time's up," she says as if she says it a lot.

"Well, that got a little heavy, huh?" Ethan Hawke, flushed and exhilarated, smiling at me, and I do it, I'll just say it right now, I swoon a little before I'm forcibly removed.

SUNERA WANTS TO TALK. SHE DOESN'T KNOW WHAT TO
do about Stewey. Stewey's on the phone, Stewey's sending
e-mails, Stewey's on the doorstep like a baby in a basket.
Stewey's got it bad. This borderline-stalker thing might be
okay from certain guys except Sunera has decided that
Stewey's problem is – Sunera always finds one thing – that his
teeth are too small for his mouth. Even as I'm talking her
down, telling her that in some cultures small teeth are a sign
of financial prudence, suddenly I picture Stewey and all I can

see are the bright white mouse teeth of his namesake, Stuart Little, and I know it's doomed.

Sunera is telling me this in the cafeteria of *The Daily*. "Half-day," she declares, as she often does, explaining why she's in a suburban area code at three o'clock on a Wednesday, four hours from date time. I'm happy to take the break, having spent the morning under headphones transcribing the Ethan Hawke tape, rewinding my favourite part several times: *And the reason for your call? Absolutely.*

Sunera's theory of reduced labour is this: when entering or exiting the office, walk quickly, even jog, if you must. Press *Ring* on your cellphone when in the elevator, then turn to your co-riders and sigh, "No time to pick up. Meeting. Relentless, isn't it?" Come in before everyone else one day, then don't turn up until 5:30 the next. Skip most Fridays, but run in every weekend and send out e-mails on Sunday during the ten minutes you're in the office, the electronic equivalent of urinating in the corner.

Sunera does these things because the actual work – the assigning, the editing, the final proofing – occupies her for about four hours a week. In part, this is because Sunera is a genius with an off-the-charts IQ. Her parents still keep her law-school acceptance letters stuck to the refrigerator with magnets shaped like tropical fruits. There are others with whom Sunera works who could fulfill their job requirements in six, eight, or ten hours a week, but they show up for fifty, eyelids purple from late nights, loudly martyring themselves at the printer. (I remember a brief blip, a moment of about six weeks a few years ago, when government ads suddenly appeared on buses and billboards: WORK SMART, NOT LONG, and people in the city took note. In the mornings, the underground tunnels that run below downtown, linking office tower to mall to office tower, loomed empty until five to nine; a yodel could really fly. The subways cleared by 6:00 p.m., Pilates became popular, and children turned to their parents and said, "Where's Nanny?" and "Who are you?"

But one day, an eager someone showed up at 8:30 a.m. and made a big noise. The boss admired the rogue sound, the tidy pile of paper that was waiting for him when he sat at his desk in the morning. The cubicle next to the eager someone caught wind, and the next morning, he let it be known that his day starts at 8:15. With hardly a breath, the subway grew pointy elbows and city skin regenerated its old grey layer and the days keep getting longer and longer.)

Sunera's father had been an economist in Mumbai. Here, he ran a magazine stand in a downtown mall for twenty-five years, the final few of which were spent serving young MBAs copies of *Wired* and *Fast Company*, shaking his head as teenaged CEOs appeared before him in flip-flops and jeans, clutching their lattes in environmentally friendly mugs, offending his sense of capitalism. "They don't even know who Keynes is!" he would shout to his wife, who rolled her eyes, sliding packages of gum into plastic bags.

Surrounded by balance sheets and pricing guns, Sunera chose words. It was the greatest accomplishment of her life, learning this language at ten years old. She could answer the girl outside the library who called her "Paki" with a cogent: "Actually, different country. Look it up." She read

Middlemarch and lost her accent, and won national awards for essays trumpeting the virtues of the Canadian mosaic. At thirteen, she flew to London to recite one to the Queen, who leaned in with her licorice breath and told her, "Lovely, my dear."

But by university, Sunera began to feel like an Uncle Tom. She questioned her desire to "pass" as some internalized slave mentality and sought out rebellion. Under the tutelage of a radical feminist German lesbian teaching assistant with impaling studs on the back of her leather jacket, she went gay for a while. But that made her even more desirable to both men and women. Her phone never stopped ringing, and soon she was delivering speeches to snow-covered campuses, screaming, "Brown, queer, we're still here!" The problem was that everyone agreed. They were brown, queer, here, and that was *totally okay*; in fact, it was encouraged. Envelopes of grant money addressed to Sunera kept arriving in the NABLATS (Network Alliance of Brown Lesbians and Transgendered Students) mailbox at the student union building, and one day, in the middle of a battle cry on the quad, Sunera surveyed the smiling, supportive white faces: "We're here, we're queer, get used to – ." She stopped. Everyone was used to it, including Sunera.

She left the stage, and read some more, lazily taking the exams for law school to silence her parents. But she deferred all the acceptances (and there were only acceptances) and took one of the magazine jobs that were waiting for her after graduation. She worked at a women's magazine, composing articles on tampons that kill and massages that save, and the opposite-of-women's magazines (not men's magazines, but magazines) courted her, even from south of the border. She considered leaving Canada. She considered it as she wrote her fifteenth piece on national identity, or Quebec sovereignty, or hockey moms. She considered it as she moved up the ranks from junior to associate to senior editor at the country's only newsmagazine, where there were just two people above her on the masthead, each healthy and nostalgic for the Sixties and refusing to die.

So she agreed to meetings in New York. On the thirty-fifth floor of a building so old that the black-and-white tiles at the entrance spelled the magazine's name under her feet, she spent a long hour dazzling an editor with her comparisons between the immigrant experience in Canada and the immigrant experience in America, basing much of her argument on *An American Tail*, the Disney cartoon about an upwardly mobile Russian-American rodent family, the Mousekewitzes. But when she really imagined packing her bags, stepping onto the airplane with a ticket in her pocket, the clouds in the sky clustered to form her mother's face: "All our hard work, Sunera! All our sacrifice and you leave us in our old age? Oh, the shame of it!"

Luckily, her younger sister was selling leather pants out of a discount warehouse in Acton, so the parental rage was mostly pointed in that direction, leaving Sunera a little breathing room once she decided to stay. And somewhere in that space, she discovered that family dinners and work meetings were both improved by low-level substances, that their steady hum was just enough to calm the wake of those tectonic shifting identities, provide some cohesion. But at the end of the day, when the magazines and talk shows ask, Why so single, fabulous girl? I think of how full Sunera must feel stomaching her family's vacillation between smothering pride and sagging disappointment because all that she's created can't be babysat. I don't think she's got much left for the Steweys of the world.

As she sits in the plastic cafeteria chair, talking about Stewey's teeth, I'm filling out expense forms with false numbers, trying to get my fire-me thing back on track. In the past week, I've missed several meetings and sat on dozens of unreturned phone calls and yesterday I propped open the fire-escape doors, causing a four-storey evacuation.

I fill in the form with six forty-dollar cab rides in two days. A receipt I found on the street for gumboots. A $200 restaurant tab (on the back, I write, "Lunch with Ethan Hawke"), which consists only of vodka and beer and of course took place last Saturday night at a stumbly table with Sunera and the rest.

Sunera opens a small silver cigarette case filled with blue and pink pills, separates the pink from the blue, daintily pops one of each into her mouth.

"Should I ask about this?" I say. "I'm asking about this."

"Mood evener-outers," she says, marble-mouthed.

"Prescriptive or street?"

"Very prescriptive. You should meet my doctor. He deals exclusively with media whores. It's like *Valley of the Dolls* in there, with laptops," she says, smiling that fluttery smile of the recently ingesting. "Interested?"

I'm a little disappointed that Sunera would engage the fleets of antidepressants that are servicing half of our industry. Her old-fashioned abuses please me more; she is the only person I know capable of disengaging an entire office sprinkler system so she can hot-box her office on an 11:00 a.m. break.

"I don't know if I want my mood even," I tell her. "I don't know if I want *your* mood even. Aren't moods kind of the whole point?"

Sunera looks at me. "Point of what?"

My cell rings: dad, from Arizona. Sunera snatches to see who I'm ignoring.

"Your poor dad," she says.

"My poor dad? The absentee landlord of fathers?"

"I know, I know, he wasn't around –"

"Oh, he was around, it was worse than that. He was the absentee landlord who lives in your apartment."

Sunera's face drops and I know she's suddenly seeing me as a sooty foundling. "Still, he's your *dad*, Max." The way she says "dad" suggests all kinds of dadlike behaviours I never saw: the bedtime, the lecture, the strong silent type. She's thinking of her own dad when she says, "You should call him back."

I'm considering whether to snap at my best friend or hug her when Marvin comes swanning into the caf with a new haircut – pointy, blond, painful – and spinning like a bottle cap in a street-corner game, bursting with a piece of gossip.

"Did you hear? Did you did you did you?" This level of Did-you-hear? requires smoking. While carcinogenic bacon as a lunch entree is deemed an acceptable health hazard here in *The Daily* caf, the room is non-smoking, all the better for my get-fired agenda, so I light up and ash into Sunera's Diet Coke can.

"Baby Baron is selling!" hisses Marvin, leaning in all gleaming and giddy. "Rumours are flying. He's selling *The Daily* to *television*." Marvin makes television, his life's work, sound like a swear word. "We're hemorrhaging money, apparently. This is it. It's the end of journalism as we know it," says Marvin, like this is a bad thing.

"How so?" I ask.

"Convergence, Max," he says. "They'll use the same reporters from TV to write for the papers, and if there's anyone left at the papers, they'll have to appear on TV. Look at me! I'm not telegenic! I'm screwed."

"You mean they'll just cut out the whole middleman 'writer' thing and let the anchor-people talk directly into computers and some guy in a room with silver walls will press buttons on this old Hal-type computer, and this machine will just convert TV into newsprint, and bingo," I put on my best evil sci-fi villain voice. "The future will be now, Marvin. And we will all be unemployed."

Sunera shakes her head. "That's not why you'll all be unemployed," she says. We look at her.

"Anytime there's a corporate takeover, the new company needs to make its mark immediately. They'll fire you to prove they're serious," she says.

"Serious about what?" asks Marvin.

"Serious about being new."

Something occurs to me: the two words most writers want to hear are not, as some ambitious young things think, *bidding war,* but *severance package.* My escape strategy may be up for some modification.

Sunera is driving and talking on her cellphone and on the radio Howard Stern is shitting all over Renée Zellweger for being temporarily fat and I'm imagining my boardroom buyout, a teary goodbye, a billboard-sized novelty cheque in my hands: Baby Baron, the Editor, the Big Cheese gathered at the long espresso-coloured table weeping as they let me go . . .

Downtown on College Street, the latest neighbourhood to moult its immigrant past and make way for sommeliers and organic grocers, a white sheet flaps between street lamps like it might be advertising a small-town bake sale. Instead, it reads, ACCLIMITIZE: SIX NEW ARTISTS in black letters. The next sign, a few feet later, says, BUS TO BLOW LOUNGE EXPERIENTIAL ENVIRONMENT. COLLEGE AND CLINTON. 7 PM, WEDNESDAY. The Ex and his new "collective." Sunera gasps, phone branching from her ear.

The Ex spent our twelve years working as a bike courier in the day, painting in the living room at night. The galleries were indifferent, the government grant agencies puzzled by his proposals. "I'm interested in painting beautiful things," I read over his shoulder before he slammed a forearm down over the papers.

"Add this clause: '. . . about my experiences being molested,'" I suggested. "Trust me. That's where the money is."

He frowned.

The Ex was a terrible player. At parties, he stood frozen in front of anyone who mattered, his eyes unfocused. He was a limp handshake of a man in public.

But this new woman, this *woman he left me for* (what picture emerges? Loofahed elbows, multilingual, a saluting ass), got him out there, I hear. I hear, and I pretend to be deaf, putting my blankest face forward. I hear that she is very well connected in the arts scene, especially for a lawyer. They spent last summer in Europe at her parents' "London flat" (the cruel casualness of cocktail conversation) with hot young British artists: the guy who puts sharks in tanks; the woman who sculpts the negative space inside bathtubs. And the Ex emerged from August with a group London show on his CV, enough to get him some press Here because it was a small success There. She must have media coached him too, because lately he's been in the alternative weeklies and *The Other Daily* mouthing a new kind of futurism, a way of "talking back to the technology that talks for us," phrases made bearable because he's boy-band cute in his woolly sweaters.

And every time I see him at a bar, or a party, or come across his new middling fame, I go over all of this again: how he got so far away. I can remember the events but not the feelings. Cool, indifferent documentation; an autopsy report. Sunera's silver cigarette case of pink and blue pills, not evened out, but dulled.

Theo McArdle, back in the day, wore second-hand striped pants like a court jester and dyed his hair a different primary colour every few months. I took to black then and fourteen years later I am still wearing black and listening to some boy-friendly Stan Getz with my legs tucked under my butt just so, accessorized by a glass of red wine and a cigarette, generally radiating a beautiful-woman-lounging vibe.

I've arranged myself so that when Theo McArdle comes up the snowy walk and peers in the sliver of window I've framed perfectly with the slightly open curtains, he'll catch his breath at the sight of this staggering creature, this jazz-appreciator, this feline catch.

But Theo McArdle is a little late and *Entertainment Tonight* is on and I really need to catch up on the news for a second – work related – just for an update on the Tom-Nicole thing, so I have to disturb the tableau and I'm slithering low down (in case McArdle should peak in, I want to be out of his line of vision) with my wine spilling just a little and I'm rubbing that into the hardwood where the Ex's rug used to be and I can't really hear the TV over the Stan Getz so I'm propping up on my elbows and putting my ear close to the speaker and that way I can hear some beauty tips delivered by that girl from the sitcom (the one with the roommate who's gay but she loves him and isn't it hilarious how her entire life is devoted to this farce of a relationship and week after week we tune in as he brings home some hunky boy from the gym or buys a ticket for one to Fire Island and she's all devastated and the laugh track gets louder and louder and louder) – so I'm like this, belly down, wine spilling, when I feel a light tap on my shoulder.

Theo McArdle has decided to walk in. He made his way to the porch, opened the door, and strode right into my living room, where his first sight of the evening is not me, gently cast in the glow of the non-working fireplace, but rather me on my belly, a pin-sized noggin attached to the television, enraptured by celebrity shopping advice. And that gentle tap – a hello, really – feels from here like the calling card of an axe murderer. I let loose a scream that alarms my hand, causing it to jut upwards, knocking the red wine into a perfect slo-mo rainbow arc that ends all over my head.

So I'm in the back of the cab, showered and wearing pink because the black is wine-soaked and I need to do laundry and my wet hair is slowly freezing into ice slabs. Theo McArdle is still apologizing and I'm smiling my no-no-no it's-fine fakey-good-girl smile. (This is going to be another mess of epic proportions, I should not go out any more, it's a sign, it's a sign.) The snow is falling and the cab is slipping a little on the streetcar tracks, and I am inside a cloud of exhaustion. I'm thinking, Can I do this, can I really just start again, do the relationship two-step, climb into the phone booth and emerge wearing my Super Self suit and hand over all the stories and little frayed pictures of my life, overload his poor arms with all the best parts of me?

I close my eyes. I don't think I have it in me any more; the problem isn't the giving-in part – I'm pretty good with the buckle and swoon – it's the giving over. What I remember about love is that it succeeds or fails on the will to concede the rest, the part that's outside the stories, outside desire, that aureole that tells you something deeper exists. What is that anyway? Some kind of self, I suppose. It's tiring just to try to locate it, let alone hand it off to someone else.

Then Theo McArdle does something. He stops apologizing. He shuts up and his silence makes me turn my head, and he's looking out the window, away from me, his breath leaving a small patch of fog. We hit a particularly slick patch of ice and he reaches out his hand and places it on my leg. His hand knows exactly where to go without even looking. There is still such a thing as instinct.

Theo McArdle can keep up. He can joke around with the waiter, but not too much. He mentions Christopher Hitchens and a book I would like to read if I ever read again. He tells me that the other day, this homeless guy came up and asked him for change, and Theo looked at him and said, Dave? They had been childhood friends back in New Brunswick, just normal friends with matching lives and now this guy lives under a pile of garbage in Tent City with his dogs and he's worried the city's going to bulldoze it for the Olympic bid, and it kills Theo to think about it. Theo talks like this, like he's unwounded, unafraid. He uses the same steady voice for all his stories, even the heartbreaking ones. When Theo was six, his older brother died of chicken pox. Theo remembers how his brother would take one walkie-talkie and tell Theo to wait in the basement with the other, listening for a signal. Hours later, Theo would find him in the backyard playing with neighbourhood kids. He remembers better things too, but being forgotten is what he remembers the most. It doesn't embarrass him any more. He was just a kid, enumerating fights and disappointments.

"It was a long time ago," he says.

Mine too, I think, but I don't mention my mother yet. I'm not above pulling her out in a silence just to watch faces stiffen, mouths purse themselves in regret. But with Theo, I can't imagine what I would say. His frankness startles me. I feel like I need to be more awake than I have been in years. I feel like I'm listening with new parts of my body.

Allissa Allan (whose column today in *The Other Daily* was on how hard it is to host a dinner party without proper rapini imports. Another burning civic issue addressed) and the New Left Ideologues are at a table by the window, and I ask Theo McArdle what he thinks of her writing and he looks puzzled. Turns out he has no idea who she is, and I love this about him.

I tell him what I know and what everyone who reads *The Other Daily* knows because she is her own source of news, and her news is this: Allissa Allan is a Torontonian born to a banker father and an oncologist mother, raised on the Bridle Path where streets once wide enough for equestrian trails now carry sports cars into the driveways of Cape Cod colonial mansions belonging to American basketball players signed to the Toronto Raptors. She grew up with a barre in the special sunroom where she practised ballet until her toes were solid as wood. She is a girl who attended a girls' school that, in the early Nineties, experienced a slight uprising after a hundred or so years of "hold your fork in this hand." The girls, with knee socks and pleated skirts and ironed hair, were listening to Bikini Kill and making out with each other, writing words like RIOTGRRL across their knuckles in black ink.

Allissa and her friends listened to gangster rap and brought black boys from the public schools to cocktail parties. Their parents smiled supportively, driving the boys to the subway at midnight and not noticing, or pretending not to notice, when they walked right back over the North Toronto lawns and climbed the trellises into their daughters' bedrooms.

In winter, Allissa Allan went to Florida and berated her parents for their complicit racism, and tried to befriend the weary Cuban wait staff. In summer, she stayed at her estate in Muskoka for two months and water-skied, dividing her literary mind between the *Cosmo* quiz and Susan Faludi.

In Allissa Allan's final year of high school, Kurt Cobain died, and this marked a change, a release from Doc Martens and lumberjack shirts, a return to slim skirts and heels and fun. She attended a small college in the States, where she dated the son of a senator. Upon her return to the city, while dining at the Allans' one night, the greying editor-in-chief of *The Other Daily*, a man not immune to the delights of breathless youth, offered Allissa a summer internship. Her articles on dog aerobics and water-filled bras were remarkably readable; she could burp them out in record time, each as disposable, as mindlessly diverting as advertising copy. Within months, she was offered a column at the city desk. She thought about privilege, then decided she could do more good than harm with a platform from which to pontificate about how a conflicted young woman in the 2000s deals with the issues of the day: sex toys, dating, the inadequacy of self-tanners. Sometimes she threw in words like *deconstruction* and *aesthetic* to keep up the paper's intelligentsia reputation, and satisfy some quieting part of herself. The public went mad for these porny little peeks, and the editors found the stories both cheap (no travel, no research expenses) and salacious – a winning combination – and they put their feet up on the boardroom table and said, Everything is in order. This is how we want our young women. No threat from below.

Her photo began to appear with regularity in the paper: Allissa consults Toronto's best liposuction expert; Allissa goes on an Internet date; Allissa invites the mayor's assistant for a man-back waxing. The editors put her pretty face on the newspaper boxes with her favourite phrase in bold font just under her bemused white grin: "It's all good."

Allissa Allan has become her only subject. I'm almost envious. She creates herself in that column; I create other people. I'm getting outdated, obsolete. We're in a time of confession, and I'm mouthing other people's sins.

I don't mention this part to Theo. Instead, I say, "Rapini."

Theo McArdle looks blank.

"That's what she wrote about today."

"Oh. I think I saw that, but it didn't look very compelling," he says. I learn something: Theo McArdle doesn't just appreciate the columnists' photos – he reads the stories.

And I'm trying to imagine what life is like for Theo McArdle, who once lived in East Africa building wells with his ex-girlfriend and misses his small town in New Brunswick where half the people speak English and half the people speak French; Theo, who suffers yearning for the moment that just went by. I remember that yearning from the first time I knew him, and this is how I want Theo McArdle to stay: sitting across from me, half-shaven, lips moving, body listening to mine. He is nothing to me yet. I know that whatever happens, I will never desire him as much as I do right now, unknown.

I remember that from the time I fell in love.

The Ex and I used to joke that we would tell our children about the band: three girls, guitar, bass, drums, amateur plodding 4-4 time less noticeable than sheer volume. We would make it a bedtime story, or a yarn to fill the hours on a cross-country road trip. I would say, Your father danced up to your mother in the mosh pit squall and said: "Excuse me, do you have the time?" This was your father's sense of humour, but your mother didn't know it yet. She thought, A weirdo, and totally gay – lanky and planed olive-skin features – and she said, "Time for you to come up with a new opener," and felt very Lauren Bacall clever, but he didn't hear her because the band was screaming loud about doing nothing for a living.

Your father was twenty, and your mother was twenty-one. Like any night, there were other people it could have been but your mother ended up with your father at 3:00 a.m. in the hot summer night, lying on the wine-coloured grass, drunk on bottles of beer. They checked each other out twenty and twenty-one-year-old style (in this order): music, film, books, beliefs (none yet, except for the bands and the movies and books, but both were hopeful that the lists would soon give rise to some scheme to live by).

In this way, they kissed on the grass, and two weeks later, he brought his army bag of clothing and his stained box of paints – a little garden – into her tiny apartment and your mother thought that the universe had turned itself inside out, had become something entirely good, and sex was a new and untried addiction and she never knew she could laugh so hard. They graduated, and moved to the city, and travelled, and got sober, and mostly they remembered that feeling of the upcoming, that push toward the next phase of the relationship, that momentum that had started in the mosh pit that was, my God, two years ago, then four, then five, then seven, then ten.

And then the part we wouldn't tell, not even to each other. How we got older and the edges of the days emerged, shark fin out of water, and the world turned right side out and dulled. We read the newspaper over breakfast instead of talking about how the night before one had shifted this way in the sheets and the other noticed, or how we had sensed each other's dreams. And all those conversations from before, about what to name the children (Clara and

Charles) and how the unbought house would be renovated and maybe we should make it official and get rings – other people were suddenly living those conversations all around, not just making science fictions about the future but building up and spreading out. Everyone got married and babies. And I looked at him one day on a street corner by a kicked-over newspaper box and said, These are just conversations, aren't they? And he said, Yes, and he burst into tears because he was, it turned out, in love with someone else and I couldn't believe I didn't know it. I, who could once intuit the very thing he desired to eat just by examining the curve of his mouth, I had not sensed this in him, that the man I lived with was fingers and toes in someone else's mind and body. I felt unsmart. I had lost my sensitivity to him. Now he wore on me like everybody else, another fatigue. That's where he had been the night I waited up until 5:30 and he came home, smoky and drunk and mad at me for asking. He had been with a woman and she had a name and the name was Elizabeth.

In that way, the matter was decided, and the we of us, the much-discussed four of us, drifted to the sphere of dead ideas, and sometimes I feel those unborn children tugging: Don't forget us, don't forget us, don't forget.

The past can be bossy. Just when it might seem to be shrinking in the distance, it waves its arms and makes itself known. But I'm ignoring the past, because after an award-winning dinner, I am in Theo McArdle's apartment.

What you most fear when first invited to a guy's place: any kind of framed car paraphernalia, like a poster of a red corvette; any reference to marijuana as a lifestyle choice, like say, a bedspread emblazoned with a leaf; an inordinate number of mom photos; push-pinned posters, especially of undeservingly push-pinned people from history, like Mozart or da Vinci; a wall of baseball hats.

Theo McArdle's apartment does not break any of these rules, but it is not like any of the apartments I've been spending time in these days. Marvin's loft (once a button factory, as he'll proudly tell you), for instance, is a tribute to vinyl furniture. Sunera's gone kind of bamboo minimalist in a momentary "Zen chic" fit she hasn't rectified yet. But Theo McArdle's running with a homier look, lots of aged wooden crates holding books and wiry brass statues that could be religious or could be bongs and fringy carpets and – my God – are those spindly green life forms plants? Needy buggers, they make me nervous.

"If I smoke in here, will it bother the plants?" I ask, and Theo smiles, hands me an ashtray with a Mexican death mask painted on it. "Cheerful," I say.

What would be the worst music he could put on right now? "Mustang Sally." "We Built This City (on Rock n' Roll)." Bauhaus. But Theo McArdle foregoes the CD player for his turntable and puts on some scratchy blues. He stands there, moving the needle from track to track to get the right song sequence to backdrop a story he's telling me about Screamin' Jay Hawkins. Now here's a guy with some slow blues voodoo who was married six times and fathered maybe sixty kids who are trying to find each other on the Internet now. Then Theo asks me questions about my work, about British Columbia, about why I don't have any furniture. He doesn't nod, but he's listening, his brow slightly knitted. He tells me that what he does in his lab at the university is pretty boring; he's solving problems, the same problems he's been working on for about a decade now. Sounds familiar, I tell him.

But what he loves is the abstraction in his field. Like did you know that, theoretically, an object can exist in two places at once? Newton was wrong. Most people are wrong. Even Einstein might have been wrong. When particles get small, everything we thought we knew about the universe breaks apart, the normal physical rules change, and you end up with quantum rules. Theo's getting excited now, really and truly happy to tell me how there hasn't been an Einstein in the quantum field to put it all together yet and make sense of all these theories, but there will be. Someone, or a bunch of someones, will come up with new rules to live by.

I take a drink. My skin's not used to thinking this much. I flip the pages of a book of Lucien Freud's paintings, all these hulking melted bodies, and I go, "Note to self: never agree to pose for a Lucien Freud painting. Not flattering." Theo's not an easy laugher, so when you get one, it's all the more satisfying.

We do a quick past-relationship rundown. I keep the director's cut to myself and give him the version I've been handing out the most lately – the one that goes: "We drifted apart" – and isn't entirely untrue. Theo McArdle has his own

problems, and she waves hello and steps into my consciousness, some English girl who's still building those wells in
Africa and here's her picture stuck to his fridge. She's clean
and skinny, and doing a really annoying thing: she's actually
standing in a field of flowers, holding one white bloom to her
nose. Sheer rapture at nature's bounty.

"Well, it doesn't look like your girlfriend has allergies, so
that's good!" I shout to Theo, who's in the bathroom.

Theo McArdle calls back, "What?"

I don't clarify because his voice – smooth then broken by
a Maritime yang, the voice of someone good – makes my
easy sarcasm, my instinctive contempt for a field of flowers,
even nastier. I can feel the lateness of the hour, though there
are no clocks in the room.

When Theo comes out of the bathroom, the hair above
his forehead is slightly wet, as if he's just splashed water
on his face. And then his leg is next to my leg on the couch
and his arm is next to my arm and what will happen? What
will happen? Breathe and still, thirty-four years old, that
warming of the hips because he's there and a long time ago
we kissed and it was pretty damn good as I recall. Then Theo
McArdle leans over and hovers on my neck and I feel the pull
of him deep in my stomach, a pull as familiar as – .

"I have to go to the bathroom," I blurt.

End nuzzle.

"Okay," says Theo McArdle, disentangling.

Theo McArdle's bathroom contains three products:
toothpaste, a sliver of soap, and shaving cream. I would add
toilet paper to the list except there are only two squares left,

which I intend to use. I get the pang that parents must get the first time their newborn screams all night: Theo McArdle is imperfect. He does not shop ahead. I feel that gut pull again and of course – it's not love, it's menstruation.

I have many things in my bag. I have sunglasses even in February, lipstick, plastic bottle of water, nose drops, Altoids container of grass, matches, lighter, cigarettes, Altoids container of Altoids, Filofax, a photo of my mom in a plastic Tic Tac case, a hairbrush. Are there tampons on this list? Are there tampons on Theo McArdle's single shelf?

I fold the two squares and of course they're the tree-hugging one-ply kind and will last me to the foyer before soaking through my skirt. Under the sink is bare except for a bottle of cleanser. Under the radiator is dust. I contemplate asking Theo McArdle if he keeps his toilet paper in some environmentally friendly root cellar, but then he might think I've taken a crap, which seems like the groundwork for a mental image that could stifle the possibility of future nuzzling. So I'm going through my wallet wondering if I can fashion a pad out of my old bank statements, feeling a kind of kinship with my Native sisters bundling the leaves but – screw that. All men should have tampons in their bathroom. It's polite. All women have towels.

"Theo!" I shout, and he comes shuffling to the door.

"Uh . . . yeah?" he asks in a little boy voice that's equal parts curious and petrified as to why a woman is beckoning him through a bathroom door (is it just me, or does one vocal note sound almost optimistic, as if to ask, hopefully, *fetish*?).

"Do you have any toilet paper?"

"Oh no, Max, I'm sorry, that's it."

New strategy. "Okay, I'll be blunt. Did the flower sniffer leave any feminine hygiene products behind?"

"Huh?"

Theo McArdle is testing my patience. "Do you have any tampons lying around?"

"Oh . . ." It doesn't matter how liberal, how hemp-clad, how sensitive New Age, how crystal enthused, tell a guy you need a tampon and he'll revert to some sniggering neck-free frat boy.

"Uh . . . uh . . . heh . . . I think I have some paper towel. Would that help?"

"Sure. Can you sew six pieces together and line it with silk?" I say.

"I'll go to the store," says Theo, and I feel a little guilty.

"No, no, it's okay. Paper towel is fine," and I almost mean it, but I have to admit, I like the idea of Theo McArdle running through the snow on a mission for me.

"Two minutes!" shouts Theo, slamming the front door.

My bum numbs on the toilet. I toss the soap sliver hand to hand. Theo has no magazines in his bathroom. I do the lean and reach for his can of shaving cream, catching up on my product bilingualism: Je me rase, tu te rases . . .

Nothing to read, nothing to hear. The music in the other room has ended. The faucet doesn't even drip. I shut my eyes for a second, skirt hiked up around my waist, shaving cream in hand, listening to someone else's apartment.

Theo's feet cutting up the front path, snapping the snow, closer and closer, the urgency of a midwife running through the backwoods.

Theo knocks.

"Should I open the door?" he asks.

I attempt a trial reach, but the door is too far and I don't want to stand up and leave a trail of blood on his floor, another somewhat unromantic image.

"Okay, come in, but it ain't pretty," I say.

Theo opens the door a crack and his big red ski jacket backs in, one gloved hand holding a package of Extra Soft Kitteny toilet paper and the other, a box of super-jumbo night pads with wings. When he's taken about five steps, he opens his hands and releases the goods halfway between us: a hostage negotiation.

"I hope that's okay. I wasn't sure what to get –"

"It's fine. Thanks," I say. His jacket stands there, back to me, just nervous talking: "I don't know why the tampons weren't actually on the shelf, so I got these and then when I was paying, I saw tampons behind the counter with the illicit goods, like condoms, but I'd already paid and –"

"Theo," I say. "You can leave."

"Right." The jacket leaves.

I remove a pad from the box. It is the length of a toy train, the thickness of a phone book. When I'm strapped in, I can't close my legs.

Funny, I'm not feeling so amorous any more. Theo's on the couch, two fresh glasses of wine set up in front of him.

With each step toward Theo, the pad makes a sound like two pillows in a dryer.

"I'm gonna head," I say, and he nods like he guessed as much.

"I hope that wasn't too weird," says Theo.

"Weird, yes," I tell him. "But also kind of lovely."

In the foyer, he helps me into my jacket. The space is crowded with hooks dangling fleece and mountain-climbing gear and so we are up against each other.

"Good night," says Theo, and he leans in and kisses me for a while. Deep and familiar, a memory loosed and warm, a kiss in two places at once, present and past.

THE EDITOR IS GLOWERING. *THE EXAMINER* RAN THEIR Ethan Hawke profile two days before the official start of the film festival, screwing us out of our front page for the Entertainment section; somehow they got inside information on when our story would run. Curious.

Still, the Editor won't kill the piece – this is *Ethan Hawke,* after all – so now I have to barf it out within the hour, and the Editor is literally pacing back and forth in her cubicle, which is two steps one way, two steps back, snorting and puffing the whole time.

There's a hush over the newsroom these days. Heads bowed, chairs lowered, soundless lips moving into headsets plotting escapes, resumés firing through the fax machine.

I am not as forward thinking. I sit and calculate my severance every few hours, logging time. Until it comes, perhaps inspired by the goodness I dated last night, I will try to be as honest a writer as possible. This could, of course, finally be the thing that gets me fired. But for now, I look upon it as a new civic duty to unshackle the public from its clanging desire to know. I intend to peel away the layers of celebrity white noise and unearth a snotty, pock-marked human being.

So I describe Ethan Hawke as a "pretentious boho weenie." I alert the world to the fact that his film on Swiss banks is a morally questionable exercise in Oscar-mongering. I put in the Uma stuff, and mention how I tricked him into giving it up by posing as a lesbian organic farmer. I tell the world that he is fat, but I grant him the word *charming*. I say: He's just a person, deluded and self-important, with occasional patches of kindness.

Hit *Send*. I watch as the Editor reads. I put my feet – shoeless – up on the desk and wait.

Then I see it: A handwritten envelope is sitting on stacks of unopened press kits. That's right: blue ink with a postage stamp in the corner. You can still get those – who knew? The determined evenness of the round cursive writing on the thin white airmail paper suggests a tracing page of lines once lay beneath.

Dear Maxime,

I live on the island with my mom who sometimes works in the city. Elaine does art at our school and she is friends with my mom and sometimes I stay with her. She told us that you were sort of her daughter a long time ago. I have seen your photo in the newspaper. I would like to ask you about your job for career day. Do you like your job? How did you get it? How much money do you make? Do you meet famous people, if so, who and where? Were they nice?

Thank you very much for your time.

Sincerely,

Franny Baumgarten

The warmth of Franny Baumgarten's one-time touch on this paper travels right up through my hand and directly into my chest, where it burns. Earnestness always makes me suspicious. A trick? A colleague trying to make me feel guilty for failing to appreciate this life? Are people sniggering, plotting, playing?

One cubicle over, I see Hard-Working Debbie dutifully transcribing an interview with a woman who is balding and has started a support group for other unfortunates. Debbie jerks around suddenly, likely because my crumpled publicity still from *Flintstones Part 3* has proven a worthy projectile, dislodging her headphones.

"Debbie," I ask. "Do you know anything about this? Who put this here?" Debbie's eyes narrow, her lips pucker like a cat's ass.

"I don't know anything about it," she squeals, and I never knew Debbie had such a piercing voice. Across the aisle, Knee-Socks Steve in Sports looks up from behind his wall of novelty sports paraphernalia – whatever keeps the world at bay, Steve – then quickly ducks down.

"Knee-Socks Steve!" I shout. "Did you put this here? Is it a joke?" He burrows behind an oversized foam football that's the precise shape of his head.

Marvin is at the fax machine, electronically begging the CBC for a job, and he makes a nervous *shhh* gesture to his lips.

"Shhh yourself, Marvin!" I scream. "THIS ISN'T FUNNY!" I put the letter in my back pocket and throw myself into my puffy coat. The Big Cheese pokes his head out of his office to see about the noise, stretching his arms, working the jaw in a yawn, yellow hair a mane around his face.

I run toward the exit as the Editor gives me a thumbs-up, a close facsimile of approbation. She likes the Ethan Hawke piece. I remain hired.

My second missive comes with the heading, "Evaluate *Your* Drinking."

Someone has seen fit to double team me this day. Franny Baumgarten isn't enough disarmament; also, I need this, I need this under my door, soggy under my wet boots. A pointed move because were the glossy green leaflet a casual find from the mailbox, I might think it a generic flyer, an unsolicited piece of junk mail. But it is clearly under my door because someone put it there to lie in wait like the cat I've resisted.

"Would you like to know how *your* drinking compares to *other* Canadians? Take this simple test to find out."

I remove the Baumgarten letter from my back pocket and lay it on the stack of magazines that's substituting for a coffee table. The flyer is green and determined. It lies in my lap, unfolded like a triptych menu at some quantity-oriented American restaurant.

What would you do?

I do this: I twist my free, faux fountain pen with *The Daily* written on the side, the one I received in lieu of a Christmas bonus last year. I give it an old-fashioned lick of the nib, which is ballpoint, and bad to lick. I spit and begin the exam.

"What was your drinking like during a typical week in the last year? List roughly how many drinks you have on each day of a typical week and add up the total."

Monday . . . Mondays are tough, I think, because Mondays are the first day back at work, so I admit it, I treat myself a little. Let's say three little V&Ts.

Tuesday . . . Tuesdays are a good TV night, and a lady must have a beer with good TV. Four beers.

Wednesday . . . Wednesday you can feel the ground shaking as the weekend lumbers closer. You have to toast the weekend! It's been so long! Come hither, weekend! C'm along! Three to five.

Thursday . . . It's okay to indulge on Thursday because Friday morning is pretty much the weekend, am I wrong? Everyone's tired Friday, why not me? Five to ten.

Friday . . . TGIF, sports fans! Five to twelve. In my defence, I try to clarify, writing, *Less numerous when drugs are available*, but the space on the form is too small.

Saturday . . . How to soften the blow from Friday night: un peu de vin. Five to nine, 'cause often I'm bagged.

Sunday . . . Sadness because it's Sunday. Have a Scotch to welcome the possibility of the upcoming week. Two to three.

Turns out I'm drinking a bit more than my fellow Canadians. According to the pie chart, this consumption of fifteen or more drinks in a week – or thirty, in my case – puts one firmly in the top percentile. Top percentile. Usually a desirable place to be, and yet it's the darkest colour of the pie, a black, unappetizing little slice. The lightest colour is a healthy apple green, for those 58 per cent in the zero-drinks category.

I'm shocked by this number. Are you telling me, Government, that 58 per cent of Canadians aren't liquoring themselves up at least once a week? Are you saying the majority of Canadian women aren't lubing the joints, warming the cockles, doing what they must to get through? Telling me that a chilly woman in Churchill, Manitoba, who sees polar bears waddle down Main Street, who glances around the shack and suddenly realizes she doesn't know the whereabouts of her bite-sized baby boy – are you telling me this Canadian woman doesn't hightail it to the liquor cabinet and suck back a wine cooler while she's waiting for the police? Are you saying the skinny Quebec City art student in Olive Oyl footwear and negligible bangs, the girl who collects antique milk bottles and hasn't eaten more than a bagel a day for three years – are you telling me she doesn't (when the roommates are at band practice, when the phone didn't ring when it should have) – are you telling me she doesn't carve an opening out of that box of Niagara-region gasoline-tinged Chardonnay her sonofabitch drummer ex-boyfriend left behind – are you telling me she doesn't just drink that shit down like a hungry puppy at the teat?

I don't buy it. People lie to the Government, because they think the Government lies to them.

(Except for Franny Baumgarten's parents. Her mother gave her a fresh blue ballpoint pen, a pristine pad of white airmail paper that felt like tissue in her hand. She sat opposite Franny, reading an historical novel as Franny wrote, her feet swinging, hmmmhmmming in a way that would be annoying on a less brilliant child but only makes Franny's mom love her more. Franny Baumgarten's mother is drinking tea.)

"Chance of negative consequences related to number of drinks per week . . ." I have a 38.1 per cent chance of "negative consequences," the kelly green spike, just slightly less ominous than those drinking fifty-one or more drinks per week. Their negative consequences are at 43.5 per cent. "Physical health, outlook on life, friends/social life . . ."

What do these brochure writers mean by this? Negative consequences?

I ponder the phrase *negative consequences* in the kitchen. I consider negative consequences as I open my cupboard and pour a vodka and tonic into a giant plastic cup decorated with a cartoon of Jackie Chan and the words COMING

SOON – HI-YA 2! I imagine really drunk people sticking knives into toasters or running lawn mowers over their feet. Negative consequences, I think, fingering the pamphlet with one hand, drinking with the other. Flipping and sipping, I get to the final page. "*Your* choices about drinking." A few options, with boxes to tick: "My drinking is fine for now." "I will think about changing my drinking." "I will reduce my drinking to a low-risk level." "I will contact my local assessment and referral centre to find out about programs and groups that can help me."

Me. Me. Me. All this first person – what to make of this? At the compound, Tree Ridington-Raymont's mom made all the girls gather on the beach to welcome Tree's period. I once had a teacher who told me a bottle cap was as worthy of study as a poem by Keats. "One plus one could be three," she said. "Each to his – or her! – own." Relative. Evaluation. Consequences. I wonder what these words mean to Franny Baumgarten.

I leave all the boxes blank.

FOR THOSE NURSING HANGOVERS OF THE TINY-quasimodoisringingabellinmyskull variety, there is nothing like an 8:00 a.m. screening of a three-hour wordless Russian/German/French co-production about Lenin. This is the film festival, and the idea of covering the film festival generates a strong response from Mohsen, who shouts after me as I leave his cab, "You have the best job in the world! Only in North America can you watch movies and get rich!"

Theo McArdle called last night to talk film festival, and we drank wine over the phone. He has booked several afternoons off work and plans to go from theatre to theatre until he finds a single ticket available. Without knowing the name of the movie or the country that made it, he will just chow down: Korean, Indian, even British. He doesn't care. He's got the hunger. I did this before, when I was a waitress, a temp, a student. I did it because I cared about Soukorov's mottled light and I liked the thawing boot smell of a winter movie theatre and I imagined some kind of small current running through the place, knitting together all the people inside, fraught and scared and laughing at the same thing.

After the *Saturday Night Fever* incident, Elaine made arrangements to have movies sent over from the mainland. Every Friday night at the island community centre, Elaine would thread the reels with her chewed fingernails. All the kiddie freaks sat upright, noses running and Salish sweaters touching, and for two solid hours there were no discussions about how we felt, no rap sessions, no consensus to be reached. Just Lauren Bacall's tucked-in waist, her unmoving sheet of hair. Darth Vader ventilating. The Black Stallion rearing against his chains. The first moment, the moment the movie started, was like a bathtub filling in a silent room. The rush of drawing hot water, the ear-stuffing volume of it, and then the stopping, the silent space before the step inside.

But it's not so much like that for critics. Critics go to press screenings in small rooms filled with other critics, cranky, caffeine-fed, light-starved, and tired. I feel sorry for the movies; surely their parents don't know the bitter sitters with whom they've placed their babies.

Day Three of the film festival and I've slept through large segments of a Mexican film, a Czech film, and something animated and possibly Japanese that starred a large, lusty eggplant. I've attended a few cocktail receptions at random embassies – Oman has a film industry; who knew? – and Sunera and I have run into several accidental parties because every bar in the city is rented out for festival events. To leave your house is to wander into the mirth, like it or not. Mostly, it's likeable.

Following the Taiwanese female ejaculation movie, I walk a few blocks to the press-only screening of a big American film, starring Nicole Kidman and a British guy. The theatre is much fuller than it was for the Japanese eggplant. I'm sitting near the Sludge Monster, the most mushroomy of all the critics, a man swear-to-God named Darcy Sludge who has been writing for the city's lefty weekly since people got lefty. Without provocation, Sludge will tell you (and I don't recommend provocation) how he knows Pauline Kael, and how he studied in Paris with André Bazin and he will tell you these facts, already unappetizing, as he unpacks a hot meal onto your armrest. Be it morning, noon, or night, the Sludge Monster carries with him a steaming Styrofoam-boxed feast in a padded blue sack. He opens it up, unleashing the stench of boiled meat. He ignores me, perhaps it's the toque I have pulled down over my face, but proceeds to engage the gentleman to his left, Indie Magazine Guy (smudged black-rimmed glasses and the exhausted air of someone who stays up night after night clicking out unread editorials bemoaning the state of film subsidies) with his analysis of a Dogme film: "It's no Fassbinder!" He actually uses the phrase *mise en scène*. I pull the toque lower.

The American critics have descended on the city with loud voices and laminated press passes swinging from their necks, travelling in packs, joshing and waving at one another, and smiling smiling smiling. Behind me, three Americans have moved on from complaining about the weather and are complimenting Canadian shopping. "They have Restoration Hardware now. It's so much easier than Cannes."

"True. They have everything here."

"Except J. Crew," a woman with a southern drawl points out, correctly.

Sludge unleashes a cartoon trail of smoky tendrils from his vat of boiled meat that circle and drift across the screen, creating pretty shadows and nausea as the movie starts.

I stay fairly awake. It's a period piece about a mother in a fog-shrouded estate and a death and it ends just as the Sludge Monster is licking at the corners of his empty container. The lights come on and volunteers with a nervous air of efficiency set up tables and chairs at the front of the theatre. A line of studio executives and publicists, shampooed and frowning, marches in from the sidelines. They're blocking their prize, keeping it concealed until the last possible moment. Finally reaching the front of the theatre, the executive crowd breaks and scatters like Busby Berkeley chorus girls to reveal the sweet hidden centre: Nicole Kidman, the Director, and Another Guy. The audience applauds Canadianly, which is to say with both indifference and awe, and not for very long.

Nicole Kidman is wearing (I write this down) a red silk Chinese dress. She is tall, with wire-rimmed glasses, half-vamp, half-librarian (I write this down, too: I could use it!). She looks at her feet, at the table, at her hands, which shake lightly.

There are two kinds of press conference questions. The first is the starfucker question, which includes queries like: Why did you do this movie? How did you get in character? Where did the idea come from? Celebs listen to these questions, and like the cartoon about the dog who only hears its name when the sentence is, Why did you eat my Christmas turkey, Bobo?, what they hear is, How did you get to be so fabulous? And that's the question they answer, tails wagging.

The second type of question happens only at film festivals. It's the Sludgey, *mise en scène*, I studied with Andrew Sarris question. It involves words like *auteur* and inappropriate references to *Battleship Potemkin*, as in: My question is for Ron Howard. Were you purposely responding to the dystopic midnight fantasy of Agnes Varda when you made *Backdraft II*? The questions are usually delivered with a French or a Polish accent, and they make everyone feel better about their lives, especially the askers, though actors never answer those questions, deferring instead to the adored daddy figure, the director.

"It was a lot of fun making this movie. We were like a family," says Nicole Kidman in a quaking Australian monotone with all the conviction of a fifth grader delivering a speech on ichthyology to her science class. "We all played practical jokes on each other. It was fun."

Family. I click through the screen on my cellphone, reminding myself whose calls I haven't returned. Elaine. My dad. My dad in a tent in Arizona.

A moustachioed little man who smells of saltwater cologne is sitting next to me fighting with his digital recorder. "Fuckity fuck," he repeats, pressing buttons, holding the box up to his ear, frantically shaking it so hard his isosceles elbow pokes in and out of my arm. On my other side, a handsome, greying woman in a black turtleneck exactly like mine is nodding beneath headphones, listening to the translation: I hear Nicole Kidman murmuring, "Just like a family . . . really good time . . ." Then Italian: "Bueno . . . familia . . ." The seats are too close together. Her headphones nearly brush my cheek, and the man continues shaking the recorder like a maraca: "Fuckity fuck." He's sweating now, sweat mixing with the aftershave; a scent like tidal pools. The woman is nodding, listening hard: "Bueno . . . bueno." I think, I could be her in twenty years.

My mind drifts. I feel a guilt twitch over the unreturned phone calls. How could I call my dad back? What could I possibly tell him about all of this?

I look at Nicole Kidman and I realize I know more about her life right now than I do about my father's. But I only know the details, the breakups and the box-office figures: names, dates, and injuries. These are the boundaries of my job, and they're closing in. My palms moisten. My shoulders shudder. I look at my right hand; it's in the air. Somehow, I can't help it; the hand doesn't care about professional repercussions. It waves frantically.

I need to know something.

"Lady in black," says the Czar. Most women in the room answer to that description, but he means me. I stand up, my heart racing a little under the collective sweep of eyes. The notebook paper clots in my palm.

"My question is for Nicole Kidman," I say.

"Speak up, please," says the Czar.

"My question is for Nicole Kidman," I shout. I clear my throat. "What's it like?"

The Czar gives Ms. Kidman a quick, apologetic glance that she doesn't catch, plucking at her water glass with her bony fingers. "Can you clarify your question, please?" asks the Czar.

"What's it like?" I'm just going for it now, just letting it all out. "I mean, when everyone thinks your husband is gay, and then he leaves you, and you're a billionaire and not untalented but in a business where talent doesn't really matter and, and, you had a miscarriage that we all know about." The strangeness of this strikes me suddenly and I say it again, "Somehow we all know about that. Every single person in this room knows and, you, and you have children, right? You have two children?"

Nicole Kidman looks up, straight at me, unsmiling, her white skin reflecting the lights of the cameras that line the sides of the theatre.

"My question is, What's it like to be you?" It's a bad question. I recognize it as such even without the Sludge Monster's little choking sounds. But it occurs to me that that's my problem; I don't know what it's like to be anyone else. I can't imagine any other life but this one. I'm being stabbed to death by my point of view. Does anyone else ever feel like that? So desperate to break your own borders, so frantic you want to smash through someone else's stomach and crawl in? Maybe Nicole Kidman knows something about this; a person who walks in other people's bodies for a living must, surely?

Did I just say that out loud?

I sit down.

The room is very, very quiet. The Czar whispers something in Nicole Kidman's ear and she shakes her head. The Italian woman moves ever so slightly away from me. Nicole Kidman leans forward, mouth over the microphone. In a girlish Australian voice, she says softly, "It's probably not that different from being you."

I doubt that, but I write it down anyway.

"Next question!"

The Royal Ontario Museum needs cash, it seems. Otherwise, why would hundreds of publicists, journalists, film buyers, and even one or two actual filmmakers be allowed to mingle with the Egyptian mummies, resting empty crantinis next to displays of Roman glass *circa* 870?

A DJ is in the centre of the gallery under red strobes, headset held to one ear, neck bobbing to electronica, music robots would make out to. This is one of the hottest tickets of the film festival, according to the free ticket that arrived in my mailbox at *The Daily*. Film festival party passes marked Exclusive and Non-Transferrable and Arrive Early are circulated like Chinese restaurant takeout menus at this time of year. Studios run off excess invitations to ensure hundreds of people are left at the door, creating the illusion of desire. The star will enter from the alleyway.

This party is hosted by an American film company, so the drinks are bottomless and back behind a red rope next to the Etruscan jewellery collection – so *The Examiner* informs me as he sprints past – Nicole Kidman is nursing a Perrier and waiting to go back to Hollywood.

The music is so loud that no one is talking, no lips move as bodies snake through one another. Theo appears, hands me a vodka. Inviting Theo here is a little like inviting him to my cubicle. I am at work, really, and usually I go alone or cling to the corners with Sunera and Marvin. But how easy it was to conjure up Theo: I called him, and he came. I wonder if everyone can see that he doesn't fit in, calm and cool in vintage cowboy shirt and jeans. I don't want to talk to anyone else, or introduce him to the media mass. He could get tainted, start talking about Screamin' Jay Hawkins, and be mistaken for simply charming, or just simple. He could embarrass me. Wait: what I mean is, I could embarrass him.

Theo mouths something I can't make out. He signals and I follow him through the crowd of men in pastel dress shirts and women in stiletto boots and black cocktail dresses, each differentiated from the next by only the smallest detail: a bow at the waist, a piece of silver at the neck. These dresses are so simple – knee-length, wispy, sleeveless – and so expensive; thousands of dollars wrapping the reed bodies of twenty-seven-year-old women. Wealth is the pulse of the city right now, and an adjacent nervousness; heads thrown back laughing loudly, eyes darting suspiciously toward the next person, as if the fun might be mugged out from under each of them.

The crowd thins until there is no one but Theo and me in a dark hall. Glass cases of Byzantine coins are lit like crusty subway tokens. A security guard steps out of the shadows, gives us a look, and steps away.

"Money is the oldest language," says Theo. "After the iconoclast period, Jesus started turning up on coins. That's him with the halo and the book of gospels."

"It seems sort of perverse, doesn't it? Jesus on a coin?" I say. "What's that thing about moneylenders in the temple?"

He nods, smiles. Theo tells me these coins are partially made of fabric.

"You are a nerd," I say. He shrugs and I'm wishing he would take one step closer, his body meeting mine at the waist. "It's amazingly cool just how uncool you are."

"I sometimes come here on my lunch. My office is just over there," he gestures toward the university campus spread out behind the museum.

"You know most people go to McDonald's on lunch, right?" Theo doesn't mind being teased.

A pocket of gigglers moves in next to us. They are a self-contained unit, moving without any acknowledgment that we share the same space. One by one, each gleaming young thing hangs its head over a case, as if examining the coins. The sporty grinner looks, then a gangly redheaded woman in a pink dress, then a man in a pinstriped suit. They are so dressed up that I think, Grown-ups. But no, they are a decade younger than me. I'm impressed by their reverence for history until I hear the redhead say, "God, my front teeth are totally numb." They're doing coke lines off the coins. This detail hits Theo at the same time it hits me.

"Let's go," I tell him. He's very still, his face darkening. Something in this look is unnerving. What if Theo has heroic delusions? I grab his hand and start walking. He walks too, but slowly, then stops and turns.

"What's wrong with you people?" he says, almost curiously, as if examining a foreign custom: *Why do locals dress this way on Sundays? What is the significance of that finger gesture?*

Pinstripes looks at Theo, completely baffled. The other two are laughing, not meanly and not at Theo, just laughing the way high people laugh.

"Show some respect," says Theo, with anger this time.

Pinstripes is surprised at the tone. Theo drops my hand, a gesture that means he might make a fist. I wonder in a detached way if I'm in the presence of a man moment, a show-down. I see the cases shattering, glass falling, a coin rolling around the corner onto the dance floor to be crushed under a high heel.

"What did you say, man?" says Pinstripes. I notice that he is taller than Theo, but rangier. I have a strange thought: Theo could take him.

"Don't be so arrogant," says Theo. Pinstripes considers this. He looks like a man whose synapses are firing for the first time in a while, trying to make some connection. And I realize at that moment that there cannot be a fight because this guy has no idea what he has done to offend Theo. There is nothing at stake for him.

"Come on, man," murmurs his friend, who is no longer grinning but looking worried, eyes darting.

Pinstripes licks his lips. The redhead muffles a giggle. The moment has gone from loaded to pathetic.

"Whatever," says Pinstripes and he turns his back on us.

I hear Theo exhale and I realize he is nervous. He is not a fighter, but he cared enough to pretend.

Then he is pulling my hand, leading me back through the robot music, the undancing crowd. Outside, we move down the red-carpet stairs and away from the party into the cold air. Drivers lean on the hoods of limousines, smoking. Theo is still holding my hand.

"Are you okay?" I ask him. He nods. He's walking with purpose.

"You were very alpha male back there," I tell him, lame attempt to lighten the mood. He doesn't say anything. "In a good way."

He stops, drops my hand again. We are on a dark foot path that leads from the museum to the university, surrounded by trees. "Those people are assholes," says Theo gruffly.

"I know," I say, but he seems strangely harsh, a different person than the one I've been imagining. Maybe I've spotted it, the self-righteousness that comes with idealism.

"They were just high, I guess," I say, a bit defensive, thinking of all the things I've done that are worse than snorting cocaine off artifacts.

Theo exhales again, and out goes that grimness from his face. He looks at me, not angry but puzzled, exasperated. "How can you stand working in that world?" he asks. His voice is steady, but I feel judged anyway. I shake my head. I nod. I don't want to think about it. I don't want to explain, reason myself into mattering to him. What I want is to think about the fact that no part of our bodies is touching for the first time since the night began. I reach out and unbutton his wool jacket, move my hands around to his back.

"Max," he says, pushing me away slightly. "What are you doing?" A question that could mean all kinds of things, none of which I have an answer for, so I pull him toward me, his waist warm through his shirt. This time he doesn't stop me. His body relaxes, and we are unbuttoning, fighting the layers until pressed to one another, tongues and surfaces moving from gentle to hard.

Theo's heart is beating through his shirt.

"Maybe you should come see my office," he says.

"But will I get free drinks? Because my work may be evil, but there are perks." Theo laughs and gives me another rough kiss.

We duck through an alley next to the planetarium. My heels slip on the melting snow and Theo takes my elbow. Formal, a gesture for a blind woman.

The university is quiet, gothic under ice. We follow the path past the Anglican altar toward the ugly part of campus, the part that isn't in the image of old mother England, but

1960s utilitarian, the cruel future of the new world. A massive grey cinder block where Theo goes every day to work.

The doors are open. On a Saturday night, a few bloodshot students mill around the atrium, drinking Coke, reading on couches in silence.

Theo runs a security pass through a small electronic box that unlocks his office door.

I don't know what I expect from science; time machines, monkeys regenerating themselves in plastic chambers. I do not expect this. Theo's office is the size of an elevator, as windowless and grey. He turns on a small chrome lamp by an old telephone, the kind with the earpiece attached by a chord. A stainless-steel desk covered in papers and a computer. Walls of books, stacked on top of each other instead of in rows.

"This room is completely depressing," I tell him.

"Isn't it?" He shuts the door and pulls out the desk chair for me. "What did you think my office would look like?"

I mention the monkeys. He laughs, circling the room, straightening books. "There are two ways to be a quantum physicist," he says. "One is theoretical physics, which means math, and the other is experimental physics, where you get to build expensive machines to test and see if the math is right."

"Time machines," I say. I pick a pad of graph paper off the desk where Theo has scribbled numbers in parentheses, and letters, and more numbers. "You're on the math side. These papers are like props from a movie."

Theo shakes his head. "I'm a neophyte."

"At everything?" I'm half-kidding, playing at movie banter, but Theo ignores the note of irony, sits down at my feet. He spins the chair until his face is next to my knees.

"I have an idea," he says. The room is quiet and hot with closed air. The lightbulb in the desk lamp hisses faintly.

Theo unzips one of my boots, determined. He unzips my other boot and I alert, my body rigid, waiting. Fast, now, he rolls down my tights, pushes up my skirt with one hand. He looks me in the face first, a look I don't recognize from Theo: a focus, control. Then he is between my legs, his tongue brushing, thrashing, and stopping, starting. I close my eyes, gripping the edges of the chair, reluctant to go over, to hand off into this perfect, forgotten release.

Outside the Big Cheese's office, I scan *The Daily* front page: STANDOFF: TENT CITY GROWING, BIG BOX RETAILER GRUMBLING.

The Big Cheese waves me in. His large, blockish hands click at e-mail, while his skull is fastened to a headset on which he's chatting as Ravel murmurs out of a Bang & Olufsen CD player on the wall, a stereo designed to look like art. The whole office resembles the interior of a sports car, black and low lit, dashboard lighting his chin from the desk. It's staggering what the human body is capable of now, how many places our heads can be at one time.

I ease down into a black leather chair that puts me several inches lower than the Big Cheese. He mutters and curses, then disentangles from all the electronic wires, runs his hands over his head to make sure he's free of plugs and sparks, spins to face me.

"So why are we here?" he asks. He is famous for speaking in riddles and rhetorical questions.

This one is easy, however. "Because my editor called a meeting," I say. I scan his desk for a severance cheque, and glance out the door to see if security is waiting to escort me from the building. Surely, with my bad behaviour of late, I would be one of the first to get laid off if the Cheese was cleaning house before the big takeover. Yesterday the Editor caught me opening a beer bottle with my mouse.

"Ah yes. She's on her way, I believe," says the Cheese. He checks his ear for technology one more time, shaking his neck like a swimmer just out of the pool. I expect a tiny silicon chip to fall out.

"What's going on with you these days?" he asks. I never know how to answer that question and the Big Cheese always asks it. Is he looking for a wacky single gal anecdote, or does he want me to throw him some story ideas, get professional?

I give him a combo: part self-deprecating personal story, but work related: "I accidentally on purpose lit a filing cabinet on fire with my cigarette. Did you catch that?"

Cheese smirks, almost approvingly, then goes blank.

"What's going on with you?"

As usual, he ignores this question. On a shelf behind him, Cheese has a miniature bust of George Orwell, sporting a Queen's University baseball cap.

"She's saying you're late a lot, and I'm supposed to reprimand you," he says, picking up a pink squeezable ball designed to release stress. Someone has drawn an angry face on it with a V between the eyebrows. The face is smudged from squeezing, mouthless. "What do you think?"

"I think I am late a lot."

"Do you want to know what I think?"

"Umm –"

"I don't really care if you're late. I don't care if you come in at all as long as your stories are filed on time and they're your usual calibre," he says. Squeeze, squeeze. "That piece on you and Ethan Hawke was very funny."

"You're not going to fire me?" I ask.

"Why should I fire you?"

"Uh . . . because I nap at the office. I'm surly. I'm . . ." I'm searching here. "I'm late a lot."

Big Cheese silent laughs. "Well, you chose the right profession. If you want to get fired for that behaviour, you should work in a bank."

We sit there, the squeeze toy wheezing.

"You know," he says finally, "you should write about your bad work habits. A column about lighting a filing cabinet on fire could be funny. Maybe you need to move more in the Allissa Allan direction, dating and mating. Girl stuff. We could sell some ads. Loft furnishings, martini mixes –"

I laugh, but he doesn't. I realize with a start that the Cheese, a man who interviewed Gorbachev in the Kremlin, is serious. My head starts pounding. "Is thirty-four still a girl?" I ask.

The Cheese sighs. "You're only as old as you feel, Max. Quick, who's the most famous Max in movies?"

"That's what Woody Allen's friend calls him in *Annie Hall*."

"You're right, Max." Cheese always asks me the Annie Hall question and looks pleased when I answer it. I wonder if he knows that the Woody Allen character hates being called Max, that it's an arbitrary, meaningless nickname.

This darting conversation alarms me. In the past, the Cheese has always been placid, sleepy even, but resolute. I know how much he wanted to run this paper. There were rumours of scheming and plotting, trips to England and confidences betrayed at the news bureau where we were working. It is a talent of the very rich and very educated to be viciously ambitious while appearing disinterested at the same time. But today, he is something different. The paper is dying, and he is desperate. Baby Baron has the attention span of a spider monkey and may already be onto the next thing: the women in Australia are much hotter than the women here, it seems. It occurs to me that I might be witnessing a man on the cusp. I've strolled into the den of someone whose dream is floating away from him.

Cheese starts rambling: "Do you know how busy I am? See that phone?" On a desk entirely hidden by papers and magazines and squeeze toys, the far left corner holds a sleek silver phone, accentuated by a moat of empty desk space around it.

"Nice phone," I say.

"That phone is a direct line between our esteemed chairman and this paper. It's a bloodline, Max. I have one at home too. Any time, day or night, the chairman can call me and tell me what to do with my paper. Include a photo of some lady friend of his on the society page. Change the font . . ." He closes his eyes. "Computers, Max. A person should never feel alone in this world." His eyes snap open. "Do you know what time it is in London, Max?"

"Umm . . . Six hours ahead?"

"No, Miss Montessori, five hours, five hours from here. Which means at four in the morning here, the chairman is up and on the computer and he's got a few things to say before I've even had a shit and a shave." He grabs the ball, squeezes once with intent to kill, then winds up and barrels it right over my head, where it smashes a wall pockmarked with squeeze-ball dents.

"It's a difficult time, Max," he says, a vague statement. I am stunned that he is speaking so frankly to me, an entertainment reporter. Either this is a testament to the complete irrelevance of my work – surely a real reporter would not be privy to an editor-in-chief's breakdown – or his own budding madness.

I think about Marvin out there, chewing his fingernails to the quick, and I have to ask, "So is the paper going to be sold? Are we all going to lose our jobs?"

Cheese sighs. "We need more advertisers, Max. People don't change their reading habits easily."

"No one's buying the paper?"

Suddenly, he's rooting through the files on his desk. Photographs of ex-wives and children rattle. He mutters, "Maybe they're right. Maybe there isn't room for another paper in this country."

A light rap and the Editor enters, drops down next to me, and sits with her hands clasped in front of her so tight she could turn air into diamonds. The Big Cheese finds what he's looking for, sheer delight on his face: "Ah-ha!" He produces an old muffin from under the papers and holds it up triumphantly. The room is very quiet, but for the masticating man in the rumpled suit.

"We received a call yesterday from a certain studio," says the Editor through her stumpy teeth. "They were quite irate about your behaviour at a certain press conference where journalists were expressly forbidden to ask certain questions. They feel you harassed the talent. Nicole Kidman, to be exact."

"What did they say?"

The Editor clears her throat. "They said, 'We invited her to dinner, and she defecated on our table.'"

"They didn't say that."

"Actually, they said shit."

The Big Cheese coughs, as if swallowing a laugh. Suddenly his hand juts out toward the silver phone and he thrusts the receiver to his ear, panicked. A beat, relief, and he puts it down.

"Still working," he says to no one in particular.

"We, of course, believe in journalistic freedom," says the Editor. "However, we cannot live under the char-ahd that these are not perilous times at the paper."

It's rare to experience a real moment. It's rare to feel like you're being thrust into a future you haven't lived before, final frame of a movie, lights on, and it's just you again. But when you're in a moment, in a real potentially life-altering situation, that's usually when you start considering the banal. The thing I should be thinking about is whether this conversation threatens the sacred ideals of a free press, or just my place within it, but what I'm thinking instead is how amazing it is the Editor will always find a way to include at least one word requiring British pronunciation in any conversation. I wonder if I could trick her into one more before the meeting is over.

The Cheese eats on.

I say, "Don't you wish muffins came in some other kind of packaging? Like that shiny silver stuff, what's it called? You know . . ."

"Tinfoil?" says the Big Cheese, like this is the most normal conversation in the world.

"Yes, but what's the other name for it . . ."

The Editor is getting annoyed, clasping and reclasping her hands, veins emerging on her forearms.

"They pulled their advertising," says the Editor. "And I want to know what you're going to do about it, Maxime."

"Do?" I ask, looking back and forth at the two of them for clarification. Neither meets my eye. Silence, and then finally the Big Cheese sucks the last crumbs of the muffin from the paper and murmurs sleepily, "Come on, Max. Just be good."

My head fills in the blanks: Good like a muffin. Good like a girl. "What are you saying?" I ask slowly. "Is this about me or the paper?"

Cheese says nothing. He balls up the muffin wrapper and tosses it against the wall where it falls to the floor, next to a small army of squeeze balls.

"Very well then," says the Editor, standing up with the air of someone who has pressing matters to attend. "And not that it's germane to anything," she says as she heads out the door, "but the phrase is al-u-min-i-um foil."

THERE'S AN ART HAPPENING HAPPENING AND ALL I feel like doing is going home and looking up ethics in the dictionary, but somehow I'm part of it and this bumpy bus ride is hurting my bones. Blow Lounge isn't a place, but a "concept," according to the flyers we're grasping, and out in this "enviro-interface" we will be "perturbed, moved, perhaps even disgusted" by six new works by six new artists known as ACCLIMITIZE, one of whom is the Ex. I did not want to come.

"Where the hell is this going? I haven't been on a short-bus since I was in the Special Olympics," I say to Sunera. We're elbow to elbow, lurching along some muddy pathway that's either north, south, east, or west of the city, if you're one of those people who can determine such things. On our right sits an amusement park, deserted for the winter. Plastic mountains glimmering pink and blue against the white sky, a stilled Yo-Yo, and naked tracks of roller coasters, teeth bared.

"Sorry," says Sunera as we hit a pothole in the mud and she lands in my lap. The two young women in front of us with geometric retro-Eighties haircuts (red and green, perhaps left over from Christmas?) lose grasp of their water bottles and scream as they drench themselves. A guy with bolts in his earlobes and a T-shirt that reads, I Want to Be a Millionaire, And That's My Final Answer! is talking to himself across the aisle, laughing and rocking back and forth.

"Is that guy insane or is he art?" I whisper to Sunera, not without admiration. She peers across me – slams me, really, as we lurch over another pothole – then shakes her head.

"Cellular implant. You get the phone permanently sutured to your eardrum, like a cochlear implant. Latest thing." I cannot tell if she's kidding.

The bus careens off the muddy path and into a parking lot, next to several other buses flanking a huge white tent. Flat, brown fields tinged with snow on all sides, and in the distance, a half-finished housing development, rows of tiny faux-Edwardian houses built from Styrofoam light enough to sprout wings and flap away. The city is spreading.

We descend: middle-aged men in fabrics too synthetic for skin older than twenty, hard lipstick-mouthed women in long second-hand black leather jackets, girls in crocheted granny hats, managers of doomed co-operative galleries and editors at art magazines printed half in English, half in French. Feet in platform zipped-and-chained boots stick in the mud. Mouths frantically puffing cigarettes, trying to get enough tobacco sustenance on this six-minute walk between the school bus and the tent, just enough nicotine to make what's coming up bearable. Someone thought it would be a good idea to expose a child to this world and there he is, a scowling toddler whose neck vertebrae are collapsing under ten pounds of dreadlocks, a sock monkey tucked under his arm.

I shove Sunera ahead of me.

"Your idea," I tell her, inhaling one last time and tossing my half-finished cigarette into the mud.

Before we get inside, I hear a loud, slow boom, like a native drum being beaten.

"Motherfucker," Sunera says under her breath.

The shiny black floor of the tent is covered with naked bodies. It's a casual scene, naked bodies like a pile of leaves lying one atop the other, a heaving, chilly (so says the field of nipples) pile of human bodies of all different colours and, presumably, languages (funding). Legs crossed, lying on their backs, sides, stomachs, tongues out, tongues in. They shift a little, moan occasionally through the drum boom.

It's hard to differentiate the good bodies from the bad bodies, which is, of course, the first thing I do whenever I see a naked body. Is that what a body looks like these days? Is that person considered beautiful? Are those gathers, those lines, those nodules and hairy patches acceptable? Could I get away with that?

Banners flap from the ceiling. Words in black on white: HISTORY. MEMORY. BODY. HISTORY. MEMORY. BODY.

"Not those old thematic chestnuts," whispers Sunera as we make our way around the bodies.

"I wrote many an undergrad paper on the shifting metonymic female body fifteen years ago," I whisper back. "Would you say that girl's fat?"

"Which one?"

"The fat one."

So we're laughing a little – is that such a crime? One of the bodies thinks so, a blonde with a tattoo of an Egyptian ankh on her shoulder. She makes a shhhh gesture, elbowing a burly black guy.

"Your oppressive gesture is purely performative, so I forgive you," I tell her, and someone behind me applauds lightly.

I turn. "I'm not part of the happening," I tell a balding gentleman with a handlebar moustache.

He leans in: "Exactly!"

Sunera and I leave the room through a slit in the tent, into a smaller space that's pulsating with house music and bus riders sipping out of miniature plastic wineglasses. On one wall is a large canvas, about fifteen feet tall, entirely black except for a small computer chip glued to the centre and a fist-sized cartoon owl in the lower left corner. I look at the tag: "Facilitate/destroy – $6,500." My God. It's the Ex. He's finally done it. All those drawing classes I paid for: "I don't mind, I really don't," I'd say, and he'd scowl and snatch the cheque from my hand like it was payment for rental on his balls that I kept in a little jar on a windowsill.

I wonder if people could tell, looking at this computer chip, that the artist once drew a model's naked back and made me cry it was so beautiful. I wonder what he did with those canvases of stars and trees and me. I imagine them propped up against a wet wall in a basement somewhere, growing toxic mould.

I do a scan for him, try to pull him out from all the other skinny tall boy-men in vintage horn-rimmed glasses.

"Did you admire the piece?" a voice croons in my ear, and there he is, Theo McArdle, working his way down my spine with one hand. I'm surprised, but relieved too. I don't have to look for the Ex any more. I am distracted.

"I believe it will require repeated exposure over time to transcend received notions of stature," I say. "Speaking of which, did you transcend space and time today?"

Theo smiles his shaggy smile. "No, but I did have some success with a problem I've been working on for three years. Did you use your wit to decimate another innocent movie star?"

I'm loving this repartee, preparing a comeback when Sunera and Marvin pop up on either side, dragging us toward a dim corner. Marvin's got offerings: a glass of this, a vial of that. I look at Theo McArdle, wondering how we fit into his day, nervous how he might see me. Just a little, I want the Theo from that other night to stop things, to draw lines. There's a moment where he pulls back, a shadow of good judgment moves across his face, then he shrugs: "What the hell. I had a good day." This is the opposite of how everyone else uses drugs – bad day, more drugs – and another reason Theo McArdle is approaching perfection.

Four coked-up people chattering in a tent otherwise filled with subdued art types sound like a bunch of cats in a bag, and that's the feeling in my head too, each thought scrambling to get on top of the last one, all pads, paws, and claws, and I'm taking in the room, eyes sweeping for the Ex and trying to imagine what I would say to him, if I'm the kind of person who could wish him well, but all I see is that aging Canadian rock star who is at every event. He's over in the corner staring at a laundry pile of stuffed animals.

Theo McArdle has his hand on my shoulder and I like that feeling, it's vaguely romantic except for the tap, tap, tapping part or is that just the drum sound leaking in from the body room?

Only it's not Theo McArdle tapping. I turn and the tapping is attached to a woman, a short woman with white hair past her shoulders, a gentle beluga smile on her small face. I can't quite put these pieces together, can't quite figure out how this face fits in this room. It's the poncho that cinches it, a Haida meets Technicolor Dreamcoat cape of blood red with a huge black raven sewn from buttons across the front, abalone squares for eyes.

"Elaine," I gasp, staring at the raven, concentrating on the buttons and threads to try to focus, keep my breath inside. "What are you doing here?"

She opens up her arms, and there it is, a big red and black raven bidding me to bend, waiting to enfold me. So I go – wouldn't you? I hand my empty wine cup to Theo McArdle and down I go, into her arms, into the distant smell of cedar and paint. I push and rock, like I'm trying to get past the bone of her neck and chest plate. Elaine doesn't laugh, or say anything, she just keeps her arms around me, hands firm on my back.

Elaine has a rental car, and as we are leaving, she offers to drive us to the city. I hesitate. At the happening, she had engaged lightly with the group, smiling politely and cocking her head to hear above the music: "I'm sorry? I didn't get that." There was nothing to get, really, just druggy chatter about the day, the bad art, the air. It's not shame that makes me want to reject her offer of a ride, it's more that I'm scared of what she might witness, and the confrontation it's sure to bring.

But I am not making this decision. "Oh, thank God. I can't bear the bus again," says Sunera, sprinting to the muddy lot.

What Elaine has is not, it turns out, really a car at all but a Rent-a-Wreck, a bones rattling, second-hand pile of crap all the jigglier for Elaine's terrible driving.

"It's been a while since I've been on a highway," she says redundantly, jerking into the centre lane for no apparent reason other than to cut off an eighteen-wheeler. The eighteen-wheeler bleats an angry dinosaur noise and speeds past, just missing us by a fingernail. Sunera screams from the backseat, grasping for her cigarette case of mood evener-outers. Theo mutters, "Okay, okay, okay," and Marvin doesn't seem to notice. He says, "Elaine, I love your poncho!"

My foot has a little inner life of its own, shaking and vibrating in tune with my ferocious lip-licking. It feels like moving confetti has been injected into my lips.

"So I've been in Toronto for nearly two weeks, Max. Didn't you get my messages?" asks Elaine, not angrily, but impatient, like she's trying to convince a child not to put her mouth over a light socket.

I answer, "Kind of."

I don't elaborate. In the backseat, Theo seems to sense that I need a way out. He says, "What are you doing in town, Elaine?"

"Representing some of the island artists at a gallery, and I heard about ACCLIMITIZE," she says, making little air quotes around ACCLIMITIZE and, in doing so, nearly sideswiping a motorcycle. "It's so great to see you, Max. Are you happy?"

Elaine doesn't exactly mess around.

"What did you think of the piece?" I ask, putting her off, but I know she'll return with the happiness question. Elaine is less easily distracted than most of the adults I grew up with; partly it's that she didn't do as much acid, partly it's some hard nut of ambition inside her. It was she alone who kept the compound running all those years after the will had run out. She made sure the food was grown, cooked, served, that the bills were paid and the children educated, if badly. When the compound dwindled down to one family, and then no one, she cleaned up the mess. She must have sold it, boarded the windows, and got ride of the garbage. I never heard the details of that transaction; it would have embarrassed her somehow, that all her work had been work in the end, a business dealing not unlike those done by her family in Philadelphia.

She stayed on the island, teaching painting in schools on the mainland. Now she cajoles the island artists out of bed and places paintbrushes in their hands. Then she takes boxes of their folk art around the country, and people buy it too, wood-carved fishermen with wonky eyes and papier mâché whales who double as umbrella stands. She is determined. If she hadn't been a freak, she would have made a good lawyer.

"I thought the piece was silly," says Elaine. "Why haven't you returned my calls?"

I make a fist and stamp prints in the smudge on the window with the curled palm of my hand. I press five dots along the smudge. "A foot," I declare. Elaine looks, swerves. Sunera screams.

"You used to do that in the van when you were a kid," says Elaine.

"What kind of kid was Max?" asks Theo.

"Oh, she was pretty sullen," says Elaine, and the peanut gallery laughs. "She was bright. Very funny, but a sad little girl."

"Jesus," I say. I turn to the backseat. "I had a haircut like a cabbage and I was living on nuts and berries. We had no television!"

"That's an outrage," says Theo, smiling. Marvin asks Elaine some questions about the West Coast and everyone listens as she yammers on about clear-cut logging and rain. A funny vibe in that car, how polite everyone is, sharp edges rounded off in the presence of a grown-up, this lulling back-and-forthlike conversation. Still, I'm sitting on my hands to keep from tapping my fingers to the bone. Every third person is flipping the finger at Elaine as she weaves in and out of traffic, going about fifteen kilometres lower than the speed limit.

Elaine drops everyone off, idling on the street until Marvin and Sunera are safely inside their buildings. When Theo gets out, he knocks on my window. The car is so old that I actually have to roll the window down by hand.

"I'll see you soon," he says, breath cold in the air. Then, more quietly, "Are you okay?"

I nod. He leans in and gives me a soft kiss on the cheek that stops my chattering teeth.

Elaine has a craving for the late-night juice bar near Theo's house.

"You need wheatgrass," she tells me.

Our waitress has an infected tongue stud (I catch a glimpse of a big red mound cherried with silver when she opens her mouth) that makes her sound drunk when she lists the specials. "We have gwaaach choop."

"Pardon?"

"Gwaach choop."

"Pardon?" She jiggles a finger, covered in Mexican jewellery, at the specials board. Squash soup. Got it.

With the poncho on, Elaine looks limbless. A platter with a silver domed cover, placed on a red-and-black raven-patterned tablecloth, a hand whipping off the dome – "Et voila!" – and there's Elaine, served up, a serious little white-headed lunch.

Or maybe it's the drugs.

"Do you remember when Dad went a bit psycho reading about Buckminster Fuller and built the yurt by the river?" I ask her, gnawing the inside of my cheeks.

Elaine nods. "He never finished that yurt."

The juice has an unwashed undertaste.

"Those are vitamins, Max. Don't look so disgusted."

Elaine tells me that my father's been wandering the States for a few years, but he comes back from time to time, unannounced, checks in with his favourite ex-girlfriend (she smiles when she says that). He's thinner, says Elaine. She tells me about people we knew, a grubby girl with two moms who married a stockbroker and moved to New York. She works in the fashion industry. Elaine tells me about the ones who stayed west: the little boy who could catch flies with his bare hands now leads rich Vancouverites on hikes over the West Coast Trail, gets up before the sun and prepares steaming cups of cappuccino in plastic mugs, leaves the warm containers outside the brand-new tents of his hikers to greet them when they wake up. This detail astounds Elaine.

She mentions parents who died. I nod, chewing my juice.

Elaine puts her hands, lightly liverspotted and soft, over mine.

"You're going to be thirty-five, Max," she announces.

"Yup."

"Your mother was only thirty-five when she died – can you imagine?"

"Not really," I reclaim my hands for my lap, where they can thumb war each other, and I look at the specials board written in five different colours of chalk.

Elaine tells me how she's renovated her home, and the coven of witches who were creating problems on the south end of the property have finally left, so there's not as much tension. She smiles when I laugh at her casual use of the phrase *coven of witches* and I have always liked that about Elaine; she can recognize absurdity, but doesn't shy away from it.

"Did you know your father's coming to the island next month? His most recent retreat is over," she says. I shake my head. I wonder if that's why he's been calling, to tell me he's going back, to invite me home. But I can't imagine an invitation from him. His voice is too faltering; it would never make it through the phone lines.

"Theo seems interesting," says Elaine. She doesn't speak to fill a silence, so I know she means it.

"What makes you say that?" I'm greedy for her answer.

Elaine cocks her head, contemplating the question for an agonizing length of time. When she is ready, she ticks off her reasons, one by one: "Because he is thoughtful. Because he is a scientist. Because he is –" she pauses. "Kind to you."

It should be thrilling, the outsider telling the story of your relationship, sanctioning the choice, spinning the details into a fairy tale. But then there's this: What if Elaine is a bad reader? How do you interpret those signs when they arrive in a drug funk, late at night, where everyone is parading around as someone else?

If we were confidantes, if either of us was more girlish or giggly, Theo would be the spark for a dirt session. I could lean in with details of the courtship, our long, strange history and the things we did in his office. I could raise my eyebrows and stage whisper, Are we too different? Do you think it could work? A riot, a purge. I wonder about those women who are friends with their mothers, if talking to your mother feels as safe as talking to yourself. But Elaine is much too serious, and I am much too cautious, and so we have lived like this, inside our strange half-worn intimacy for decades.

I tell her instead that Theo worked in Africa, and she lights up. As Elaine eats, we gather information from one another, Elaine because she doesn't like to leave any situation unresolved (and I am a situation), and me, because seeing her, I'm suddenly hungry to know what the mood is like in the west, if the ferries are making scheduled runs to the island yet, how much closer spring is out there. Though she asks, I avoid as much as I can this other life, my life in Toronto, which seems watery and temporary next to her old woman life of buildings and friendships and solitude.

Food cleared, we split the bill, and as I'm moving to put my coat on, avoiding her gaze, which is sure to be loaded, she leans in, grabbing my wrists right out of the air, her grip strong.

"Max!" shouts Elaine, shaking my hands. I blink and stare at her fingers on my wrists. "I'm so glad I ran into you. I'm so pleased we could spend time together, Max, but let me say something quite frankly, and take it to heart, my dear,

dear child: I think that something is ruining you, and you need to get yourself well."

Purple black night, slabs of headlights pile and fall on the empty walls. Elaine is asleep in my bed, offered to keep her off the highway toward an airport hotel, and I'm here in the living room in a slippery sleeping bag on a leather couch and the two materials are at odds, sliding me slowly toward the ground, a reminder that I should buy cotton sheets and wooden furniture and bamboo blinds, block out, keep in, comfort.

(Franny Baumgarten asleep under a clean white linen duvet.)

My head aches, the tinfoil taste of drugs in my mouth. Elaine breathes through the walls; raspy, a man snore. She's losing her defining girlishness. Elaine never said: I will be your mother. Unlike the other mothers, she never spoke of motherhood or the goddess, never asked for worship. She could not have children of her own, my father once told me, but I never saw her saddened by this. Her life was large, and adventurous, and she shared it with anyone who needed it, without expectation of return. If I kept my distance, it was only because I imagined all those adventures might not include me.

She always seemed tiny, perpetually clad in flowing robes. Robes were everywhere on the island. Grown-ups in soft Japanese silk, or down on the beach, burgundy and monastic in garments left behind by the monks. I would put one on, dragging its train around the muddy garden, knotting the belt and muttering my favourite word, surreptitiously learned from a contraband Christian *Archie* comic book: "Hairshirt."

Before all that, we – proper family we, mom-dad-me, we – lived in a rented stucco house, on a road about twenty minutes from the main street of Squamish, a town that looked like it elbowed in and the mountains just moved apart, leaving a lightweight little village right in their seam.

Mom taught English to the women who arrived from Gujarat and Rajasthan with parkas over their saris, and Dad fixed cars, built porches, patched ceilings. Anything with tools.

Then again, that's just what I was told after. I don't remember them working or being apart from me or any absence, but there must have been separation. She must have gone off and come back every day. Death makes you forget those spaces. They are small in comparison.

I do remember the dying part. I remember doors shutting and a long, slow silence descending that lasted two years, my seventh and eighth. Someone gave me headphones to attach to the record player so I wouldn't hear her vomiting. Now come the legends, here they come: she wore red flannel pyjamas she'd sewn herself, covered in floating hockey players. My father hauled oxygen tanks and bedpans up the stairs. I crouched a floor below in the living room listening to Jimi Hendrix on the fishbowl headphones, creeping around like a grunt marking the perimeter, ducking under stairwells and into the basement as the living room and kitchen filled with dirty dishes and garbage, and I watched my father move with a speed I had never seen, not before, not since. He ran like he couldn't see me crouched there, ran into town to bring back brown paper bags of medicine, ran to the basement for his tools to fix the car, ran to the sink, the toilet, the bucket. He would take her wherever she needed to go, wrap her in a blanket, walk her slowly to the truck, a little impatiently because she would laugh and wave and he was a bit annoyed, as if she wasn't respecting enough the seriousness of the situation, as if this was his burden alone.

The treatments made her sicker. From the window I could see her gather herself before she came back in. She straightened the scarf around her head, an intake of breath, a steeling before she rose from the wheelchair to walk the steps to see the daughter. *She puts on a brave face.* I heard this expression and put it together as a new superhero: Braveface! I drew her in red pyjamas and a cape, smiling and beckoning toward a team of flying hockey players; they couldn't keep up.

I think of this now and I can't believe how young they were: my mother was thirty-two when she was diagnosed with cancer, my father thirty-one, ages I've drifted through already. They spent those years in secret conversation with one another, my mother glancing at me with sadness, turning silent or, worse yet, forcing a big stupid grin. My father was happy to wall the family in, asking for little from the town, but people came around anyway. Good people, said the funeral director. But are people good? Are people good to bring food in plastic containers? Is it good for house-wives, flesh spilling over the waistband of their polyester pants, to arrive with brooms and dustbins and sweep in corners that had never been swept, commenting goodly: "Well, this is awful terrible, awful terrible." Were they referring to my father's housekeeping or the thing upstairs?

Mrs. Aleksiuk with her Tupperware containers of beet soup, brushing my hair so hard my eyes watered. "There now, ready for church."

We arrived just late enough so everyone could see us from their seats, prayer books in laps, Mrs. Aleksiuk marching me toward the front. I was a prize, the orphan-in-waiting, a good deed in a pink sweatshirt, hair unknotted and smooth for once.

Before, when the town was at church on Sundays, my mother and I went walking up and down the streets and she gossiped about each house: "That's the Millers'. He's a bank clerk and she's diddling the bank manager."

"That's the Hodsons'. She came from North Vancouver money and left it all for mountains."

"Now that" – she would say, in front of the Polnocheks' garden of wet colours – "is a beautiful house. Those people have some love to show, don't you think?"

I remember the small, sanctimonious ways of little towns and I think that there was also real goodness, real genuine goodness that still comes up in my throat when beckoned, lingers like a recent taste. In warm weather, I would leave my parents and sit on the front porch, spelling words on my teeth with my tongue, one letter at a time – b - r - a (molars) v - e – back and forth for hours, my escape hatch. The young woman who worked at the drugstore saw me, and she took me to her one-room apartment above the drugstore to watch television and feed me Kraft Dinner. I was happy to be distracted. I breathed the air and it didn't smell like hospital chemicals. I exhaled and breathed again.

And then, my dad's face in the door, terrified, "Where were you? Your mother was worried sick." (*Worried sick*. Had I caused this? Had I welcomed it, brought it into our home by running down the street too far ahead, by reading under the sheets with a flashlight, by stepping into traffic? Had I worried her cells to split and bunch in her veins? Would I worry her to death?)

When my father began calling people to notify them about what was going to happen, he often said, "She was tired. She was tired from looking after Max and me, and working too hard. She could make an entire soup for the week with just a hambone and vegetables from the garden." (I tired her out. I tired her out . . .)

This was his version of her, the earth mother with her hands in the soil, but she liked crap too. She fed us packaged noodles with shrimp powder just as often as homemade soup. She smoked and drank and swore. She had a temper so bad she once spit in my father's face, something I had never seen a human being do, though I learned about it from a picture book on camels. Then she collapsed weeping on the kitchen floor and he stormed out the back door.

But in between, she was dying, and my father was making up for it, rebuilding her with his stories. It seemed false to me, even so young. He began to seem like a liar, stroking photos of the two of them swimming in lakes I'd never been to, marching in protests for issues and wars resolved when I was a baby. I found this version of my mother foreign, and it made me miss her more. I didn't know yet that a person could be so varied; I liked the silly parts of my mother, the way she stuck her tongue out behind the back of a mean postal clerk, her sometimes lipstick. My father scoffed at the church women with their manicured nails and doilies, things I thought were pretty, but soon, he was winning. Everything was serious all the time now. Machines hooked to my mother wheezed on her behalf. She was neither self any more; she had holes in her uterus, a whiffle ball where a baby should be. She didn't know we were fracturing.

But I knew. I knew things I shouldn't have known because when the sickness moved in, I became invisible. I could walk through walls, curl up in closets, and listen. I could put my finger down on the phone cradle, slowly release the buttons, and listen in silently while upstairs my dad muddled through conversations with doctors and lawyers, crying without shame. In weeks, I learned I didn't even have to sneak, that I could just pick up the phone with an aggressive click and listen in: "Analgesic . . ." "Morphine . . ." ". . . normal?"

One day, on a whim, I broke my imaginary perimeter and walked upstairs. I drifted past a ball of sheets in the hallway, pushed open the paint-peeled door. I expected to be chastised. I expected to be flesh again, but my borders had been false: I was still invisible. I stood right in the room where my mother lay on the bed, inflated with sweat and dreaming in a bald head. I stood and watched her for hours and no one noticed, my father jogging in and out of the room, down to the kitchen for ice chips that he made by smashing the plastic bag with a hammer over and over, then back upstairs to place the chips on her slack tongue.

And she got better again. Her dying was like that, a series of retreats and returns. It dizzied me.

The treatments stopped and she slowly walked, her footsteps overhead on the second floor, soon padding down the stairs into the living room, where she looked around and noted out loud how things had changed: a table out of place, a lamp in a different corner. I moved objects at her asking. Sleeping Beauty awoken, again and again. Her hair – her long, straight brown hair – grew back in little corkscrews. "Touch it," she said. "It's like a poodle."

My creeping days were over. My mother had a sense of where I was at all times. In a sleeping bag on the front porch, her reading glasses (a new necessity, as if all of her was weakening) around her neck, a toque on her head in May, me up in a tree, silently watching.

"Max," she would say, without looking up. "Come down from the tree, please."

Someone gave her a television. It sat in the corner of the living room, the screen covered in plant tendrils.

"Let's read *The Secret Garden*."

"I'm too old for *The Secret Garden*."

I got cruel.

"I don't want to come down from the tree," I said. "Your hair feels gross, not like a poodle."

I refused to touch her outstretched hand with its easy-to-tear skin. I sat in the chair farthest away from her. I was a spy, not a daughter; tribeless, getting orders from the bottom of a shoe, like on that TV show. "Track your suspect," said the voice in the shoe. "Only when she's been back seventy-two days will you know she's staying." Seventy-two; my two favourite numbers, the round happiness of two; the severe rightness of seven.

I watched from windows and trees for seventy-two days until spring came. Her hair was finally longish, down around her ears now, and she looked beautiful again, her high cheeks neither sunken nor overblown. She could catch me. Day 73, she climbed the same tree from a different angle and grabbed my foot. Terrified, I howled like a stubbed toe and she laughed and laughed and my father brought us lunch to the rotted picnic table with only one bench. We sat in a row, my father, my mother, me, eating sandwiches off paper plates, shoulders touching in the summer, our limbs sighing with relief where they met.

RIGHT UNDER THE SPEAKER IN THE USUAL BAR there's not much to say or hear, really, just drinks to be drunk and so I have drunk some. Sunera has decided not to leave with me but to stay, holding court at the back of the room, surrounded by a pair of unpaid, awestruck interns from her magazine. On my way out, I brush by Allissa Allan's table, and she reaches out a hand to block my exit.

"Max," says Allissa, as if we are friends. "How's the film festival going?"

I look at her, at her low-cut white blouse, her asparagus body bent into the wire-backed chair. Her crowd tonight is leather-clad vegetarian types, faces obscured by clouds of smoke. I lean closer to examine Allissa Allan's flawless skin. I swallow a very real temptation to lick her cheek to see if it really does taste like a cold apricot. I stick out my tongue, thinking, I might do this, then catch a glimpse of myself in the mirror above the bar – a giant puffy coat, a tall toque, a tongue sticking out: a very ugly totem pole. I straighten up, muttering, "I've had a few beers . . ."

Allissa Allan gives me a concerned look.

"Do you want to sit down?"

But it seems I am already sitting down, squeezed in between Allissa Allan and a guy I recognize from TV, my puffy coat cushioning both of them, airbag style. I saw this guy recently on a cable show plugging his book on happiness. Drinking martinis and shopping wasn't the problem, he said, but part of the solution.

"Your friend digs that Situationist shit, huh?" I say to Allissa.

"What?" there is a speaker at her head too. Instead of answering, Allissa Allan shakes her red ringlets and delivers a speech that sounds prepared.

"Listen, Max, I wanted to tell you, I know that there's some kind of perceived rivalry between us, perpetrated more by the promotional departments at the newspapers than by us," she says. I lean in and take a sip of her drink. Allissa Allan is one of those people who talks with her eyes half-closed, a look that resembles sex and is, I think, kind of a hit with the men. The advantage for me is that through those sleepy bedroom eyes, she can't see my not-so-sly sipping of her Cosmopolitan.

"But I wanted to tell you that I don't buy into it. I've never had anything but admiration for your work. I think you're a scream," she says.

"Me too," I say into my collar, beginning to sweat under the down.

Then she says it, shouting directly into the canyon wrinkle that's formed between my eyebrows, like she might get an echo if she's loud enough: "When I was in university, I read your work. I always hoped that somehow you could mentor me." Allissa widens her eyes. "I think women have to stick together, don't you?"

I consider the word *mentor* and I see the Editor's pointy teeth.

"I'm not sure," I say. "I don't know that many women." I stand up, held to the ground by my boots.

"Are you leaving?" she asks, and I cannot tell if she is being sarcastic when she says, in lieu of goodbye, "Hot date?"

Snow falls, maybe the last snow of the season, muting the noise of College Street late night, the stumbling bridge-and-tunnellers on the sidewalk cowering under the hot-dog vendor's umbrella. Five years ago, this street was mostly textile shops and Portuguese bakeries. Then neighbourhood bars where old men congregated for satellite soccer gave way to lounges with neon signs, then lounges went out of fashion and became clubs. Still, the Portuguese women hold their ground, displaying buttons and zippers in their windows while next door a gourmet delicatessen features kumquats and gooseberries in theirs.

Someone must be really anxious to find that next Einstein because Theo has been working late the past week, even sleeping in his office a few nights, which seems tragic, or impossible ("Under the desk?" I asked, joking, and he said, "Yes, sadly.") Of course, Theo could be capable of sleeping elsewhere. I think of the flower-sniffing ex, and the baby frosh who swarm the university campus, their dimpled backsides winking above the waists of their jeans. I should wean myself from Theo, or the idea of Theo, the possibility of him.

And yet here I am, a block south, on another street of renovated Victorians. I stand on Theo's sidewalk for a while, kicking patterns in the snow, measuring exactly how pathetic I am. Then I lean down, roll up a ball, and chuck it at his apartment window. Nothing. Nothing means another and another and I'm a little wobbly, it's true, but there they go, the snowballs knocking at the window until out he comes, Theo McArdle, barefoot on his porch wearing long johns and a ski jacket. I'm drunk and sad, I tell Theo McArdle, only I say it like: "Hello!" and he opens the door for me, half-asleep still.

Theo apologizes for the malfunctioning radiators and I walk to the bathroom toward soap and hot water and I look in the mirror: I am grey pink, old chewing gum. I am thirty-fucking-four.

In Theo's bedroom I pull a soggy cheque for $333.45 from the pocket of my wet puffy coat, reimbursement for my fudged expenses from *The Daily*. Instead of getting fired, I'm getting paid.

"Here," I say, bouncing the wadded-up cheque off his chest. "Maybe you can give this to your friends in Africa, the well-diggers. Seriously, do something good with it."

Theo looks puzzled.

I take off the puffy but keep everything else on – socks, cold jeans, hot sweater, crawl under his hideous lime green madras quilt. Theo hands me a glass of water.

"Did your mom buy you this quilt in junior high?" I ask, bleary.

He drops his jacket and stands at the edge of the bed wearing long johns and nothing else, but I couldn't tell you too much about Theo McArdle's body because he takes what amounts to a running leap and lands under the quilt with me and I can't stop laughing. He kisses me, soft, then fierce.

"You taste like the colour red," he says, and I start giggling. Then Theo McArdle's hands are manically rubbing to warm me up and I am trying to get undressed without resurfacing from the bed into the cold air.

"Seriously, I have synesthesia," he says into my neck. "Do you know what that is?"

"Is it contagious?" I ask him, and he laughs, which I interpret as no. Then he starts telling me how the more advanced synesthesists feel colour and see music and taste emotion. With Theo, it's mostly taste that seeps into his other feelings. So when he kisses me, he says, kissing me, I taste red.

Then I shush him, make like a 1940s film diva with stones in her cheeks – "Dahlink, don't speak" – and we kiss, and I apologize for being drunk and he says, "Maybe you're not drunk. Maybe this is the way you always are and the rest of the world is drunk." He's kidding, but I hate this idea, and he catches my look, and says, "Hey, it's okay, it's okay." Theo is propped up on one elbow, his hand moving and my skin rising to meet it. And then he's inside me, both of us loosening our sounds. The self moans, then gives way to cries that sound like desperation, the end of the self, lamented with a shout. We stay like that, eyes open, locked, sober until the shudder and the sigh. And when it's over, I sleep as if underground, terrified, thrilled, finished.

A WEEK HAS PASSED SINCE THEO MCARDLE ACCEPTED my snowballs. He has been locked in his cell at the university, polishing his theories. I have been in a film festival funk, half-awake through press conferences and roundtables, filing daily eight-hundred-word profiles of stars culled from nine-minute interviews in hotel rooms. The articles slide from my hand to the keyboard, hardly a moment of mediation from my brain: anecdote ("She sips a Diet Pepsi clasped in fingers topped with chewed fingernails, the one un-manicured portion of her otherwise perfect body. She looks like an unusually tanned corpse laid out in a coffin, and then she smiles . . ."), summary of current film (". . . but this is the movie that will make you forget those past three box office flops . . ."), unusual biographical moment with authorial reference ("How did you know I worked with handicapped animals back in Iowa as a teenager?" she laughs, waggling her ragged fingernail at me. Then, she grows serious beneath her tan: "I still care deeply about those animals, especially this one sheep, Andy . . ."), end anecdote ("And so the publicist whisks her away to the red carpet, and she leaves as she came in: a mystery, a construct, a star").

The Editor had the idea that on the front page, right below the lead news story, I should have a daily bold-face column listing the restaurants, bars, and clothing stores frequented by visiting celebrities. The column, right above my headshot, is called Schmooze-fest 2001. My writing is lazy, and often sarcastic, but not so mean that I could get fired before the paper is sold. It's a delicate dance I'm doing these days: I need to come off as just crazy enough that I'll be one of the first people on the To Go list when the new owners clean house, but not so crazy that it happens before the new owners sign the papers. This matters because if I'm too lazy, too mean, too awful – all the things I've been trying to be, without much effort, the past month or so – and I get fired by The Cheese, I'll get two weeks severance pay. But if I'm excess, if BFD Television sees me as just another piece of redundant, downsizeable flesh, that's the lottery. Then I get a month's salary for every year I've worked at *The Daily*, which is six months of pay. Six months is enough time and money in which to . . . to what? I get stuck here. Make a movie? Lie in my bedroom? Scenarios float through my head as I sit in my cubicle, wrist tendons hurting from typing.

At night when I collapse under my covers, I miss Theo's cold bed as if I had slept there half my life.

And now the festival is ending, and I am outside BFD-TV headquarters, huddled in the cold with the other smokers, making a quick call before a TV appearance for a film festival roundup. Theo picks up immediately.

"Quick, tell me a joke," I say.

Theo doesn't hesitate. "How do you get two hundred Canadians out of a pool?"

"How?"

"'Okay, everybody out.'"

"I've heard that before, only they were Belgian," I tell him.

"It's the only joke I know," he says. "I've had it at the ready for twelve years." For a bit he lets me complain about the film festival, and then he gets quiet.

"What's going on?" I ask him, and I run through a mental list of possibilities: flesh-eating toxins; terrorist threats; the blonde in the field.

"There's a possibility that a university in England might be interested in what I'm working on," Theo says. Then, quickly: "But it's unlikely."

My pulse quickens. All that skittish, flirty energy between us evaporates. I get it: Theo is trying to warn me. "When are you leaving?" I ask.

"Max," he says, almost exasperated. He anticipated that I would think the worst. He knows me that well already. "It's a long shot. I only mention it because I got a call today."

"Congratulations," I tell him, and I mean it – he impresses me – but it sounds sarcastic even to me. I see him waving goodbye from a train. Dr. Zhivago.

Then details: the project, post-doctorate research in London, a position of some repute. I nod and try to sound supportive. Really, what claim do I have on Theo McArdle? My God, how desperate am I to attach my suckers to him at this early stage? I disgust myself.

"What time is it?" I ask him. I am late. Theo says things, calm things, comforting things, and warns me that he is going to be busy again these next days, nothing personal. I hang up and head into the rainbow-coloured lobby of BFD fuzzy-headed and achy, like I haven't slept in weeks.

BFD-TV is a national broadcaster with a do-it-yourself aesthetic. Their Toronto headquarters, in the heart of downtown, are built of glass so passersby can watch plumber-butted cameramen and VJs with noserings doing their jobs through the windows like those live mannequins department stores sometimes hire. When celebrities come to town, BFD closes off the street, encouraging teenage mobs to weep on the sidewalk. Television interns stand on a platform above the crowd raising their arms in the air, signaling when to scream. This scene occurs several times during the film festival, blocking traffic, and though everyone complains – "Fucking BFD. Fucking tourists" – we are secretly a little proud, not only that the celebrities have bothered to come, but that this clenched city can undo itself, get hysterical and unfettered, even if it only lasts a minute or two.

For this, their morning chat show, guests sit on bright couches covered with animal-print pillows. I'm sinking into a green couch while across from me on a red one, our host, Trish, is encouraging us panellists to speak our minds, to really say what we want to say about how great the film festival is, to not hold back just because the network is one of the festival's sponsors.

Mr. Happiness, the champagne philosopher, has been invited too, nestled in between me and Allissa Allan, gripping a hardcover copy of his self-help guide to better living through philosophy. Happiness's soul patch quivers under the studio lights.

He says, "Trish, I would like to reiterate that I'm an academic. I saw one film at the festival and it was in Swahili."

Trish flashes a twinkle smile and pats his hand. "Ree-laaax," she says, closing her eyes, breathing in an exaggerated, yogic fashion. "We're just going to have a good conversation about the film festival." She exhales through her mouth – "Oooh" – opens her eyes and pats Happiness's hand. "You just tell us what you think and voila! It's fun!"

I usually like to smoke a big bowl before occasions like this, but this morning, I woke up feeling queasy, like I needed a few dozen saltines to absorb the bile in my stomach. I should warn her.

"I'm with Happiness over here, I'm not feeling –"

Trish waves her hands in front of her face, abracadabra style. "Please, please, PLEASE. We're live in two minutes." She leans in toward her whining, bobbing, too-talking heads, her blond hair stiffened into corgi curls, and she's not so chipper any more. In a wicked stepmother voice: "Don't forget: This is *fun*."

And five, four, three, two –

"Welcome to my esteemed panel," she says. "So is it just me, or was this year's festival better than ever?"

Allissa Allan lets loose a party-girl whoop and says, "The parties were fabulous. I mean, let's face it, it's all about the parties!"

Happiness attempts to go deeper: "I do wonder if we don't project our cultural malaise onto such events, Trish. Perhaps the festival functions as a Bakhtinian carnival wherein participants are released from their everyday roles, freed to engage in the world as the taboo Other, if only for a few days, becostumed for the Bacchanalian festival! But alas" – I really think this guy just said "becostumed"; I really think he said "alas," but you'll have to rewind to make sure – "only for fourteen days. Far, far too short a time before returning to their workaday lives."

Trish swings around. "Maxime?" she says. I swallow hard, a sour ball in my throat.

"Trish, I fell asleep at several of the screenings I saw this year," I say, and then I just go off. "Otherwise, I attended a lot of mainstream crap that will get released in theatres anyway, festival or no festival. I went to a couple of parties where I was held back from the actual celebrities by a rope, which was probably a good thing since I was so drunk, something very embarrassing might have taken place had I been allowed to mingle."

AA and Happiness laugh overly boisterous television laughs. Fired up, I continue: "In between, I saw one or two decent films that will never get distribution. There might have been gems, Trish, but with more than two thousand movies showing, how could I possibly be expected to find them, or talk authoritatively at all on this or any other issue?"

Silence ribbons the couch, joining us together probably for only a second or two but television has its own physical laws and it feels more like ten, fifteen, twenty days. Then Happiness peeps, "Here, here!" outdoing his "becostumed," and AA giggles, and finally, Trish leans forward and says, "Maxime, that's why we love you! Cheeky girl!"

A WEEK AFTER THE FILM FESTIVAL CARNIES PACK UP their tents and roll out of town, I am walking through Yorkville on my way to a screening, one without festival lights. I pass paper stores selling hand-pressed gift cards, boutiques of Italian designers selling sequined and silk maternity wear. The hotels have dropped the extra security they felt they required during the festival, leaving their roundabout entrances looking vulnerable, barely guarded by men in top hats who chat with each other, a little defensive as they hold the door open, aware of their ridiculousness.

The day is icy, as if the weather, too, feels it has nothing to prove now that the celebrities have gone. Limousines are parked in garages, the restaurants and bars are open to the city again, the dull, Protestant city.

I'm hungover, looking for a coffee. I decide to cut through one of the big hotels to save myself a minute and a half of cold air. As I'm leaving through a back exit, I'm halted by a row of black garbage bags open at the top sitting just inside the door. They are stiff at the sides, as if containing boxes. I am, for some reason, compelled to peek through the openings, goaded to do so by all the wealth that visits these rose-coloured halls. What if a socialite has seen fit to throw out boxes of extra clothing, or the hotel is upgrading their electronic goods and these are bags of computers or stereos? I know what I'm hoping will be in the garbage even as I glance around the empty hall (it is not so becoming to paw through garbage) and lean in: I am hoping for things that are not adequate for the rich, but perfectly fine for me.

My dig disappoints. The bags only contain paper. In one, hundreds of press notes for movies that held their junkets in this hotel. In the next, photos from the movies, stacks and stacks of black-and-white and colour stills of actors weeping and jumping off bridges, waving their fists in courtrooms, kissing. And then, in the next few bags, newspapers. *Dailies*, in fact, distributed in all hotel rooms to inflate circulation numbers. Industrial-sized garbage bags full of unwanted *Dailies*. I pick up the top issue. WEEK FIVE IN TORONTO TENT CITY STANDOFF. BIG BOX RETAILER VERSUS ANGRY

HOMELESS. Editorial, page A7: *Sorry, street people: Our city backs business.*

And below the colour photo of a squatter, there's me, with my hair shorter because the picture is three years old. I am just barely smiling. My final report from the streets has the hed: FILM FESTIVAL BEST EVER.

Oh, *The Daily* and its predictable hectoring, its endless bad judgment in pursuit of being different. I feel a sudden pang of sadness for the paper where I work, the way you do when naïveté comes off as brute force; a child smashing a ladybug. But then, there's my face, my words, my body in ink. A wave of illness. The photo shouldering my headshot is of a young man in a torn sweater that looks hand-knitted. He is angry-eyed and certain, sitting in the rubble of Tent City, planting himself there like a flag.

THE WEEKS PASS, MOVING US TOWARD SPRING, AND MY

patterns change. I sleep at Theo's house two or three times a

week, and we see daylight together. One morning we walk

through Chinatown and another we take the ferry across to

Ward's Island looking at the ducks freezing in the pond. The

city is still new to him and it looks weightier to me now,

older through his eyes. Often I sleep in his bed while he stays

up late at his kitchen table, trying to advance his research so

the university in London will take him. I wake up fitfully,

needing his body, and hating to need him, turning my back when he gets in bed, keeping just a few secrets from him.

I take a cab from Theo's apartment to find one of the *Daily* boardrooms converted into a makeup room: we are making a commercial, a plea with the public to remember us. Beneath an oil portrait of Baby Baron, gazing into the distance like a teenage widow out to sea, the cherry-wood table can barely be seen through jars of colour and triangular sponges.

"Honey, I have to ask, Is there something wrong with your skin? Are you . . ." the makeup lady arches her hands in front of her stomach over and over, like she's caressing a basketball.

"Fat?" I ask.

She mouths it, dirty-word style: "Pregnant."

I take the hand mirror she's offering. My forehead is covered in tiny white bumps, cheeks dotted with pixels, and, to the right of my nose, a big, honking zit looks like it's trying to escape by digging out from the inside.

"I don't think so. I'm just stressed," I offer, because it's the thing to say to anyone – the Editor, Elaine, Mohsen – who asks that small, loaded question: How are you?

The makeup lady is excited to have a challenge. She's right up in my face, breathing synthetic fruit gum breath, spackling over my hideousness.

One time on the compound a bat flew into my hair and stuck, wings flapping until my dad cut it out with safety scissors, leaving a bald patch at my temple. It feels like the bat has returned, pulling at my skull. A man's distressed voice is attached to the brushes and clips, "Hmm . . . What can we do about *this*?" "This" means me.

As they gloss me over and smooth me out, hair guy and makeup lady have a conversation about the foreign correspondent who sat in the chair before me.

"I'm like, honey, if you know you're going to be in a nationally televised commercial, at least have a little squeeze session the night before and try to get rid of those blackheads!"

Hair guy shrieks with laughter, deleting a chunk of my scalp with his brush.

"Voila," says makeup lady.

"Not bad," hair guy agrees and they stand back, looking at my skin, my hair, my strategically covered ears.

Marvin pokes his head in the door.

"Ohmygod!" he says. "You look great!"

I stare as the rest of Marvin enters. "What are you wearing?" Marvin is sporting some kind of giant orange nylon snowboarding outfit. Massive rectangular pockets drip off his chest, hips, and thighs; the whole thing gathers, balloonlike, at the ankles. "You don't like?" he asks, a touch irritated.

"I don't not like, I just don't get it." And I mean that, truly.

"The pockets are for water bottles, so you never have to leave the dance floor."

"Is that a burning issue for you?"

A man enters the boardroom. A middle-aged belly hangs over the edge of his expensive black belt, and I wonder if there was more fat before and he's proudly showing off how little there is now, or if it's a new belly that he hasn't acknowledged yet. The people he passes scatter and lower their voices.

"Maddy?" he asks, standing in front of me, giving a let's-go handclap.

"My name's Max."

"Perfect. I'm Philippe, the director. Has anyone told you about our little project here?" He punctuates "little" with a chummy grin, making sure I know there's nothing little about any of this.

"Last gasp advertising?"

Philippe laughs phonetically, like an ESL student reading it off the page: "Ha! [beat] Ha! [beat] Ha!"

He gets serious. Philippe puts his hands on the armrests of my chair and boxes me in, face to face. His cellular implant dangles from one ear, swaying when he smiles.

"We think that what makes *The Daily* unique is that it's all about words. Words and people. People and words. Do you get where I'm coming from?" He smiles.

"Mmm . . ."

"You create those words, and this commercial is a celebration of you, the wordsmith. Hell, I know I couldn't do it!"

Hair and makeup murmur approvingly.

"I write about celebrities," I tell him. "I think you could probably handle it."

I'm the eleventh writer Philippe has filmed today.

"You dig Bird?" he asks.

"What did you just say?"

"You dig Bird, you know, Charlie Parker?" Let me just mention something: Philippe is not black. Marvin shoots me a don't-freak-out look. I answer back with a can-you-motherfucking-believe-this? glance.

"Yes," I say. "I've been known to dig some Bird."

"Great! I'm going to play a little Bird, you're going to sit in a chair, not unlike this one, and just move around, feel the music, let it flow through you, wordsmith!"

Philippe marches me through the office. Ad Sales, shiny in a new Armani suit, looks up from his cubicle, smirks, looks down. Up-Talking Heather hovers nearby.

In the corridor by the elevators, surrounded by white screens and lights on stork legs, I'm placed on a tall revolving chair, light monitors held up to my face like Meryl Streep being checked for plutonium in *Silkwood*. Philippe claps his hands together, jogs over to where I'm sitting, and puts his hands on my shoulders, gives them a shake. His hyperactivity is having a strange, inverse effect on me. I can feel my blood pressure dropping suddenly, a deep-sea plunge. "Are you ready for this?" Philippe shouts.

"No."

"Great! Let's rock 'n' roll, people!" Philippe claps again, and the Charlie Parker starts up. I sit in the chair stock-still, trying to breathe.

"Okay, Maddy, give me a whirl. To the left, to the left!"

I try to revolve, but the chair won't move.

"The chair won't move," I mention.

"Cut!" Bird is silenced. A minion whisks me away while Philippe pushes and tugs the disagreeable chair. I walk toward a table of Oreos and ice water, where I am swiftly intercepted by makeup lady.

"Watch the lipstick. Don't drink any water," she tells me. "No time for touch-ups."

"Maddy! Can you come back over here, honey?" Philippe leads me back to the chair.

"We have a problem," he tells me. "The chair's not spinning."

"I know."

"We're going to have to improvise. I need you just to move your body, just twist your body as if the chair is spinning."

"Are you kidding?"

"And cue Bird, and ROLLING!"

I sit very still.

"Come on, Maddy! Turn! Turn!" I shift a little jerkily to the right, looking at the masking tape X above the camera lens. "Other way, Maddy! Turn! Go! You're a revolving chair! You're a revolving chair!" My butt catches on the seat, but I make it over to the right, eye on the X. Philippe shouts, "Left! Left!" and I try to move as smoothly as possible, rotating herky-jerky on this not-rotating chair. "Centre! To the centre, Maddy!" screams Philippe and Charlie Parker is wailing and my heart is in my toes now – no, it really feels like it might have stopped altogether, just kind of pushed out through the bottom of my shoe. I close my eyes and shake my head to get it started again, like a self-winding watch.

"Nice! Very sexy, Maddy! Very sexy!"

And that's when I fall off the chair.

Unbeknownst to me until this very minute, there is a nurse's room in *The Daily* building. No nurse, of course, but there are some bandages and a fire extinguisher. It's quite pleasant in here, lying on a twin bed covered in a soft blanket, looking out a window that touches the branches of a tree. A tree. I had no idea there was a tree in the vicinity of *The Daily*.

Marvin sits on a chair in the corner with a laptop, clicking and chatting breathlessly, outlining his strategy for when we get laid off. Marvin is talking about taking his winnings to Spain and writing a tell-all about the inner workings of *The Daily*.

"Do you think anyone would want to read that?" I ask him. "No one even reads the paper. Why would they want to know more about the thing they're already not interested in?"

As soon as I say it, I regret it. Marvin's eyes fall. I'm snappy because of his certainty. He has somehow managed to come up with a plan, even a bad plan made while shopping for parachute suits and gathering phone numbers for meaningless sexual encounters. I should be proud that he truly adores his life. Where is my joy for other people? For people I love, even?

"I'm sorry, Marvin. It's a good idea," I say, and that's enough. He perks up, smiles, goes into detail about the beach in Spain, how the wine there is cheaper than bus fare.

Marvin's phone rings. He picks up, makes some sounds, and hands it to me with an apologetic wince.

"Maxime?" It's the Editor.

I put on my weakest voice. "Yes?" I cough.

"Are you feeling any better? I understand you're in the infirmary." She says in-fir-*mary*, and I don't even think that's British pronunciation.

"I fainted."

"I understand that," she says, and it occurs to me that the Editor never says "I know," just "I understand," a nod, perhaps, to the complexities of our profession, or a fear of libel. And yet, when I think of her rushing in all directions, pointy face slicing through doorways, she is one of the least understanding people I've met.

"We have an issue, however, with the deadline on the *Vogue* piece," she says. She could have said "pubic hair" piece, as it's an article about how the new issue of *Vogue* includes a spread of several celebrities looking tufty in low-waisted jeans.

"What time is it?" I ask her.

"Two-thirty. Are you well enough to get it to me by four? I wouldn't ask, but news wants to flag it on the banner, and they need to know . . ." She trails off, and I wonder if she's a bit ashamed that she might be compromising my health for an article of this particular scope.

I cough again, with purpose, and then say, "I'll do it." I'm not sure why. Not doing it would be a nice red mark in my file, the kind of thing that might spur a lay off, and Marvin – who covers television, after all – assures me BFD-TV and Baby Baron are drawing up papers as we speak. But maybe I have retained some modicum of pride about my writing. Maybe not working is scarier than this simulacrum of work. Maybe I'm the prisoner in the Sydney jail, carving her name in the stone.

Marvin hands me his laptop and I log into my work file. I already spent a half-hour on the article this morning, so I've gathered quotes from a pair of academics interpreting pubic hair's historical meaning, and one comment from a fashion director in Canada. *Vogue* won't return the calls of *The Daily*. It takes me twelve minutes to complete the piece, but I won't send it until exactly four o'clock. Until then, I'll sleep, which I need to do suddenly, my eyes closing as I type the final period.

Marvin removes the computer from my hands and turns out the light.

"I fainted last week," I tell the doctor. She nods, tightening the grip of the blood pressure cuff. "And I'm tired. Really tired."

"How are your periods? Regular?"

"Absolutely never," I tell her.

"Any concern you might be pregnant?"

"Absolutely always. Why does everyone keep asking me that?" I ask.

"Who else asked?"

"The makeup lady." Doctor doesn't want details. She asks questions, scribbling hard in her file, questions about sleep and diet and exercise. We agree all of the above are good ideas.

"Drugs? Alcohol?"

"Are you offering?"

Doctor isn't much for smiling.

"How much do you drink in a week?"

"I'm in the dark green pie," I tell her. "I'm over the limit."

"Drinking can affect your periods. It can also affect your mood, and your life in general."

She hands me the same green brochure, the one from the door, italicized letters "Evaluate *Your* Drinking," and a Dixie cup to pee in.

"Have you thought about what you'll do if you are pregnant?" she asks.

Sure. I don't think there's a woman alive who hasn't run through every single what-if scenario, moved the pieces around and back again a hundred times, playing mommy like you did as a kid.

I've thought about a Downsy baby born somewhere in my forties, when I'm alone and unemployed, and how the two of us will move into a shelter and I will carry our belongings in a plastic shopping bag down to the food bank for white bread and Kraft peanut butter handouts. I've thought about abortion, fetal sacs sucked out of my stomach with bicycle pumps. I've thought about adoption and whether I'd hire a detective to find a baby I might have handed over years ago, a wrapped package in pink that grew human limbs like mine.

I've thought about it, flipping through pregnancy books for no reason, thought about how I wouldn't know how to change diapers, or what to do with the unceasing cry, and who would I ask about this stuff, when it's just me and my turkey-baster baby living in the same apartment I'm in now, Marvin the donor dropping by every other Sunday, stale with last night's club sweat.

I've thought about being married to a brilliant, beautiful man who's off making gobs of ethical money all day long to line the nest, a Frank Lloyd Wright nest on a drizzly Pacific Coast where I write children's books and eat brown rice and tofu and lie on my polished hardwood floors with teddy bears and the perfect silky baby kicking on her quilt. The father will take me in his arms and say, You're a great mother,

Max. (Because everyone's life is lived in anticipation of the great love. No one says, She died without the great love. They say, She had it, fleetingly, and she lost it, or tragedy struck before it came to life, or she came close, and was too stubborn to recognize it, dressed up like it was in that stupid outfit. But everyone wakes up because of the great love. The vibration sets us off each morning, one sock at a time, homing toward it.)

Pregnancy and motherhood are separate states to me somehow, bordered with explosives. When my period is late, sometimes I'll take an Aspirin and think, Is this the thing that's going to make a hypothetical fetus blind, or flippered, or sad? The condom breaks and there it is: my small, angry AIDS baby. I join support groups and appear on television, bags under my eyes, AIDS baby sleeping (a lot) in a papoose while I rage against the injustices of underfunding for MWAB (Mothers With AIDS Babies).

But I can't picture anything real. When I try, here in the doctor's office, to conjure up an image of myself with a child, my own arms holding my own child in my own apartment in my own city, I come up with white space and static. I do not know how motherhood looks.

"I've thought about it," I tell the doctor and she doesn't ask anything else.

Sunera once did something so bad that she lied about it in her journal. She opened to a blank page and wrote: "Regular Tuesday. Not much happened." But in fact, that very day in grade twelve, she stole an exam, a biology exam that had haunted her, kept her up at night, churning. She couldn't keep track of the names of the grasshopper parts, the butterfly larvae, the transformative bugs with all their legs and antennae and plush organs. The diagrams overwhelmed her. She did practice tests with her father: he drew the grasshopper in his perfect draughtsman's hand, trained as a cartographer in the Indian military, made perfectly straight lines for her to fill in. She wrote: Hind leg. Belly button. He was not amused, gave her a whack on the ear that sent her reeling.

So she was angry, and she stole the exam, and she did better than she would have because of it, and she won a scholarship to university. She told me – and she hasn't told many – that this was the day her life changed because she tasted what she was capable of, and it made her strangely fearless. She didn't feel guilty, she says, almost empowered. And yet she just couldn't write it down in her journal – "Regular Tuesday. Not much happened."

"Why do you think you didn't write it down?" I asked, even though I knew.

"Why do you think?" she asked back.

I remembered a course I'd taken at university on the Bible. I was nineteen and I had never read the Bible before. The professor would say the name Yahweh over and over, slightly pious. All semester he said it and every time he did it conjured two images in my head: a bloody, rotten corpse nailed to a cross, howling; and a kid chewing gum on one side of his mouth, making that sound, "Yahweh, Yahweh, Yahweh!"

"Because of The Word, I guess," I said. "Because of God."

Sunera smiled small, but she never answered.

So here's what I can't admit yet, here's my stolen bug test.

Early in the festival, I hit one of those nights when nobody's picking up and I called Theo McArdle and he wasn't picking up, which meant, in my imagination, that he was busy changing his mind about me.

Sunera was pretending to work all night and I couldn't even get Marvin and when you can't get Marvin on the line you begin to wonder if something went out somewhere, if someone reached up and unplugged a satellite. I put on music from the Nineties and tried to bounce around up and down just me and the leather couch, a one-person Nirvana moshpit (these were the moments in which I used to read), and then I danced past the newspaper and I saw the date, and I did the number thing, the thing I did when I was thirteen, fourteen, fifteen, calculating really fast the days and weeks and minutes from when my mom died, or the amount of time until her next birthday, or the age she'd be if she hadn't died, and I could see that two days had passed since the twenty-seventh anniversary of her death. I didn't even have to get out a pen and paper for that calculation. So I drank a glass (or three) of wine until there was just enough in me that the wine started pulling, wanting to be close to its own kind, and I started feeling dangerous. I took my longing to the College Street corner where media brides in high heels tottered through the slush, past thick red ropes blocking the movie theatre where some film festival thing had the street all backed up with limos and cabs and cameras sweeping their lights back and forth so it all looked like ship lights underwater. I was wading through this, arms up to ward off body blows, and I spotted Ad Sales, huddled by the entrance of a Portuguese bakery. Bad magic, the crowd parted and there he was, tassel shoes soaked in the snow, smoking a cigarette, a window of dusty plastic birthday cakes his backdrop. The thing with him is that from the ankles up, he's damn cute, in a Ben Affleck, alcohol-swollen, super-het way and I was feeling generous.

"Hey, don't I hate you from somewhere?" I asked.

"You're drunk," he said.

"You're in advertising," I said.

Ad Sales laughed. "Haven't done you in weeks," he smirked. "Pardon me, I haven't *seen* you, is what I meant to say. How's the inner conflict going? Still self-loathing?" He began beeping from the waist. Checking his pager with one hand, he flipped open a cell with the other. "Wassssup? . . . right . . . I'm on it . . . out."

"You'll get brain cancer," I said. "Plus, why do you need the pager when you have the phone? I don't get that."

"Max," he sighed, putting one hand on my shoulder. "I have a secret to tell you. Lean in." I leaned. "Really, lean in," he said.

He moved his mouth next to my ear and breathed, "It's okay to make money. It's okay to be successful."

He brushed my cheek, a cat batting a shadow. Then he kissed me, not friendly but mouth open, into the belly of the whale.

"Hey, hey," I said and he looked at me without any regret or shame, totally blank. That's Ad Sales for you. He's a Buddha, really.

"We're the same, you know?" he said, pulling a joint out of his crocodile-skin wallet.

"That's bold. There are about twenty TV cameras two doors down."

He shrugged, sparked up, asked, "You know how we're the same?"

"Impulsive? After the rush? Cowardly?"

He laughed.

"Precisely." He passed the joint and who am I to deny my body a little respite?

"They want you to be nicer, you know."

"Who?"

"The movie companies. They think you're too hard on the industry." The crowd cheered a black stretch limousine. Paparazzi flashbulbs lit Ad Sales's face, a kid in a sleeping bag with a flashlight.

"The industry is hard on *me*," I said. "I spent two hours of my life last week watching 'NSync in Imax."

"Hey, I kind of liked that one."

I looked at Ad Sales, and he smiled. "I'm kidding. I haven't seen it yet." How does Ad Sales remain so unequivocally male in these sexually porous times? He really owns the

Rat Pack dominant bonobo angle. He leaves the cave and gets the dinosaur, which is why it was worrisome when he lowered his voice and said, as he did, "Let me take you home."

I checked my cellphone – no call from Theo – and I agreed to a martini, knowing there was a clause in this agreement.

I did hesitate, I'm almost certain. It did cross my mind not to act this most predictable script, but I have never been very good at making pacts with myself. I am better at regret. I wish I had been certain and adult and fearful of easy bruises.

Ad Sales picked the bar, one of those places I didn't even know existed, the way you don't see your neighbourhood clearly when you're living in it – all the car repair shops that suddenly appear the moment you buy a car.

Ad Sales said something to the bouncer, and we stepped into a cave of music that sounded like ring tones competing. He propped me against the bar and leaned across to give the bartender in a leather bra a kiss, saying something I couldn't hear. She looked at me and laughed. I took the drink.

Shimmering in a red silk blazer, the host of a late-night TV show on BFD called Pop, as in "culture," came cutting through the crowd with a microphone and a cameraman. "Maxime, from *The Daily*!" he cried, and the camera light clicked on, a prison-yard spotlight flushing me out from the dark corner. "Any thoughts on this year's festival?"

I drained my martini. "World-class city, my friend." Only I think it came out martini-massaged: "World-class shitty!"

The hair nodded. "Exactly! Thank you, Maxime!" He moved on to perkier prey.

Ad Sales told me how he was waiting out *The Daily's* collapse by not so secretly working on a new Web site that will deliver cakes to your door, because what you really want the Internet to do is provide a human touch. What you really want is an electronic facsimile of your mother's Sunday-night desserts, directly on your doorstop.

"Why not call the company In Lieu Of?" I asked.

"We have a name. Are you ready?"

"No."

"Cake dot com."

"Catchy."

Ad Sales passed me a new drink. "So many dumb fuck companies have gone under that we can get the equipment for cheap. We're picking up an entire office of Aeron chairs and a pool table for three hundred bucks from a dead-in-the-water startup."

Something about all those barely worn chairs, and all the twenty-somethings who went back to being baristas at Starbucks and living in their parents' basements in suburbia — something about Ad Sales's tasselled toes casually slung across the furniture of broken dreams and his own adolescent confidence that nothing bad could ever happen to him — it was just too bleak to think about. So I stopped thinking. And when he asked me for the second time, I didn't say yes or no. I bobbed along. It was easier, and we went to his apartment and we kind of fucked, and it was mediocre, and I climbed in a taxi as the sun came up, my contact lenses seared to my eyeballs.

Bug test.

That was almost two weeks before the first time I slept with Theo McArdle.

And now it's this scene.

The doctor goes, "It's positive" and I go, "You mean it's negative," and she says in her dull scientist voice, "That's an old joke."

WHAT YOU DO IS . . . YOU GO FOR COFFEE AND THEN you think, Can I still drink coffee? You get on the subway platform, swim forward through the people, just trying to make a place to breathe, and stand in that space and do it, thinking, Can I still ride the subway? Should I get a car with four doors and a baby seat and an alarm system? And then you think, What, all that car to drive to the clinic to have this thing removed? You start running your inadequate pea brain backwards through all the bad things you've done that surely crawled right up into your cells and bred infection and you want to call someone, you want to tell someone, but what would you say? You have run out of repartee. You think of all the time you wasted watching when you should have been remembering what you once knew: how to start a fire with hands and twigs; how to sleep in a snow cave. You should have surrounded yourself with old people and listened to their tales of survival, really listened instead of jotting them down for later. You have entered your thirties without knowledge and you want it in a pile of sticks, a river, your bones.

You miss the train, you miss the second train, you miss the third train, but you still have this little space on the platform; no one's trying to take it from you but that's not what you want. What you want – of course this is what you really miss, most of all – what you want is your mother.

My parents were touched by the music of their time and in thrall to the clothes, but they were far away from revolution. For people like them, middle-class Canadian kids from medium-sized towns, the Sixties and Seventies were an exercise in long-distance sympathy. They hitchhiked to Vancouver and protested when a twenty-one-year-old Black Panther named Fred Hampton was shot in the head by police in Chicago, thirty-five hundred kilometres away. Back home in northern British Columbia, they traded stories about the Weather Underground and my mother fed a few draft dodgers hiding in the mountains, but there was nothing worth blowing up on the three sidewalks of Squamish's Main Street. Anger was carefully distributed, not exploded. My mother painstakingly typed a letter to the local paper about the bombings in Cambodia and walked downtown to drop it off by hand, a gesture so sweet it makes me angry to think about. The day it was published, my father cut the letter out and stuck it on the fridge with a magnet where it stayed until its edges curled. She had signed her married name.

I was young, and remember this time with the staccato rhythms of home movies we never took. I suppose I borrowed the stories, maybe from magazines I read later, or photographs belonging to someone else. What I have stitched together as my own, the setting I have chosen for my parents' life, is a revolution of haircuts and temporary, chosen poverty. Probably there was sex, and definitely there were drugs. But for them, as for most, things weren't that different than they were for the old man behind the ancient cash register with the bell on it in the hardware store, not that different from the women in orthopedic footwear making their way to church. The days went on in pursuit of enough money to live on, and enough love.

For my parents, it could have been 1942, but it was 1965. They meet comically: he is spending the summer living in a cave on the north shore of Vancouver, surveying for the government. One day he slips and falls in a river wearing his long army pants and though it's warm, he is cold from the water; his wool undershirt drapes off his frame, a sagging wire hanger (and in the way of children, I have filled in the details that my father never revealed, and that my mother took with her when she died). He returns to the cave, wraps himself in a sleeping bag. My mother stumbles upon him by accident. She is out picking berries with a group of young women from the community college where she is training to become a paralegal at her parents' behest. She becomes separated from the others, and they are glad to see her go: her endless talking about places she is going to visit but has never been, about war and fictions. She reaches the mouth of a cave, and instead of hurrying past, she stops, moving closer to peer inside. She is fearless, even when a bear rises in front of her. Instinctively, she thrusts the ice-cream pail of berries forward – An offering? A defence? – but she does not move or scream. Part of her is terrified, fearing for her life as the thing rises on its haunches, expands and hulks toward her. But part of her is exhilarated too, thinking, Finally, *something is happening.*

Then, in an instant, she sees that the beast is just a person in a sleeping bag, a young man with matted shoulder-length hair and a long, concave face. He sees her too: a woman who defends herself with an ice-cream pail of berries. A woman who explores caves. They fall in love, and she spends the summer going back and forth between his bear world and hers. In the autumn, she doesn't return to school.

He is playful with her in a way he will never be with anyone else, was never before, and has never been since. He tugs her long hair and watches with pride when she speaks her rapid speak to other people. She teases him gently, curls up on his stomach while he reads, and sings to herself. He laughs a wide rolling laugh in her presence that no one else ever hears.

But later does come, and this part isn't story; I witnessed it. My father leaving piles of squirming bait on the kitchen counter. My mother yelling. His jaw set in anger. Her voice through the walls, high-pitched, girly, and desperate. Hours of yelling through which he was silent.

For days, he would disappear to the woods and during those times she brought people into the house, friends and neighbours, with records and cigarette smoke, doors to the front porch opened to the street, always an invitation. (The adult questions only come up later when they can never be answered, and at the strangest times. I am twenty, undoing the belt buckle of a man I don't care for when the varying currencies of sex occur to me, and suddenly I think, Were there lovers among my mother's group?)

When he came back, forced to attend these parties, he sat in the corner, sketching onto notepads things he would build. He glared at the women in flesh-coloured pantyhose, their husbands with sweat stains under the armpits of their dress shirts. My mother welcomed all of them, any of them, and often.

So my parents were not just this two-headed creature so praised at her funeral. They were separate too, and sometimes hatefully. And I get confused because I remember also the whispered laughter, the two of them with their hands clasped walking toward my schoolyard to pick me up. The dance of two people cooking together, a small squeeze of my mother's shoulder, her smile.

This was marriage for them. Thirteen years of youth. I still don't know if it was normal, if love blackened can still be love. But for them, I think it was. I hope so.

IN THE CENTRE OF KENSINGTON MARKET, AROUND THE
corner from the Cuban coffee shop and the dry goods sellers
with their barrels of beans and cured meats, is a small park.
In the summer, hippie girls play bongos underneath the
maple trees, their boyfriends swinging from monkey bars. In
the winter, small ponds of ice form next to the slush-covered
sidewalk, and the benches are home to the occasional sleeping
body wrapped in blankets and newspapers. Today, they're all
empty except for one, where a man is waiting for me.

At a distance, the Ex is still himself, rocking back and forth, looking up at the sky from under a mint green toque. If you didn't know him – and I still know him, I realize, closing in on his bench, even after all this time not knowing him – you would think he had a Discman on. I used to tease him that he was autistic, put my hand on his leg at the movies to stop his body swaying when things were exploding, people dying, any kind of climax.

He sees me and the firm set of his jaw goes slack with pleasure. Then, immediately, his eyes narrow defensively. This was always the problem with both of us: We could never decide how happy to be.

"John," I say, the first time I've said his name out loud in a year and a half.

"Max," he says, and smiles, exposing a new chipped front tooth. This jars me; he has anecdotes I've never heard, the one about the chipped tooth. He stands up and gives me a hug that I can barely feel, weak through our thick jackets.

"Do you think it's getting warmer?" I ask, thinking, This is the first thing you're going to say to him? But I can't stop myself. "I hope it's getting warmer." He does this thing he used to do: tilts back and blows air, watches how white he can make it. He swore he could tell the temperature that way.

"John," I say again.

"Max," and we're both laughing now, which is strange. I can tell, even from his hug, John is still: tall, skinny, sombre, the person I love the most in the world.

"So what's going on? Do you want to go for a walk? I only have about an hour," He talks, as always, in a slightly high-pitched voice.

"Back to the girlfriend?"

"Yeah," he looks guilty. Good. It was never her fault, this inevitable dissolution, but it still pleases me to imagine her protesting our meeting. Maybe I was the source of a fight between them. All of this means I matter still.

"You had to sneak out?"

"Not exactly sneak, but she's not too comfortable with it."

"With what?"

He squirms and sighs, always in action. "How you could be friends with an ex."

"Are we friends?" I ask this seriously.

"I hope so. I mean . . ." he fades.

I sit down on the bench, suddenly tired. The snow is melting. Wedges of snow, the detritus of city blowers, form an ankle-high wall around the park perimeter, a grey, mottled wall stained with exhaust and urine, human and animal. John sits next to me, both of us consciously not touching and it feels strange that I don't lean just an inch and put my head on his shoulder, his thin hand around my waist; how much time in my life I've spent in that position and then you have to unlearn it, another useless song lyric clogging up the brain.

The park seems to be shape-shifting, inviting spring. A blade of grass is pushing up through the melted snow right before our eyes.

I take a breath and blurt a question that's rattled around my head for so long I don't even hear it any more: "What went wrong with us?" Suddenly, it's important to me to understand this. An entire unexplored universe could reside in the answer.

John kicks the cement with a salt-stained boot and moans a little. Then he says, like he's reciting an instructional manual in fast motion, "We were unhappy. I was depressed and you were always pushing . . ." He slows down, reconsiders, and adds, "Then I fucked up. I fucked it up. But we were both miserable."

I hate this answer. It's true, and useless. I see myself standing by the clock on the stove waiting up all night, imagining him with her, or some her I didn't know existed yet. It still knocks the wind out of me. I regret starting this conversation, my pathetic hope for some kind of resolution. I am immature, the kid who refuses to heal because she likes the bandages too much.

"But we weren't miserable in the beginning, were we?" I ask. I need him to remember too.

"No," he says, pulls the toque off and runs his fingers through his hair. It's longer, a little lighter, as if he's been somewhere warm. His glasses are dirty.

"And now you're the one with the big career," I say. "I saw your pictures at that show –"

"Oh yeah. You probably thought it was bullshit?" It's a question, not a statement.

I answer slowly. "I guess I prefer your paintings, but this seems like it has an audience."

He laughs. "Very diplomatic."

His laugh is so lurching and familiar that I have to ask it, I have to get right up into that gaping bleeding wound, slip around inside its tissue, and ask, "Do you ever think about me?"

John moans again. "I can't win, answering that question." I jab him in the ribs. My hand on his body.

"Of course I do," he sighs. "Max, we grew up together. When we split, I lost a big part of myself." I'm surprised to hear him talk like that; I wonder about this Elizabeth, about what reserves of emotion she's opened up in him, if she has a normal family to visit on holidays.

Then I think suddenly, aggressively, Why does she get him? I look at his eyes, the dark lids, the handsome pull of his mouth. What he is not any more: young, open, mine. We said everything to each other once. He knows more about me than anyone I have ever spoken to and in that way he's like an extension of me that I lost the password for, a database functioning somewhere else out there, all knowing and totally separate.

I have so much to tell him, but this comes out: "I heard a thing on the radio the other day that we're supposed to be a full ten years behind our parents." I picture John's parents in their suburban split-level. Their polite Christmas gifts: picture frames and candles. John's adolescent surliness in their presence, his stingy way of refusing their advances and invitations. All through our twelve years, I still had to call them Mr. and Mrs.

I go on: "When our parents were our age, they had kids and houses and jobs for life. We still live like we're in our twenties. Isn't that weird?" John pulls the toque down over his eyes, then back up.

"Maybe that's why I've been eating so much candy lately," he says.

Babies named, children raised. I remember when he moved out and I was beat up with missing him, and I couldn't get used to that feeling of ghost limbs, that he couldn't possibly still exist because he couldn't exist without me. I told Sunera: *It's like he's dead.* She looked shocked: *But, Max,* she said, *your mom is dead. How can you say that?*

I couldn't tell her that I was secretly glad for a new loss. I didn't want to seem callous, to say what I was thinking, which was that this loss was almost worse. It was worse because there remained some semblance of hope, the body hadn't been found, the missing posters still flapped from the poles.

"I'm kind of glad you called back, actually, even if it took a while," he says. "I wanted to tell you something."

I know what it is. You just know some things, because he has the steely demeanour he gets before a cruel statement, as if it will hurt him more than it could possibly hurt you, and he has to shut down to protect himself, and that shutting down will protect you too; he will shoulder the burden. He never knew this habit just made me more frightened.

"You're getting married, or you're having a baby," I say, partially to release him from having to say it, partially to prove that he's still mine, and I know everything about him. My breath makes a light smoke. Maybe spring is coming; think about that. Think about that. In a tighter voice: "Or both."

He relaxes, always grateful that I would be hurt before he had to do the dirty work. He picked the right person, forever hurt.

"We're getting married," he says. "I didn't know if I would ever want to get married. You and I talked about it so much . . ."

Did his sentences always trail off like that? Was he always this incapable of completing a thought? I put my finger to my forehead to pinpoint the banging – right above my left eyebrow – then I laugh.

"It's important to Elizabeth. She's more traditional than you are," he says fast, defensive, and then annoyed that I'm making him feel defensive. "You know, I never really bought the whole marriage thing from you. It just didn't seem like you would ever really follow through. You're too . . ." He's flapping his hands in the air, frustrated, looking for a word.

I set my face.

"Too?"

He shrugs, drops his hands. It's not his place to make pronouncements about me any more.

"I think I'm going to go now," I tell him, and I stand up, feeling an enormous tug of fatigue dragging me down to the ground. I brace myself with one hand on the back of the bench: So that's how it might be then, nine months of bad footing.

"You never told me why you called," says John, standing up.

It would never occur to him that my news could be as profound as his own.

"I'll tell you some other time," I say, stomping the slush from my boots. This statement is habit, but out there in the park it implies some kind of future, and there isn't one.

We stand there, and I'm wondering if I'll get a goodbye hug, and it occurs to me that we might never meet again. He does it first, just bends a little, and I know where to go. I put my face in his neck to smell him. Through the frozen wool of his scarf, I do.

EVEN WITHOUT A WATCH, I KNOW IT'S TOO EARLY FOR anyone else to be at work. The parking lot is nearly empty when the cab drops me off, the sky just beginning to brighten and frighten off night. I buzz through security, past an empty reception desk. Even Ad Sales isn't in his cubicle.

7:30 a.m., says the clock on the wall. I haven't slept in thirty-six hours.

I kick through the Diet Coke cans and lower my chair as far as it goes. Thirty-six hours without Diet Coke, without smoking. Not even a drink. Thirty-six hours in the same corner of my bed, staring at the same patch of ceiling, not weeping and moaning, but waiting.

Since John left, I have never spent that long in my apartment at one time.

When my back got numb, I showered and called Mohsen to drive me up here. A new patch of ceiling.

I smooth out the prescription pad paper with the number of the abortion clinic, place it next to the phone. On the other end of that number are fetal vacuum cleaners and armed protesters lying behind bushes waiting to shoot doctors.

Way off in the distance, far from my cubicle, is a window and through the window is a dripping orange sunrise like the start of a children's book.

Who is the father? Will the baby arrive with tassels on his feet, a tiny beeper on his waist? Will he be soft and sleepy-eyed, a little bundle of empathy, a baby who knows how to get out of time and space? "Have you thought about your options?" asked the doctor. My options right now don't seem so different from the same ones that got me here.

And then this: A small version of Theo for the rest of my life might be something I could live with. It's the big version I can't picture: a father with a child on his shoulders. A homework helper. The three of us digging sand. Surely there is more to it than these movie fragments, but what do I know about fathers? My father, it is clear to me now, went mad during my childhood. He had always stayed just enough in the world for her, but once she was gone, it was like watching someone walking away in slow motion, down a staircase, descending into something liquid. He put aside that depression during her life, and welcomed it after.

At the compound, my dad would vanish for days at a time. He and Elaine were sometimes a couple, sometimes undeclared, but it didn't matter; I spent the nights without my father on a foam mattress on the floor of Elaine's room, unable to sleep. I needed the sound of my dad's breathing through the wall of the two attached bedrooms that were ours in the motel strip.

He would return days later, fish roped over one arm, hosing down his boots, hanging the catch over the back porch of the dining hall. He walked right by me, eyes on some invisible point off in the distance. First the walk to the shower and then to Elaine's bed, where he would lie alone and recover from his solitude while she worked in the garden.

One time he returned with a glass orb, an old fishing buoy covered in seaweed. He loved that orb, shined it with vinegar and made a nest of wood chips for it to live in. Parents would get stoned and pass it around, nodding at their reflections, babbling on about Meister Eckhart and the skeletons of America, believing that shit as if the Eighties weren't jogging by in bright white Keds across the harbour.

Our schoolbooks were stapled-together sheaves of paper mimeographed in the city, long pages of purple ink. The typewriter at the compound had a temperamental E that rose high above the other letters. When we used the textbooks left behind by the Department of Education on their yearly visits, other people's mothers would sit with black felt pens, inking out the sexist parts.

Some kids couldn't wade through the muck. A little boy named Erik fell weeping when he read of the Viking pillages, white, male, and Scandinavian as he was. A little girl with a shaved head did a presentation to the learning circle, declaring that Capt. George Vancouver had set foot on our island, but because there were no natives to butcher here, he moved on to Vancouver Island, and that's why we weren't living in the capital of British Columbia. The mothers murmured their approval, reminding us that one version of history held as much veracity as the next, that every moment should harbour a creative act, even spelling was an art form.

When we were driven to school gymnasiums in North Vancouver to take our tests at the end of each school year, these children – the converts, the believers, the ones who, in regular classrooms, would be brown-nosers and apple-bringers – did badly. I did well. I got older and I learned how to hold the books up to the light and see past the black lines. There was a vast library at the compound where I read about victory, and it was just victory. Clean. Declared.

By grade ten, I asked my father if I could go to the mainland for the rest of high school, taking the school ferry and the city bus back and forth. He put down his nails and boards (what was he building anyway? The whole compound was in disrepair, gopher-hole-sized spaces in the floorboards and nails protruding; a little girl sliced open her bare foot on a rusty bolt and had to be rushed to the mainland for a tetanus shot). This was in the time when his pupils were so dilated that it was like looking at a plastic baby doll with black circles of ink for eye sockets. He rubbed his forehead so hard I thought he'd pull skin off.

"Okay," he said finally. "If that's what you want."

I did. I wanted alligator shirts and acid-wash Levi's and one pink plastic earring in the shape of a cube and fingerless gloves and school dances and strawberry-flavoured coolers and joints fat as thumbs.

I learned quickly that if I got off the bus a little early on the way to school, I could go to the Park Royal Mall. The theatre there had matinees and restricted movies and a serene old woman at the counter who never checked ID; she could barely see through her one watery blue eye. I cut class for movies, and for worse, but mostly for movies. Sometimes I stayed out so late that I missed the last boat back and Elaine would come across in her outboard motor to find me waiting on the dock, bra in my pocket from a drunken fumble.

After one of those evenings, I lay on the mattress on her floor, trying not to close my eyes to keep the room from spinning. Elaine came in from the bathroom smelling like grapefruit soap and crouched down, handing me a rainbow-striped Guatemalan woven wallet with a $20 bill in it: "Mad money." She explained that a woman should always have a little money to protect her, money to wake the water taxi owner and get home, money to let her get angry, instead of sucking it up. The idea chilled me, as if without this twenty-dollar bill, I might be forced to do something against my will: "No, it's okay. I'm not mad. I'll stay." Money to keep the bad at bay.

The kids at my new high school lived in mansions in the hills of North Vancouver, glass and cedar A-frames and bungalows with swimming pools. I blended in easily, dropping television references to win their favour, learning sarcasm and meanness to keep it.

Grade twelve was the year they carried university catalogues with them like accessories. One girl, a thin, boneless blonde who took great care to care very little about anything, complained that she would wake up in the morning and find applications on the pillow next to her, placed there by her anxious psychiatrist father. My own father nodded when I showed him my grades and said, "Good, Max," handing the report card back to me. He looked puzzled when I thrust it at him again. "You're supposed to sign it." I said.

"Oh yes. Like a very important legal document," he laughed. He thought everything that was serious in the real world was silly, but the real world fascinated me. Some nights I slept in my friends' houses in a guest room, or on a couch next to a television as large as a wall. In the morning we would have fresh-squeezed orange juice and scorn whatever grown-ups passed through the kitchen. In principle, nothing excited us. When the sun set, we went to the beach to smoke and flirt with boys we hated.

Most nights I went back to the compound because these parents, while ridiculed, still held sway somehow, and the girls needed to be in their own beds by midnight or police would appear, flashlights in car windows at the dock or in the liquor store parking lot. I was jealous of these moonlight rescues orchestrated by fathers protecting their daughters' virtue.

Somehow, with very little effort, I earned As, and this mattered to me, though I could tell no one: not the girls competing to be dumbest, not the mothers at the compound, competing not to be competitive.

The spring of grade twelve felt endless. The frail friendships of high school fell apart once and for all, as if everyone knew there were only a few months left, and gave up pretending. I had final exams on my mind, and was plotting my escape, fashioning a raft out of university and scholarship applications.

One afternoon in my final months, I attempted to study at the long slab of table in the dining hall. Two little girls jammed twigs in their hair and danced around screaming, "Chicken, chick chick chicken!" The doors were flung open and the sun was warming the mothers on the porch, a pair of them smoking and giggling, looking out at the water, the other islands hunched like grey whales on all sides. I knew the cold tang of that water, the naked midnight swim off the dock with everybody laughing and Elaine smiling at me, saying, *This is the life, huh?* And for them, it was heaven, and I was going to leave it, and never come back.

I hadn't yet told my father that I was leaving because I didn't want to be hurt when he didn't mind. But it seemed that now, spring was upon us, and that meant momentum, and change. I walked across the wet field toward my father's room.

I had an essay in my hand, typed on the compound's large electric typewriter. What was the subject? Something about poetry.

I planned what I would say: *I'm going to university. You won't have to worry about me any more.* But that was wrong; he never worried. Something different: *It's time for me to leave. I'm ready for you to let me go.* Wrong too; he had never kept me. But it would suffice, and the drama of the words pleased me.

I opened the door to his room slowly. My dad lay on his side on the bed, facing the wall, socks dangled from his toes in a point. I knew he wasn't asleep by the easy breathing.

"Dad," I said, my heart racing. He rolled over onto his back and looked up at me milkily. We were breathing two different kinds of air: Mine was thick with anticipation, the electric chaos of expecting a fight. His was dull, flat-lined. Then, instead of the rehearsed speech, I thrust my essay out in front of me, surprising myself. "Dad, will you proofread this for me?"

He took the pages in his hand and flipped through them a long time, with unusual deliberateness. I wondered if something I wrote struck him. Watching him read, I felt dizzy with optimism. That's how it was with him: I swung between hope and disappointment, a violent oscillation.

And then his hand dropped. The papers drifted to the floor and he said, "Max, I took something a while ago. It's hard for me to focus."

I bent quickly to gather the scattered pages, face burning.

"I'm sure it's great," he said.

I stood up. The paper was out of order. Hatred surged in my gut. I loathed him for his dumb stillness.

"I'm leaving," I said, quickly, hoarsely.

My father nodded, eyes half-closed. "Mmm," he said. "Can you wake me for dinner?"

I stared at him, eyes hot, then turned to go. As I turned, I spotted the glass orb on his dresser, a random thing he'd found in the ocean and been so proud of. I removed it from its woodchip bed. I took it in my hands. My dad watched, a look of defeat already crossing his face. I lifted the ball over my head, held it still for a moment. He closed his eyes, and so did I. Release. Glass sprayed up into my jaw, my bare legs pocked with blood, drifting downwards.

Are you sorry? I wanted to scream it, to puncture his calm, to bruise him awake. *Are you sorry you left me when she did?* But I knew he was only sorry for one thing: Sorry that she died first.

I didn't scream. I said nothing, and neither did he.

I walked to the door. I thought of all the things that were ahead of me: I would wet a tissue and clean the blood from my knees and ankles. I would take an airplane east and read and work and live in buildings with central air conditioning and dishwashers. I would be gone, and in the grip of that thought, I didn't want to turn back but I did. I saw my father looking at me, not moved, but afraid. It was one of the last times we were alone together.

I kept Elaine's mad money zipped in the top pocket of my army surplus backpack when I left. I took that wallet with me my very first night at university on the other side of the country in Kingston, Ontario, my bags unopened on the floor of my residence room, following a train of people to the four-block-long downtown. I sat in a smoky bar designed to look like London, with a red English phone booth in the corner and a bobby hat for tips. The kids I sat with came from places I couldn't picture: upstate New York, Montreal, Toronto. I bought them a round of two-dollar Molson Drys; it came to twenty-two bucks with tip, and I was happy to hand over the soggy bill at last.

ONCE A MONTH OR SO, SUNERA THE GOOD DAUGHTER stays at her parents' house for the weekend, helping her mother cook and shop for the unending series of family weddings. I take the College streetcar east, past Regent Park, a city of government-subsidized high-rises with cracked windows and small, proud rowhouses built around gravel-floored parks. With the snow melted, a few people have laid out blankets to sell their things, as if they've been waiting to unload them all winter. The streetcar stops in front of one desperate yard sale manned by an old black woman squatting before her offerings: a foam-filled lion won at a fair; faded T-shirts laid out flat; a plastic toaster with a burnt, raggedy chord.

The streetcar continues through the crowds of the city's second Chinatown and, finally, Little India. I open the window an optimistic crack and the smell comes first, cardamom and ginger. Stalls of purple orchids, battered saris on plastic torsos attached to store awnings, twisting in the wind. The women stand in clusters, plastic shopping bags dangling from wrists, voices overlapping loudly against the Bollywood soundtracks blasting from the video stores. The men stand apart with their legs planted wide, smoking, talking to each other, rarely glancing at their wives and daughters. A few women have taken off their winter coats, and here and there a sausage-arm pushes through the gold-threaded sleeve of a sari into this freakish warm air. The weather is an anomaly, first taste of the spring that will come in a few weeks. Skin has returned.

Sunera's mother opens the door and peers up at me. "Sunera, Maxime is here!" she shouts. She gives me a kiss on the cheek and takes my coat, perusing my black turtleneck, jeans, black boots combo with a sigh of disappointment. Sunera's mother scares me. She starts every relationship from a place of disapproval; her daughters will inevitably let her down; the food placed in front of her is bound to be terrible; the man at the grocery store is robbing her blind.

The house smells like milk tea. Sunera's father sits in the living room surrounded by piles of newspaper, the snouts of his slippered feet resting on an ottoman. He looks up, makes a grunting noise, a waving gesture, then returns to the papers.

"Girls like black," says Mrs. Singhal, irritated. Mrs. Singhal prefers to pack her snowman body into red overalls, a pink T-shirt, and white, no-brand running shoes: a toddler's clothes.

"Mummy, leave her alone," says Sunera, looming over her mother, twice her height and half her weight. Sunera is wearing a hot pink sari disco-balled with tiny mirrors. A thin gold chain disappears up one nostril.

"You look beautiful!" I say.

She raises an eyebrow, does her best Bollywood voice, half nodding, half shaking her head: "I am a good Indian girl, yes?" ushering me upstairs.

"Sunera, don't forget about the flowers! You must pick them up by four o'clock." Sunera shoves me up the staircase. Her mother follows, still talking.

"Okay, Mummy!"

She slams the door, basically in her mother's face, but somehow she does it politely.

The walls of Sunera's childhood room are covered in adolescent obsessions: Model UN participation certificates in cheap frames on the wall, a poster of The Velvet Underground. I touch a yellow push-pin and wonder what happened to my childhood things, to my mother's things, and I remember how stark my walls were, in the barracks, the van, how every bat and ball and book belonged to everyone and no one. Then this: my mother had hoops of silver dangling from her ears.

What happened to her jewellery? Somewhere, that silver still exists.

When Sunera announced that she was moving out right after high school, her father read the papers and her mother ranted and cried, Why must you go to school so far away?, even though it is only five hours from Toronto to Montreal. Mrs. Singhal threatened to turn Sunera's room into a sewing room, but her anger came in fits and spurts and she could never finish the conversion. She doesn't, in fact, sew at all and for her mending needs likes to visit her friend the tailor on Gerrard Street where they talk for hours while the tailor sews a single button onto a wool overcoat. But the idea of a sewing room seemed right symbolically, so Sunera's rolltop desk houses a high-end electric sewing machine that's still in the box. She shoves aside bolts of silk and kicks at balls of yarn until there's space on the electric flower-patterned polyester bed throw. We sit cross-legged on the twin bed, each of us perched at opposite ends like we're about to play cards, and my knees click and burn. It's been a long time since the learning circle. Sunera's skirts spill over the edges, her neck poking out of the melting folds, treading water in a big pink puddle.

"My cousin's wedding is in two weeks and my mom's gone apeshit with the shopping," says Sunera. "What do you think?" She puts her hands together like Shiva, does that side-to-side head-weaving dance. Then she pulls the gold chain from her nose.

"Glue," she says and pretends to flick me with it. She pops an evener-outer, a pink pill that looks like baby Aspirin. "Want one?" I do, but I don't.

"Which cousin is this?"

"The one from Scarborough. Remember my birthday? You met her. Tall?" I nod, but Sunera's family gatherings are packed with brilliant, beautiful cousins and sisters and second and third cousins ranging from twelve to forty. The only way to tell them apart is by the varying levels of disappointment their mothers exude.

"She's never met the guy," says Sunera. "She's lived here her whole life, he's fresh off the plane from Delhi. Interesting power dynamic, huh? He has to give up everything for the woman and come here."

"Is it a money thing?"

"No. He's a successful computer programmer back in the motherland, but his family wants him in the New World. The fantasy endures," she says, hopping from the bed. In one fell swoop she opens the window, places a bolt of fabric at the crack at the bottom of the door, lights a stick of incense jutting out of a mottled houseplant, and reaches under her pillow for a pack of Camel Lights. It is an elegant routine perfected from years of practice.

"Smoke?" I shake my head no (pickle baby puckers up its fish mouth: thank you, mama), but damn it looks good there in her hand. It's the look – grown up, certain – that I miss more than the taste right now.

Sunera leans back, rattling the bedframe. "She's twenty-seven. She lived with a white guy and it turned to shit. She can't meet anyone she likes in the city. You know what she said? She said, 'How could it possibly be any worse?' And you know the strange part?" Sunera drags. "I found myself going, 'You're right.' I mean, why not? I don't see a lot of successful relationships either." She laughs. "Maybe I should ask my parents to hook me up."

I don't say anything. I'm thinking: I haven't talked to anyone in three days. Sunera looks at me, mistakes my broken expression for concern, and adds, "I'm kidding, by the way."

"Everyone's getting married," I say, picking at flowers on her bedspread.

"What? Who else?"

"John."

"Get OUT!" Sunera kicks me in the shin in disbelief, ash flying all over the pink waterfall dress. So I give her the scoop, all the best details about meeting John in the park and the green toque, the girlfriend anxiously waiting at home. She says the right things – how the new wife is probably a nightmare, how he's such a mess and a bad artist and how I'm better off without him but aren't I glad I loved him then? All the perfect kind things that always roll out of Sunera so easily. Then she says, "What possessed you to call him anyway?" And she looks at me with her dark eyes and she is like some goddess of friendship in that stupid dress, and I start crying. I lose the fight with gravity and flop right over in a big wet pile.

"Max, what is it?" She's stroking my hair and I'm coming undone on the layers of pinkness, snotting them right up.

"Snot . . . dress!" I snorfle, and this makes me cry even harder.

Sunera smiles: "I hate this dress. I truly hate it. It's pink." She passes me a handful of dress. "Blow."

I sit up, wiping my face on the pink, and then I take a deep breath and I tell her. I say it out loud for the first time.

"Pregnant."

And then the second thing: "And I'm not totally sure who the father is."

We sit quietly for a minute, me choking on the snotty dress. Finally, Sunera says, "You slut." And I laugh, which I haven't done in a long time.

She asks me what I'm going to do. I say the one thing I know for sure which is that I don't know. She leans over, takes my hand in hers, and says, slowly and clearly, "I'll help you out if you want to keep this baby, and if you want me to drive you to the clinic for an abortion, I'll take you." A strange thought comes to me: Sunera will be a good mother one day.

Monday mornings at university always brought a queue at the health centre, a long line of morning-after pill poppers, young women in Doc Martens with long johns peeking through jeans, or ponytailed jocks. I've taken those pills, twelve hours apart, because the condom broke or I couldn't quite remember if the condom existed in the first place. I never got pregnant, somehow, despite my reckless-ness, and yet the girl who always used birth control, who was into double duty, backup, insurance (the condom never without the foam, the pill never without the condom, the diaphragm never without the jelly), is the girl who goes: 'Oh my God,' and you're holding her hand in the bathroom over a little blue stick and then waiting in the waiting room to take her home after the operation, rubbing her back as she sleeps on her side. If it's that arbitrary, then why bother? I've thought that: *Why bother?* I've even said it: *We don't need to. I'm safe.* Safety; the blunt edge of children's scissors that can still poke your eye out.

One time, shouting in the corner of a bar, Sunera told me her story. She shouldn't have been ovulating, but it was the night her boyfriend first said I love you, and she thinks she just laid an egg right there. Her body said, I'll show you love, pal, ten days early. Stranger things have happened. It turned out Sunera and the guy didn't have the same idea of love and she was twenty-two and just out of university, working her first big job and living back at home in the half-sewing room. Her mother went with her, demanded that she stand right next to the machine, a whirring globe dangling from a post. She body-blocked the machine so Sunera didn't see anything when she looked except for her mom, frowning and nodding, frowning and nodding.

"Do you ever think about yours?"

Sunera shakes her head. "No, honestly, I don't. I know there are people who think, Oh, it would be four now, it would be eight, but I never do. I know it was the right thing for me then."

I look over at Sunera's childhood bookshelf: *On the Road* beside *Alligator Pie* beside *Anne of Green Gables*.

"I think I never quite believed I could get pregnant," I tell her. "I've gone this long."

Sunera laughs, raises my hand to her lips for a little kiss. "Who knew you were human?" She gets up. "Let's have some fun."

She opens a small pot of henna, the colour of cedar stump flesh.

"Isn't it just for brides?" I ask, as she tickles the top of my hands with a long thin brush, starting at the centre and working her way out – a nature documentary where everything is sped up and becoming – a vine gives way to bud, bud to petal, petal to blossom.

"Today it's for friends," she says.

The interior of the streetcar taking me back west is entirely covered with newspaper images: politicians shaking hands; a Tent City squatter peering out from a refrigerator box; rock stars squinty with guitar face. And alternating these front page images, in very fuzzy black and white, are some of *The Daily's* esteemed columnists: the Loony Libertarian; the Crotchety Conservative; the Sultry Society Lady. And underneath a fringe of dark hair, eyes down as if ashamed, or on the cusp of fainting, me. The Celebrity Chick. The final frame of the car reads: *The Daily. Think It Over.*

A plug of a woman enters one stop after me, green hospital scrubs on short legs jutting out from a long black winter coat, slightly frayed at the cuffs, two plastic bags substituting for a purse. But for a pair of kids making out, the streetcar on this Sunday afternoon is nearly empty, and yet the woman in scrubs chooses to sit right next to me.

She stares at my henna-ed hand and asks, "Going to a wedding?" There's a foamy trace of Spanish in her voice.

"No, no," I say. "I'm, uh . . ." I'm looking for the word. "Appropriating."

She doesn't respond, just reaches out a finger, cold and callused, traces the lines on my hands. I'm not big on public touching, but I don't pull away because the way she's moving her finger, it's like she's trying to pull something out of me, deep under the skin, and she's staring and tracing, very still.

Quickly, quietly, as though we are old friends, she starts telling me a story, a fairy tale of sorts. I might repeat it one day in a dark room to help a child fall asleep. I have been rehearsing.

The woman is named Mercy and she is a nurse. This is the first true unbelievable fact. Mercy came from Guatemala. In the dirty wars her family was killed off, one by one. Twenty-five years ago, she hid in a shipping container in the hull of a liner. When the lights of San Diego came into view, someone tapped the container and she climbed out. Dozens of people dove into the harbour, swimming to safety; from a distance, they must have looked like luggage being tossed overboard.

It was arranged that she would hide in an empty truck travelling to British Columbia to bring lumber back to the United States, and she hid under a cot in the cab (they never check the cab, only the back), her clothes still wet, and crossed the border safely. She jumped out in Vancouver and took the American money she had sewn into a plastic bag in her bra and traded it for Canadian dollars. With that money, she bought a bus ticket to Toronto.

She learned English and went to night school, living in a basement with friends of relatives from home. People were coming and going all the time, Guatemalans, El Salvadorians; the windowless basement was an unofficial shelter. She worked illegally in a hotel, cleaning uniforms and stained towels, until she made enough money to get a lawyer, and the lawyer got her papers. She had seen the piles of empty blankets in the basement, all that remained of those who had been tapped in raids at the restaurants or on the docks, people sent home, and she wasn't going back. She would live above ground, legally, become Canadian.

Mercy studied medical books by flashlight. One of the comings and goings in that basement left her pregnant and she gave birth to a daughter the day after she took her entrance exams for nursing school. She named the daughter Maria.

With five hundred extra dollars a month from the government and a job cleaning offices at night in the Bay Street financial district, Mercy and Maria got a bachelor apartment in a sky-rise at St. Jamestown, a collection of towers with optimistic names: the Halifax, the Vancouver, the Montreal. St. Jamestown was built in the Seventies so swinging singles could live downtown and walk to work, but the white professionals only stayed a few months, edged out by groups of immigrants bringing their families one by one from far away, all to live together in apartments no bigger than a bus. The families – big, loud, always working – lived side by side with the gangs and junkies who wandered over from Regent Park. They stayed in St. Jamestown for years, and every single time she entered its teeming corridors, Mercy thought, St. James, brother of John, disciple of Jesus. On the swings in the playgrounds sometimes Maria's foot brushed syringes with the sole of her shoe as she went up, up, up.

Maria and Mercy's neighbours were Somalian, Indian, Chinese, and the hallway walls were wet with steam from cooking. Maria's favourite food, at three years old, was samosas.

Mercy became a nurse. She took Maria and they moved out of St. Jamestown, to a building at Yonge and Eglinton with a doorman who would check in on Maria while Mercy worked the night shift.

Maria was smarter than everyone else in her class. She grew tall and beautiful, with long black hair, and by fifteen, she had a job selling clothes at Club Monaco. She won a scholarship to university in the northeast United States. Mercy was terrified, but she let her go. They talked on the phone almost every night and Mercy sat alone at Maria's graduation ceremony, delirious with what she had created.

Maria returned to Toronto and moved back into Mercy's apartment. The two stayed up late, talking through the night. One evening Maria came home from her job working at an investment banking firm and said, 'I've met someone.' His name was Vikram and he was a banker too.

Mercy didn't know what to make of this handsome young man who showed up at the apartment with daisies in his arms and scrubbed clean the chicken-stuck pots without being asked. She watched him watching her daughter. He never interrupted Maria. Many of his sentences began: "Maria thinks . . ." and "Maria said . . ." He beamed with pride. He brought Mercy mulligatawny when she was sick.

Maria loved Vikram's family. She came home from his parents' house in Richmond Hill, a bedroom community of subdivisions known for little except the city's best Chinese food, with all kinds of stories about small cousins and old aunties. Maria cracked Mercy up with her tales of meddling visitors from southern India who used the bathroom tub to soak fresh stems of curry leaves smuggled into Canada.

Mercy was often alone. She took extra shifts to fill the time that she used to spend with Maria. She steeled herself for the inevitable, and when Vikram arrived one day while Maria was at work, Mercy knew why. She couldn't say anything but yes, of course, though a small poisoned part of her wanted to slap him and lock the door. I have had so much change already, Mercy thought, feeling sorry for herself. I can't take any more change.

But she did. She took it when she sat up that night with Maria, who couldn't stop laughing, mockingly dangling her hand in front of Mercy's face and saying, "So anything new with youooo?" The engagement ring sent off sparks.

The day before the wedding, Mercy drove Maria to Richmond Hill. The house was small and identical to the houses around it, and Mercy couldn't imagine how all those people Maria had described could fit. When the door opened, she saw how they did it: everyone was touching, small arms around big legs, skin hip to hip. Vikram's mother, Kaly, grabbed Mercy and put her in a place of prominence, high on a chair by the fireplace. Kaly explained that this wasn't a traditional Mendhi party, because Maria wasn't Indian, and Kaly said, happily: 'We get to be more than Indian now!'

As the girls painted each other's hands and sang, Kaly told Mercy about her work as a counsellor in a high school, and slowly, Mercy's anxiety floated away. She loved to be feted. When Maria's hands were perfectly embroidered, she kneeled before her mother and her mama-ji, displaying her wrists and fingers, which looked like they were blooming. The women cried a little.

Maria had asked if Mercy wanted a Catholic wedding and Mercy guffawed. There would be two weddings. A Hindu wedding and a secular wedding. The morning of the Hindu wedding, Mercy was at Kaly's house stringing up rows of purple orchids while Kaly hummed and braided her youngest's hair.

Vikram and Maria rented bicycles at a sporting goods store near Mercy's apartment. They wanted to cycle to the waterfront and spend some time together. *Alone*, said Maria on the phone to her mother, but she laughed as she said it.

Following Yonge Street southbound, sound is hemmed in by an overpass; on a bike, it is like travelling through a tube of white noise beneath the earth.

Maria had her hands over her ears and watched Vikram go across first. He looked back at her and shouted something. She made a face: *I can't hear you.* She moved forward and then a car turning right onto the expressway ramp plucked her bicycle up, a circus elephant grabbing a toy with its trunk. Maria flew through the air, landed directly in the centre of the very same crosswalk she'd been negotiating. The light turned red. All the cars stopped. It was so polite: no beeping, no bumpers touching, motionless.

Vikram dropped his bicycle and ran back toward Maria. Just before he reached her, the light turned green and one car – a blue SUV – surged forward, pushing him several feet until it stopped suddenly. This all happened in the tail end of a second, it seemed: people opened their car doors and went forward to look at Vikram and Maria. They were bodies now.

Kaly took the call. She turned to stare at Mercy, laughing in her high chair. Mercy felt something, a door had flung open and shadow flooded in, and she turned slowly, thinking, Don't look. It's better not to look. But she did, and the look she saw on Kaly's face was one she recognized from years in the hospital, a look like the smell of rubber gloves and disinfectant. All my life has come out of me, said Kaly's face. All my life has ended.

On the drive to the same hospital where Mercy worked, chauffeured by a nephew, the women said nothing.

The day-shift nurses were clustered in admissions when the two mothers entered. "Mercy . . . ," said the head nurse softly. Mercy began to scream. Kaly patted her on the back, and went to see her son.

That night, Mercy returned to the apartment and pulled the blinds. She told the doorman not to let anyone up to see her. He piled flowers outside her door and removed them when they began to rot. When Vikram could walk, he came over, opening the door with Maria's key. He found Mercy lying in bed and he turned on the light. She saw that his face had changed: a small petal of pale scar tissue was stamped in the centre of his right cheek. His other eye was wet, open but closed. He leaned on a cane, like an old man.

Vikram packed up Mercy's things. He put a quilted coat around her nightgown and one by one, he rolled socks on her feet. She leaned against him and he carried her like that, Mercy on one side, his cane on the other. They shuffled past the doorman to Vikram's car and the doorman wept.

In Richmond Hill, Mercy was given her own room. She had displaced a few young children, it seemed, as the room was covered in posters of Britney Spears and Backstreet Boys. Mercy remembered Maria's phases: New Kids on the Block and Milli Vanilli. Kaly brought her tea and sat by her bed, reading, while Mercy memorized the number of links on the pocket chain in Nick Carter's jeans. Below that was a small shrine to Ganesh, grown dusty with child neglect.

Vikram's father brought Mercy food on a tray, toast and tea. She stayed in bed a long time, and it was like that dream that everyone has of stopping the clocks.

One evening, Mercy looked out the window at neutral September, the green yard rolling into night in foggy shadows. Downstairs, the family murmured and she missed her village in Guatemala like she had never missed it before, a fist in her back turning, turning. She envied Kaly her statues and shrines, her unspoken certainty that Maria had already returned as something better. Mercy stared at Ganesh in the corner and remembered her idols, her beads and crosses left at home, and the endless depths of belief possessed by her own mother, a drunk. For a day, she lay in bed and hated them, all the devout women.

And then she didn't.

She awoke one morning to snow soft against the window. Here I am again, she thought. And that was enough.

There was no epiphany to report, just the forward turn of one era, a break in the continuum to be noted later, and by others. This time is finished and so something else would take its place. That she could live with.

Mercy put on jeans and a sweater from the pile of her clothing that Vikram had carefully folded, resting on top of the pine dresser. She went downstairs where music quietly played, everyone in different corners doing different things, watching television, eating, children scribbling in books. Kaly had asked the crew to turn down the volume, and they had.

Kaly saw her, and rose from the table, her reading glasses low on her nose like a cartoon animal. A hedgehog, Mercy thought, and she smiled. It hurt her face to do so.

Mercy moved home, but her life changed. She spent her weekends with Vikram's family. She cleared out Maria's room and took in a boarder, a young Japanese student. This made her stronger, she felt, and Kaly helped her distribute Maria's things. Vikram kept the ring.

Unfortunately, the Japanese student proved to be a TV addict and a food thief. Mercy asked him to leave (his angry ESL reply: "Go fuck your own self!"). Watching him walk out the door – and only because she, Mercy, had asked him to – she felt all powerful. She left the apartment and moved to a small house in Little India.

Mercy tells the story with such perfect timing that it ends one stop before she gets off, leaving just enough space to appreciate my stunned silence. Mercy looks at me, smiles, and her lips pull back to reveal a set of perfectly straight ivory teeth. Only then do I suffer a flash of doubt. I imagine her riding the streetcar day after day, targeting someone alone and worried looking, adding details, whispering into a new ear, a private turn-on.

I should tell her good luck, or thank you, but I don't. She picks up her plastic bags and walks out the train doors, thumping with the stocky rhythms of the short. She descends at Queen's Park to a boulevard of hospitals and emergency rooms. I strain, but after a moment, I can't see her any more. Still, I imagine that on a day like today, the beginning of spring, the awnings are sure to shelter patients in hospital gowns with IVs in their arms, grazing fresh air or smoking, frowning as if they're going over a major event in their minds again and again.

SLEEP CALLS, BELLOWS, BEGS. I PULL THE BEDROOM curtain and push aside clothes, moist towels, magazines until I get to the quilt. I climb beneath in my jeans and sweater, my head so deep in the pillow I dream I'm eating feathers. It seems impossible that it's only six weeks since Elaine slept in my bed. Can that be true? No calendars, no watch. I sleep.

When I wake up, bright climbs through the window, morning or afternoon. I hang the towels over the curtain to cut the light and climb back in bed. When I wake again, pushing up through the covers for air, it's submarine dark.

My bag is ringing, or my phone within my bag, which I locate by ear in the bathroom. I open my bedroom door to light. Daytime again. On the edge of the tub, I pick up the phone's glowing blue dictates: Nine messages. Theo. Sunera. Theo. Elaine. Editor. Editor. Marvin. Theo. Editor.

I speed-dial.

"Where are you today?" the Editor asks.

"Sick," I tell her, at which point I realize it's true, drop the phone, and throw up in the sink. When I pick up the phone again, she's still on the line.

"You really are sick," she says, mildly surprised. "Are you too sick to fly to L.A. in the morning?"

I'm silently trying to quell the storm in my stomach.

"Maxime? You know what I'm talking about? The Jennifer Aniston junket. I need to confirm when you'll be filing."

L.A. Things I've agreed to.

"Friday," I whisper and I hang up, rest my cheek against the cold sink. The phone rings again: MCARDLE. What could I possibly say to him right now? What words could I use?

I listen to the message: "Hey, it's me. [pause] Theo. Do I need to say that? I'm feeling a little like a stalker with all these calls. How about doing me a favour and calling me please so I don't arrest myself? [pause] I don't know . . . If this was New Brunswick, I'd say, 'Okay, boys. See you later.' And then I would." Click.

I assume this is a folksy Maritime expression I don't understand but not long after, when I'm in the bathtub rereading my drinking brochure, there's a knock at the door.

I pull on my bathrobe and shimmy along the wall so as not to be seen through the front bay window. But if I hide behind the foyer door and crane my neck a little bit, I can see him: Theo McArdle on my porch.

"I see you," he shouts from the porch, matter of fact.

I open the door.

"I'm sick," I tell him.

"That sucks," he says. "Can I come in? I'll make you feel better." He raises his eyebrows in a joking, salacious way that makes me think of Ad Sales.

I don't hesitate. "No," I say.

"Max, what's going on? It's been a week," he speaks firmly but in a soft voice, a voice of concern. Concern has always made me recoil.

I'm thinking, *All that I am not telling you,* even as I say how busy I am, and how I'm going to L.A. and it's just not a good time. *All that I am not telling you.*

"Why won't you look at me?" he asks, again in this voice. So I do, I meet his gaze; my eyes flitting, his holding fast. But my body pulls back, keeping distance. Theo is standing on the porch, wind-churned and handsome from the cold. I'm in the foyer, hugging my body to keep my bathrobe on.

This standoff lasts a beat, and then Theo says, "Let me come in. I'll make you some tea –" He makes a move to get past me, but I block the door.

He stares at me, a little disbelieving. I can't bear it, those clear eyes. I imagine them set in the face of an old man. I imagine them set in the face of a baby. What provocation, what turn of events will end this short, blissful cycle of new sex and the slow learning of one another, I wonder. Is it happening right now? From inside the thought, I suddenly ask, "Are you leaving?"

"Do you want me to?" He has misunderstood me.

"For England," I say. He lets out a low groan, almost a growl.

"Is that what this is about?" He is angry. "You're waiting for the inevitable collapse."

I shake my head no, but I say, "Yes." I mean it as a joke. Theo knows better.

"I'm right here, you know," he says, almost snappish, as if it should be obvious. Of all the things he could have said, that's the one that seems cruellest because it's the one I believe the least. Tears well.

"Max –" he says, and he moves toward me. I hold out my arms stick straight and shake my head. All this time I've been waiting for him to disappoint me, but of course I'm the disappointment.

"I can't talk to you," I tell him, tears coming fast now as I move backwards into the house, my arms still out in front of me.

I shut the door and slide my back down the wall, hands around my knees, head bowed. He knocks. Then he waits a long time. Maybe a half-hour passes, maybe longer, and the sun begins to go down. The hallway is cast in darkness. I hear his footsteps down the walk.

I've been told that Los Angeles has neighbourhoods of spoon-faced Mexican children where limes grow on trees, but Los Angeles to me is hotels and the airport, window glimpses of blue sky between fingers of palms.

The studio pays for these junkets and those moments of California daylight as they pay for the plane ticket and the brushes with celebrity. The breakfast buffet is swarmed by TV chicks with flammable up-dos and overweight middle-aged journalists happy to be away from their wives, grown men clad in free baseball hats and sweat-shirts inscribed with last week's junket – *Big Mama* 3, *Daredevil* 2.

The Canadian writers huddle together. "So, Max, when will you be running your Aniston piece?" *The Examiner* asks in a voice that's supposed to sound casual but hits the upper registers of a cheat. I concede all information.

The star entertainment reporter for *The Other Daily* is a hunched, aging man with hair like an acorn capping a smooth nut head.

"I understand Golden Productions isn't too pleased with you, Maxime," he says. "I understand you said some-thing on a panel that upset Nicole Kidman." He sounds almost admiring.

The alternative weekly has sent Sludge to trap Aniston too, and he has cribbed an entire jug of fresh-squeezed orange juice from the buffet, which he's drinking through a straw. "More interesting than that is what I heard." No one leans in because of the juice gale he's shooting into the atmosphere, but we do cock our ears.

"BFD Television is trying to buy *The Daily*," he says with a slurp. Heads whip my way. I shrug.

"I don't know anything," I tell them. It's true.

There are eight of us around the table, adjusting our tape recorders, quietly test-test-testing although at this particular table there's a lot of un, deux, trois and ein, svei, drei. Map-sized plastic tags dangle around our necks, in case we get lost and need to be returned to our home countries: BELGIUM, JAPAN, SPAIN, otherwise known as Team A. I've been placed at the foreign journalists table by some publicist who finds Canada exotic; it's flattering, in a way.

"Dinner last night was crep," says Australia, a man who doesn't trust the nametag to convey fully his nationality and has topped off his cliché with a floppy Crocodile Dundee hat. "Last year we went to that steak place and this year it's some Tex-Mex crep."

Japan nods. "Is more cheap this year," she says. Japan pulls out a PalmPilot. "From Eddie Murphy junket!"

The table moans with envy. Sure, we're bunked out in four-hundred-dollar-a-night hotel rooms with spine-conforming pillows and baskets of foot softener, but where's the free technological equipment? This movie sucks.

"So Team A," I say. "Do you guys think we should get a mascot or a cheer or something? How about, like, a viper, or a manatee?" Team A ignores me.

A publicist scurries to the table, a single bead of sweat miraculously balanced on his brow, jutting out like a pea.

"The producer will be first, followed by the writer, then Ms. Aniston," he says. "Anyone need anything? Espresso? Chai latte?" Damn straight; everyone needs something and when the snacks arrive, the table devours and conquers.

Here's the thing: most entertainment writers earn very little money, and even less prestige. These men and women who have been flown here from all around the world live, most likely, in one-room haciendas, grimy rez-de-chaussée apartments with mouldy bathtub grouting, their desk drawers stuffed with thumbed copies of *Hello Magazine* and half-completed movie scripts of their own. Something in them wanted this; proximity, if nothing else.

The sadder ones, though, are those who truly loved the movies once. They thought they could make a living – *best job in the world* – writing about movies and that writing about movies was a way to write about love and dying and laughing. But slowly, they were pushed toward celebrity profiles and diets and dating stories, and these ones have kids to support, alimony to pay. At the next table, there are two: the stooping Spanish man and the shrivelled British woman, identifiable by the novels in their laps. So they know what it means to write about celebrity for a living – the wearing down, the dulling – but they do it anyway. Those, I admit, are my favourites, the broken-backed ones.

The producer is ushered in, an oily creature in squeaky loafers that warn of his approach. Italy launches the first question: "Do-a you-a love-a the movie?" Why yes, the producer loves-a the movie. Everyone worked together 110 per cent, it was like a family – "Familia!" he says for the benefit of Italy – and this project mattered because no other movie like it has ever been made before and no, nobody on my movie is a diva. I don't turn on my tape recorder or take notes or ask questions and eventually, no one else does either. This is too much of a PR crapathon even for Team A. We sit in silence, staring at the producer's hands, wondering about all those gold rings keeping his fingers from touching. Looking uncomfortable, he signals the publicist and is removed.

The publicist returns cross.

"Listen, you're expected to ask questions. We do keep a list of who's participating," he says. This means we might not be invited back, the same way people who write one too many negative pieces (the actor can never appear too stoned, too fat, too stupid) aren't invited back and the same way no one on a junket writes negative pieces because the editors need the movie companies to advertise and just thinking about all those unspoken rules, it's too much like the compound, too much unsaid, and I feel it all of a sudden: language, thick and liquid, curling around us, prying at our mouths and pens, trying to get out, and us, too cowardly to use it.

A thought sends panic streaking down the back of my eyeballs: *If I have this baby, I'll have to teach it how to speak.* And it will look at me to see what I've done with all these words, and what will it see? What will it see?

The screenwriter has a patina of morning over his skin, eyes encrusted with sleep. According to the press notes, the writer went to Harvard. He answers questions in three languages, one of which is Japanese, so let's give him bonus points and call it three and a half. Looking from face to face intently, he describes the film like this: "I think that slowly all of us are shying away from intimacy. We're shying away using clever cynical devices. If you look at films, any truly emotional moment is undercut by a cynical moment right afterwards," he says. "I think that the way we lead our lives, all of us, is prone to unhappiness because we're taught to want things, we're taught to think we're not complete without something, and unhappiness, like a background drone, pushes us not to feel because what we feel is unhappiness."

Australia yawns, adjusts his hat.

The Estonia journo gets up and scampers to the buffet for a muffin.

This is my job. Work used to mean digging and building and days dictated by sun and snow. This is some new kind of work, a steady magnetic hum of tape recorders clicking and the electroshock of computer screens. The publicist is the one organic component, huffing and puffing, circling the table, kicking at the carpet with his heel, scribbling the names of non-participants on his clipboard, consulting the stopwatch attached to his wrist.

"By jolting the audience into a strong emotion, you can make them feel. By feeling the unhappiness we reclaim back our humanity with all the imperfections that make us human," says the screenwriter.

I hear myself speaking before any editing instinct takes over. "No offence, but this is a romantic comedy about a Manhattan career woman who inherits twin babies when her maid, Imelda, is deported. Do you really think it's a film about emotional intimacy?"

The publicist leans close to my nametag and scribbles hard on the clipboard.

The writer nods, turns even paler.

"You should have seen the first draft," he mutters.

The panic has turned to pain, lodged itself between my eyebrows. I rub my forehead. The writer is removed and Jennifer Aniston approaches, tanned collarbone sharp enough to slice cheese. She sits, adjusts her tank top, shakes her hair that hangs like medieval chainmail over her face. Two bottles of water – one sparkling, one flat – and two glasses appear in front of her. The screenwriter, it occurs to me, was not offered water.

Several journalists laugh loudly for no reason. Tape recorders slide toward her. Aniston's hands rise slowly to her face, and she parts her hair, looks out at us with a small, tired smile.

"Hi," she says quietly.

A starting gun. The questions fly. "Do you-a like-a the Brad Pitt?" asks Italy.

"Will you make the baby with Mr. Pitt?" asks Estonia.

And I'm thinking, Jennifer Aniston in the part of . . . somebody's mother.

That screenwriter is wrong. Unhappiness isn't a jolt; it's a dull, ignored ache. You can go years without acknowledging it, decades even. But it does find you. One day, finally, it just marches up and demands your attention, a feral child slapping at its captors. This pounding above my eyes then – I think it's grief, and grief demands to be taken seriously. Grief demands air to breathe. Nothing can breathe here.

I stand up. I place my tape recorder, my notepad, my pen in my bag. I put on my jacket.

The publicist materializes by my side. Faces turn.

"I can't do this," I say. The publicist is wearing a nametag; I never noticed that before and I suddenly think of all the publicists I've met over the years whose names I never bothered to ask. The publicist's name is Adam, and Adam scribbles furiously on his clipboard.

"Good luck with your film," I tell Jennifer Aniston, who nods, and then I push through the room, a swimmer dividing the pool.

I write the Big Cheese an e-mail. I tell him I've left the junket early, that I can't do junkets any more, that no paper should do junkets any more, and I actually type the word *integrity* with the same fingers that are used to typing the words *glam* and *hot* and then I tell him I'm taking a break, that I'm tired and I'm taking a break and he can fire me if he wants to, but I need to sleep.

Send.

At a time like this, there's someone you should call: Father A or Father B, men who are somewhere right now, thinking about the weather, their thinning hair, men who don't know what they've started.

But instead of making that call, I dial my travel agent and she can do it, and I dial Sunera and she says it's a good idea, that I should get away, nothing has to be decided right now. That's true because I saw the pregnancy wheel, the pocket-sized plastic wheel dotted with a calendar, and the doctor spun it and said, "Five weeks, but with your irregular periods, you'll need an ultrasound to confirm. You can get a clinic abortion up until fourteen weeks, but if you want an early term MVA, then you have to go in under eight weeks."

"MVA?" I pictured being strapped in the front seat of a car like a crash-test dummy smashed by hot twisted steel.

"Manual vacuum aspiration, with plastic instruments. Early term abortion." My doctor says everything in the same monotone: "Spread your legs. Pee in this jar. My husband left me. Plastic instruments." Until now, plastic instruments meant recorders, Schroeder's piano, a kiddie drum.

In the hotel room, I throw cassette tapes in a backpack stained from barely remembered trips to Europe, a kid's thing in my grown-up hand. Why don't I own luggage? I wonder what Theo McArdle thinks about abortion, what his ex-girlfriend thinks, the one on the refrigerator. I wonder if Ad Sales has a hidden Catholic past and will buy me a ring from shotgunweddings.com or join the picket line at a clinic. Underwear, toothpaste, bottled water, cellphone just in case I want to be found.

The taxi becomes an airplane, the airplane becomes a bus, bus becomes a ferry. Within these different vessels I'm asleep, face pressed up against the glass on the plane, doubled over into my lap on the bus, resting on my backpack-cum-bed on the ferry. I've never needed to sleep like this in my life, as if the thick rubber hands of a mobster are holding me under cold water.

I wake up against a coffin box of life jackets on the deck of a small ferry. Inside, a stand sells outdated magazines and key chains of plastic whales. I buy a *Daily* from an acne-scarred teen cashier who spends his days floating back and forth in this boat, the West Coast equivalent of a job working at a highway doughnut shop. Every single person in the lineup is wearing a brightly coloured Gortex jacket so that all together they resemble a cluster of grounded balloons. My jacket is black, my black boots ringed with salt stains.

On the front: TORONTO LOSES OLYMPIC BID TO BEIJING (Editorial, A4: *Why human rights is not the issue in China*). Also, the economy continues to boom, there's still nothing wrong in the world, the new president is actually the new president and below the fold, good news: they're working it out, Tom and Nicole, they're doing what's best for the kids, splitting up their estates, trying to simplify, clean up their lives. Yoga is helping.

And on the second to last page of the Toronto section: the big box retailer hired bulldozers to clean up Tent City, and in the end, the residents didn't have the walls to stop the ploughing. The lot is bleeding chemicals into the lake, but no matter; the earth is being primed for the second largest hardware store in North America.

The Other Daily has chosen to showcase a story that my esteemed paper neglected to cover. There, in prime front page real estate, is Baby Baron, dapper as ever in a taut blue suit, only he's got handcuffs in place of his cufflinks. COOKED BOOKS? the headline reads. AN HEIR DISGRACED. *The struggling broadsheet with a proudly conservative stance is certain to be sold or cease publishing within weeks, say insiders . . .* Baby Baron was bankrolling some very big parties all around the globe on the paper's dime, it seems. Shareholders are not charmed. Somehow, there is no surprise in this ending. Pundits predict that the media boom will silence, the newspaper warriors will disarm, and the industry will enter a depression. The Brits have begun booking flights home, airlifts to safety or more interesting wars.

I already feel severed from the paper, bored watching the explosion from afar. Then some old gossip sneaks into my head about Hard-Working Debbie from Life. Her husband is a deadbeat dad who left her with three kids. She's older, late-forties; who would hire her now? I go outside for some air.

This is the first time I've looked up in a while, streaks of cloud, mist skimming the islands we're floating through, rocks like planets on all sides so close you can see the barnacles marking the tide line. We're big and blocky, but we move sleek, purring engine and seagulls dipping down, the smell of rotting seaweed and old rain. I steady myself on the rail. Beauty is so unfamiliar it feels like anxiety to me, and all around are Japanese tourists clicking away on video cameras and digital boxes as small as decks of playing cards. A middle-aged man sits on a bench with his laptop open, maybe describing this scene right here right now to his daughter in Taiwan, San Francisco, Moose Jaw.

I think I would rather be asleep. Being awake is the dream where everything is too bright, sound comes screaming, the veins on the leaves too pronounced, the edges of the sky curling like wax paper. I look at my hands, shaking lightly, an addict in withdrawal. It feels like my whole body is expelling itself, making room for this new one.

These rare B.C. skies make me wonder, How did my singular childhood take place in so many eras? The commune was caught perpetually in the Seventies while I lived my teenaged life in the Eighties. My mother died in 1974, but the photographs in my head make it look like the Fifties with sepia-toned housewives in shapeless shifts and men in baseball hats. The Squamish funeral parlour was stuffed with uneven rows of banquet hall chairs, black vinyl seats, and vases and vases of wild flowers. Later, I saw the bank manager stacking and loading those chairs into the back of his car, returning them to the town's only branch. Still, there weren't enough places to sit; thickets of people covered the back and side aisles. The whole town came out to watch my mother's funeral. I could see them when I peeked out from behind a curtain that separated the "family area" from the mourners. I was pretending to be a star in a dressing room, a Bette Davis idea of what a curtain could mean. In my pink velvet dress, my only dress, I felt girlish and breakable and excited, my breath high in my chest, aware that I was about to make an entrance.

They filed in – grown-ups whom I had never seen, and some familiar: the casserole-deliverers, the post office lady, my third grade teacher, Mr. Defflert. My mom knew the post office lady? I wondered about my mother's secret impact on the world. I had only ever seen her in relation to me, and as she died, in relation to my father, who seemed to need her so desperately. But here they were, adult men and women who had known something of my mother that I never would.

I realized that I had never spoken to her the way that adults speak to one another, the respectful teeter-totter of language, the comforting, musical back and forth of it, heard as I leaned into her waist while she chatted with someone she knew.

Weeks after the seventy-two-day remission, she got sick again. She would not come downstairs, though my father said it was a question of could not. So every afternoon I went up to her room. She took up less space with every visit. I sat next to her on the bed, answering endless questions, me talking and talking, trying not to look at the tubes snaking up her nose and into her wrists, tubes I believed were shrinking her, sucking her dry. I described every tiny detail of my life: how I got the twist-tie to stick into the Plasticine to make the spider paperweight, what Johnny Gundy did with a stick to Jeff Zivic, how I would improve the Narnia books if I wrote them myself.

And now all these adults filing in reminded me how stupid my concerns were. How bored she must have been with me. For the first time, I sensed a boulder-sized space coming toward me. I would never have grown-up conversations with her. She would never know what I became. I was alone. Somehow, in the plume of activity that masked her dying, this had never occurred to me until now, looking at Mr. Defflert's bearded face, the bush of it dragging so low it merged with the tufts of hair poking out of his V-neck sweater.

The room buzzed with bodies, the sound and smell of lavender and tea, old women fussing over my father, who did a marionette slump in the front row. Something felt stripped away, flesh off a chicken bone, and I stood stock-still, eight years old, uncrying, knitting a blanket of shame out of the seconds passing before my mother's body appeared. I dug my fingernails into my arm, thinking, How could I have been so stupid? How could I not have realized that while I was only watching, everything that mattered had changed?

ELAINE'S HOUSE IS A SYMPHONY OF COLOUR, A BIG, cymbal-crashing, incomprehensible, modernist German symphony. Far down the road, it rears itself: stained glass in pink-rimmed windows and rainbow-coloured wind-socks on all corners as if a big gust might pick the whole house up off the ground and turn it into a kite. Trees on all sides and then, where the trees end, more trees.

The path I'm walking, the path that brings the house closer to me, is muddy; it's been raining (B.C. weather report joke: It's raining, been raining, or about to rain), but it's warm out and the white crocuses are balled and ready, the first hydrangeas hanging their heads, a garden on the edge of being wild and green and bent because Elaine never believed in controlling flowers.

I pause outside of this house, which is the house Elaine built with more of her inheritance, after I was safely gone from the West, after my father took off for good, when she briefly became a lesbian. This house is on the other side of the island from the compound; neutral ground, then, and I'm grateful for that because this is the house in which I will see my father for the first time in seven years. My outline of a father. He is, like it or not, the top of this genetic rope my baby is climbing and I'm here to get his version of things.

A bumper sticker on the front door reads, NUCLEAR FREE ZONE, and before I can knock, a small face appears in a crack in the doorway. "Do you have any cruise missiles with you?" it asks.

"No," I say truthfully.

"Ballistic missiles?"

I pat my backpack to check. "No."

"Guns? Red meat? Hate lit-er-ature?" She says the last word like she's just learned it.

"Franny, be good!" Elaine scoots the child – a blur of blond and skinny legs – out of the way and opens the door to throw her arms around me.

"We're so happy you could come. Oh, Max, it's wonderful." Elaine's eyes water.

"Who's this?" I ask and the creature scurries off.

"One of my students, Franny Baumgarten. She's staying with us this week while her mother's in the city. I was hoping it would be a madhouse here, but sadly, it's just the immediate family, plus Franny." Elaine makes little air quotes around the world *family*. "Did you see your father on the way in?" asks Elaine. Franny hovers behind a large plant.

"*The* Franny Baumgarten? I owe her a letter."

Elaine has old stained-glass windows inside too, leaning against the walls, some suspended with chain, their rotting wooden frames barely intact. Any wall free of glass is covered by woolly weavings dangling from curtain rods; if you lean back in this house, you risk being cut or cuddled. Elaine shows me where I'll be sleeping, in a spare room underneath a horse-sized loom.

Franny Baumgarten awaits us in the living room, perched on a stool, feet dangling, poised behind a harp three times her size. She misinterprets my glance as a challenge, narrows her eyes, and begins to strum frantically. The result is like a box of bottles dropped in an alley for recycling.

"Franny! Please respect the quiet!" Elaine shouts.

Franny hops away on two feet, rabbit-style. The stained glass rattles.

Elaine shakes her head. "I don't think one should own anything more valued than a child's pleasure, but I *would* be sad if one of the windows shattered. I think I'm getting too attached."

"Elaine, you live on an island. You're not attached to anything." She beams; this is a high compliment.

"Go see your father. I think he's nervous." As soon as she says that, my own nerves scurry across my back. *Father*: this is not a word that rolls easily off my tongue. In the beginning of our relationship, John used to tease me because I never mentioned my father. He thought it was curious and, after a while, sad. I tried to explain: He didn't want the part. My childhood was a collective experience, so how could he have been definitive, singular? John kept waiting for me to put my head in his lap and cry. Later, he didn't find my reticence that amusing; he called me cold, and said I could never really give in to anyone. "Work it out, Max," he said angrily, slamming the door (and this disapproval links to another one: Theo on the walk to the university that night, confounded by me. "What are you doing, Max?")

I know that if he can, my father will be outside. I walk to the back of the house, and there he is in this fenceless yard, bent over scraps of wood, hammer in hand, building a small house, a miniature of the big one. It's too large to be a bird-house, too small for a tool shed.

There was always something about his hunched, thin frame that looked like an old man even when he was young. Now that he's older, the body matches the face, cheeks lined and drawn. He is wearing shorts and the skin around his knees hangs in sagging parentheses. My father, who lives his life like a boy floating down a river, is now in his sixties. He straightens and turns, offers a little wave. I wave back and immediately trip on a two-by-four. I throw my hands forward and fall into a near-perfect push-up position, knees on the ground, belly protected from impact by my straight arms. It's the opposite of thought. My father offers a hand to help me up.

"She's a little clumsy," he murmurs, like he's remembering something. This I had forgotten: My father is without metaphor. He is all observation, no judgment. Maddening then, it's comforting now, if only because I know it so well.

He pulls back to look at me, picks a weed out my hair.

"Weed," he says. I nod.

"Hi, Dad," I say. I would like his eyes to well up. I would like some kind of buckling, but his face is composed, his eyes alert. More alert than I remember them, ever.

"Hi, daughter." It's a joke. At the compound, no one said mother or father, but Joyce and Richard and Anne, all things equal.

I don't know what to say, so I gesture to the small house. "What is this?"

"Oh, this," he says, like he's never seen it before. "This is for Franny to play in. It's a replica of Elaine's house. She's even going to fire some stained glass for the door." He picks up the door, recently cut and dusted with wood bits. He holds it in front of him, between us. It comes up to his chest. An empty square where the window will go.

"Would you like to help me hang the door?" he asks.

"No," I say. Then, seeing his eyes dart, it occurs to me that Elaine was right: he is nervous.

"I don't know. Do I?" I say. "What are we talking about here?" He just wants me to hold it, turns out, while he slides the hinges together.

So this is our first meeting in years, the two of us on our knees in front of a miniature house, speaking only of nails and levels. Like this, the afternoon gets cooler and turns to dusk.

"Do you eat animals?" Franny Baumgarten is sitting in the middle of the kitchen floor with a zoo of stuffed animals in her lap while Elaine and I prepare dinner: tofu steaks and couscous. Seriously.

"Yes, but not stuffed ones." She giggles. She holds up a crudely sewn, floppy-eared, blue checked thing that could be an elephant or a mouse. I'm not sure what she wants from me.

"Cool," I tell her.

"It's for yooooooooooou!" she shouts, and she's having a good time with that long o sound, up and down and around and around, until I snatch the thing out of her hand in an effort to shut her up.

"My God," I say, fingering its Frankenstein-stitched sides, its lumpy glue-whiskered mouth. "Did Elaine buy this for you?"

Elaine comes in from the back porch, arms laden with basil pulled from her garden.

"Are you still buying toys from Tards-R-Us?"

"Max," says Elaine. "They're mentally challenged crafts-people!" But she's smiling a little in spite of herself.

Franny Baumgarten stands tall, animal minions at her feet, then sprints out of the room, abandoning them. A television clicks on in the living room and Elaine shakes her head.

"I'm sure you never thought I'd have a television," says Elaine. I rinse the herbs in the sink, swirls of mud on the white enamel.

"Oh, I don't know. I suppose it's inevitable. Everyone has to enter the real world," I say.

"There's your problem," says Elaine. "Television is not the real world."

Franny Baumgarten screams, "MAAAAX!" from the living room and Elaine and I run in, dripping basil stalks in hand, hurtling toward the inevitable ripped limb, the dangling eyeball, the masked abductor, whatever horror might be on the other end of that scream.

Franny and my father lie on the floor in front of a tiny black-and-white television set. There, on the screen, is an ad that looks like a music video with trumpet-heavy jazz horn blowing and quick cuts of burn victims and tornadoes and wartorn villages and actresses walking the red carpet. Interspersed are more familiar faces, and that's jarring at first, to see the hard-done-by gaze of Debbie from Life, Marvin's powder-bronzed cheeks – and then, for a brief brief moment, there's me, and I'm tossing my hair and glancing over my shoulder, sort of smouldering, sort of ill.

"*The Daily*," says a deep male voice. "Think it over."

"Think it over," repeats Franny Baumgarten. Basil juice drips down my wrist. Who was that fetching woman? Some secret me bred in a Petri dish.

"Curious," says my father.

"Sultry," says Elaine.

"That must have been just before I fell off the stool. I look a little woozy. I remember, I closed my eyes for a second and . . ." Franny Baumgarten begins pummelling Elaine backwards into the kitchen.

"Max, sit down," says my dad. I lower myself, attempting to cross my legs, basil on my knee, and something makes a creaking sound in my thighs.

"Jesus, I hate sitting like this," I say. My dad, on the other hand, sits perfectly upright. If you put a magic carpet under the guy he'd be up and off, sending you postcards from Egypt in a matter of seconds.

"Did you perfect that move in the teepee in Arizona?" I ask. My dad smiles. I get all tucked in, limbs in line, and I'm sitting across from him. I'd like to be at a more casual angle – this seems somewhat confrontational – but it might take several minutes to extract myself. So we sit.

"I've read your work. It's very funny," he says. "And very dark." I'm a bit taken aback; it's not like my father to evaluate.

"Do you still love movies?" he asks.

I don't say anything. I'd forgotten how his voice sounds, slightly muffled, like he's talking through a cloth soaked in chloroform.

"When you used to disappear to the movies when you were younger, I always wondered if you actually liked movies or if you liked the reprieve they provided. Elaine can't stand movies, you know. She thinks they take you out of the world." He raises an eyebrow at me.

"Dad," I whisper, "are you making fun of Elaine?"

"I love Elaine, but she's a bit of a flake."

I laugh.

"Before you leave, we need to take a walk together," says my father. It isn't a question, it's a command.

I look at him, the lines in his face dividing him in pieces, sun-worn provinces. "You sound . . . ," I hesitate. What is it, exactly? I don't know yet. "Different. What did those Hopis teach you?"

My dad laughs a snort laugh, inhaling instead of exhaling. "Two years of cognitive therapy in Tucson," he says. "Very expensive."

Within a week, I am used to it here. I am forgetting. I sleep in the shadow of the loom. Elaine is weaving Philoemelia in three panels. The rape, the imprisonment, the escape. I sleep under the story of her rape, which Elaine, ever the optimist, has chosen to weave in very bright pinks and yellows.

I start each day with my head over the toilet, and then I clasp my hands together to keep them from shaking. At night I dream sometimes of a girl baby, sometimes of tails and fangs and giving birth to rutabagas and husks of corn. But my afternoons, once school is out, are spent exploring the roads with Franny Baumgarten. She's taken a shine to me, and likes to lead me around, chattering, kicking at tide pools on the rocks and crushing life forms whenever possible, encouraging me to do the same. I'm slower than she is, flopping along in my father's gumboots, too big, and

Elaine's raincoat, too small. The headache cries out for booze, but I don't indulge.

There are often dogs out on the rocks, and they lumber over uninvited until their owners appear, low on the beach, calling for them, nodding at us. After a few days, the nods turn to waves. Finally, a middle-aged man and a woman approach us. Franny hugs their dog, a freckled mutt just slightly bigger than her. They are curious as to who I am, though they know Franny's mother. Their prying is gentle, like a couple piecing together a mystery they're reading out loud. I can tell I've been the subject of speculation on the island, the strange woman with Dolores Baumgarten's daughter. When I mention Elaine, they brighten and murmur affection. "You're the ex-stepdaughter," says the woman, and I'm surprised, wondering if Elaine refers to me that way, unused to being called anyone's daughter. I imagine Elaine saying this phrase casually, maybe on a boat deck, or in the bank on the mainland. *My ex-stepdaughter.* She says it almost as an afterthought, or as the easiest way to explain what we are to each other, and I like this. The "ex" suggests a complicated history, one we have somehow all survived. "Yes, I'm the ex-stepdaughter," I say. In the upcoming days, people on the rocks smile at us more easily, pleased to have an explanation.

Soon the baby dreams stop and my hands shake less and the headaches loosen and I'm dreaming of places I'm already in. I'm dreaming of the roar of the ocean, the spray plumping up the pages of my book, the useless red fabric of the raincoat sopped to my skin as I walk. The dreams are friendly, and without symbols. When I wake up, my breathing is shallow, and I'm grateful for the lack of subtext.

So my dad's gone all cognitive therapy on me. He's got these little recipe cards that he drops around the house like an Easter bunny, little white cards with daunting typed phrases followed by ellipses: "I need . . . When you . . . I felt . . . If you . . . I will . . ." We're supposed to fill in the blanks, I guess. Elaine ignores the cards. Franny uses them to construct a fan with glue and staples.

I stand in the kitchen fingering one: "When you . . . I feel . . ."

Through the window, I watch him hitting planks with his hammer, two-by-fours dangling over the edge of a sawhorse. Franny zigzags behind him, a red towel tied around her neck, nails hanging from her mouth like fangs.

I push open the window, knocking dusty cacti and vitamin bottles that line the ledge. *When you ignore a small child, I feel like poking your eyes with a fork.*

"Franny! Take those nails out of your mouth!" I shout. She skids to a halt, looks around confused, then locates me in the window. She smiles so widely the nails fall from her jaw. My dad continues sawing, oblivious.

Elaine is suddenly next to me. She has a great knack for appearing out of thin air. I didn't even know if she had feet for a long time because her robes dragged on the ground, like she was just another mushroom extension of the earth.

"Where has he been all this time?" I ask her.

Elaine wipes her hands on a dishtowel and goes to the cupboard atop the refrigerator. On tiptoe, she pulls down a plastic container filled with postcards and photos, bills, keys. She removes a newspaper clipping, smoothes it on the kitchen table. *Volunteers build housing for needy in record time.* It is a small community paper from San Francisco with simple, high-school yearbook layout, the kind of thing a street person tries to sell. The article is dated three years ago. The photo is of young men and women, younger than me, standing with their arms linked in front of a flat-roofed bungalow. On the edge of the grinning chain is my father, head slightly bowed, smiling sheepishly. The article identifies him as "a hitchhiker from Canada," one of many non-locals ("a surfer from Australia" "a Kiwi student") who showed up one day answering an ad for help and stayed several months.

"How did you get this?" I ask Elaine.

"He sent it to me," she says.

The clipping surprises me. In his travels to the woods, my father was always stopping to trap and construct lean-tos from the brush, always lining his caves carefully with leaves and tarps. I would encounter them sometimes on my own wanderings. Building housing for other people seems like a version of that, but it's hard to imagine him finishing one of the houses, nailing the last board, closing the door. What's stranger is that he sent this article to Elaine. I never knew him to look for approbation of any kind. It was as if he needed my mother so profoundly that when she died, he shut off the valve and stopped requiring anyone. I always assumed this is why he and Elaine never worked; she was ever forgiving of his isolation, but in the end, he didn't need her forgiveness.

And yet, moved by pride, my father took the time to cut an article out – a slightly self-aggrandizing article – and send it to Elaine. He managed to stamp and address the envelope. He opened a mailbox in San Francisco and dropped it in. I'm struck by jealousy, and for a moment I think it's because he has never sent me such an envelope. But that's not it; if what he wants is engagement, Elaine, with her praise and enthusiasm, is the person to go to. I wouldn't come to me either. So the jealousy is something else and I think it's this: even my father is able to need people now. It is a skill he never taught me.

"Then he was living with the Hopis for a while," says Elaine. "He's a nomad, really. If it hadn't been for your mother, he never would have stopped moving."

Before the illness: my father and I, walking home before dusk. He spots it first, lifts a finger, and points at a shape lying on the road, stomach swelled from illness, quick, small breaths. My father says, "Wait here." And I wait with the deer. It looks past me, hazy and poisoned.

I don't remember ever being scared, even looking at this great dying thing. Nor was I sad, really, just curious: Who will miss this deer? What got into her veins? Why did she come here to lie down? Where was she going before she fell? I believed I could ask these questions, and there would be answers, and those answers would make up for the awfulness of dying alone, stomach ballooned like bellows. I was young enough to see order, even in disorder, to have faith in reason.

I sit in the front seat as my father shoots the deer, so it's just a sound behind me. He lifts her carcass into the truck. I know that we will return home and my mother will squeeze my shoulder, looking at the deer with concern as my father drags it into the garage. We can't eat her because of the poison, but my father will take the skin and sell it. Money comes from anyplace, and sometimes no place, but there is always food for the three of us somehow.

"Are you two back together?" I ask Elaine.

"God, no," she laughs. "But we matter to each other. We know things about each other."

"Like what?"

Elaine considers the question.

"Well, this is probably not as profound as you might wish, but did you know that your father's hearing is terrible? He probably didn't hear you yelling at Franny."

A pang: there is so much I don't know about my father.

Elaine is going into the city, she tells me. She has a doctor's appointment, and she's made me one.

"What for?" I ask her.

"This is a small house, Max. If one person is throwing up every morning, everyone knows about it."

Things happen to make a person plug in. A sudden midnight slap awake, a cold breeze through the window that tells you no one else alive feels like this. I know that I only exist because other people tell me I do, so I flip a switch and suddenly I am accessed, hacked, entered. My cellphone is in the corner, adapter plugged into the wall under a basket of wool. It blinks to life with green words in the dark: 13 MESSAGES. Thirteen messages from the same five people: Theo McArdle, Sunera, work, Marvin, Ad Sales. I listen to their voices, and for the first time in days of rain and wood, I miss words.

Back behind the loom is an IBM clone the size of a small airplane, but wired for e-mail. I hunker down, listen to the ring and static bouncing back and forth – there and the earth, there and the earth – and I'm thinking about how I have virtually no understanding of things like e-mail, cellphones, electricity. What is it that I could teach a child? What will I tell the alien toddler with the tear-shaped head that I'm bound to give birth to, the one who holds my hand and says, "What's e-mail, Mama?" I'll have to say, "Well, there are tiny men the size of the stem on a thumbtack, they live inside the computer, and they run through giant pulsating underground veins . . ." I like the Flintstones answers: the ancient birds who play records with their beaks. Fleshiness appeals.

Subject: what yr mssng
From: Marvin
This is an actual e-mail that came around today:
<<To whoever felt the need to steal my Maple Leafs calendar . . . I'm heading to the drugstore at lunch to pay another whopping $3 for another one.
I'm just wondering, should I buy two this time or do you think the one you have now will be enough?
Steve Rogers, Sports>>
I hope you're alive. Do they get proper news out there, or do I have to go over the gruesome details of Baby Baron's fall from grace? The assistant blew the whistle! He had

photocopies of everything, cheeky little bastard! I hope I get to be an anchorman. Would BFD supply the clothes for free? If not, I'm practising my Spanish, soon to be chillaxin' on the beach.

Come home soon, wherever you are.

XOXO M.

Subject: Me
From: expandyourwealth@cake.com
FYI Max, you may never hear from me again because the paper's collapse spells opportunity for some of us. I'm taking Cake.com to New York for an American IPO, fuck this non-Olympics town. You should think about getting down there too. Boom times, my friend. Boom times.

Subject: what's going on. . . .
From: SuneraS
Wonder how you're doing in the great outdoors.

Things are fine. Birthday party for Stewey last week. Thought of you. Theo M. was there, cute and earnest, good in a crowd. Misses you and is confused. Held my tongue; ne t'inquiètes pas!

Can't imagine how you're holding up. Please call me anytime – collect! Turn your cell on, bee-yatch!

I have good goss.

So it's night before the cousin's wedding and all the women are together at my aunt's house singing eating etc. Deadly ritual, turns out, b'c I woke up in the middle of the night with this stabbing in my stomach. Ridiculous, like something trying to chew its way out. Called a taxi and waited on the curb so that if I fell down dead, it would be in a public place.

Get to the hospital and lying on this gurney in the hall, I start throwing up. Charming, non? They're equipped for this sort of thing, and the pans start coming out and in between heaves, I notice that the person who's been rubbing my back and changing these vomit-filled pans is a not unattractive male nurse. Yes, male nurse. Not my type, really, blond and generic, but cute (170, 5'10). Funny too. Got one of those big bear faces. So kind. (BTW, it was the dhal. Half the ladies were green for the bride's special day.)

Best coincidence, M, is that the next day, I'm at this wedding factory – fifteen weddings at once in this hideous hangar covered in taffeta and fairy lights; nauseating – and guess who's in the hall one over? Nurse boy. Could not be shitting you less. His cousin's getting married to an Indian! We've spent a fair amount of time together. 'Kay, every night (deets to follow in person).

And bigger news: I'm getting promoted. One of the boomers sold some tech stock at the right time and he's off to start a bookstore-café so I'm moving up the masthead. Never thought this would matter but I like it. I have some ideas, might shake things up a little. Remember *Partisan Review*, best magazine in history? Me neither. Never read it, but read about it (there's a bumper sticker for you).

Anyway nurse guy is a little straight edge – not so into the pink pills etc., but more from a medical than a puritanical p.o.v. Will you come home now so you can meet him and fall in love too?

Subject: none
From: Theo McArdle
Where did you go? Sunera said west and I said, no way, not without a call.
Some questions:
1) Are you feeling better?
2) What was going on the other day?
3) About London: Nothing is decided yet. (I realize that's not really a question.)
4) But that's the exciting part, isn't it? (There's your question.) There are newspapers in London too, though you might have to write about the Queen. And the university could still reject me. Or they could accept me and I could reject them. Anything is possible.
Been considering you and Nicole Kidman. Did I ever tell you that I think you're a pretty great writer, even if I don't quite get the subject matter? But I think I might know why you hate your job. It's a principle of quantum physics. The act of observing something happening causes a change in the thing being observed. Different worlds, yet we're up against the same shit. Funny.
And 5) Can we have sex again please?
TM
PS – 6) Soon?

TODAY I TURN THIRTY-FIVE. I KNOW THIS BECAUSE I'M woken by Franny Baumgarten whispering in my ear with her scentless child's breath: "Happy birthday, happy birthday, HAPPY BIRTHDAY!" Then she looks at me very seriously.

"You have to go to the doctor today," says Franny Baumgarten, who is wearing an adult-sized T-shirt. It hangs to her knees, sloping the slogan: HERE TO SAVE THE INDUSTRY.

"Yes, I do." I reach for last night's water glass on the ground next to the futon.

"Are you sick?" asks Franny.

"No." I sit up and rub my eyes. I keep a pile of saltines nearby at all times to slow my churning belly. I eat two.

"But maybe?"

"No."

"But you have to go to the doctor *on your birthday*." This is clearly unfathomable to Franny Baumgarten, who begins pulling at the loose threads on Elaine's tapestry, threatening to undo it.

"And also your mother died," she announces.

"A long time ago," I say. "Your father died too, huh?" She pulls at a string, wipes her nose with her free hand, dances a little.

"Yes, but I don't know him, so it's not so sad."

"Really? I think that might be sadder."

Franny looks at me, eyebrows squirming, puzzled.

"I guess so. Sometimes I feel bad I don't remember."

"Do you remember anything about him?"

She ponders for a moment. Then: "Don't move!" She runs from the room, pulling that piece of yarn with her, slowly unravelling Philoemelia.

"Franny," I call after her. She runs back in, huffing and puffing, holding in her hand a photograph. A clear blue swimming pool, a handsome young man with a proud brow, his chest dripping with water, is linked at the hands to a toddler in water wings. She floats on her frog belly, grinning at the camera.

Franny leans against me, warm. "I remember he taught me to swim."

"He looks like a good guy, Franny." She points out some

things about the photograph: Her mom took it. Her water wings are orange, and she outgrew them a long time ago. Her father didn't know it but there was a lump in that wet chest. Smoking is bad.

"Do you have a picture of your mom?"

I make Franny fetch my bag, thinking how useful kids are. I dig around, and Franny peers inside. "Cigarettes!" she whispers, so no grown-ups will hear.

"I quit. Seriously." I realize that's true: when did I last smoke?

I pull out the Tic Tac case that holds a black-and-white passport-sized photo of my mom. She has a small-town bouffant and a tight-lipped smile, as if she's afraid to show her teeth.

"She was younger than I am now," I tell Franny, and then I point out some things to her: how my mother never actually used her passport because she never got to go anywhere outside Canada, how she hated having her picture taken, how she got this done in a photo booth in an old drugstore in Vancouver that was torn down to make way for a McDonald's (I made that up years ago but what can you do? Some stories just endure).

I'm holding the picture of her father, Franny is holding the picture of my mother. The yarn lies in a pile in the centre of the room.

"Wanna trade photos?" I ask her. She considers the proposition.

"No," says Franny Baumgarten. "I like mine."

I take a water taxi with Elaine to the mainland, and we walk the newly cobblestoned sidewalks of the harbour town toward the doctor's office. It's one of those days that's neither hot nor cold, the streets patchy with sun. The ferry town has acquired a patina of fake rustic quaintness – Ye Olde Fudge Shoppe – that breaks down after a few blocks, the town reverting to its natural environment of strip malls and parking lots. The doctor's office is between a nail salon and pet-food chain.

This doctor is all twenty-five-year-old Doogie Howser genius brimming with West Coast cheer, telling me how he works in rural communities one week a month and do I know what it's like for the Haida and he's actually asking me this while he's buttering my stomach with clear jelly and rubbing a cellphone-like machine back and forth really hard, like he's trying to pull the thing out of there with some supermagnet.

"How specific can you be, using this? Can you tell to the day it –" I stumble over the word *it* because I've never been able to call children he or she until the ability to shuffle a deck of cards emerges. "Was conceived?"

"Conception took place five weeks ago." I do some math.

"Not, say, seven weeks?"

"Five."

"But how do you know?"

He points at the screen where a black-and-white fingerpainted sea lulls and rushes.

"Science," he says this with wonder in his voice.

So now I know. Now I know which late-night huddle made this life. My nerves tingle with anxiety while the smudge floats calmly in its sea. I should call its father, now that I know the number to call. I feel my heart jump, but I'm relieved too, just to have an answer, even if it's a terrifying one, even if it resolves nothing.

"How much time do I have left to make a decision?" I ask.

The doctor is as moved by my plight as he is injustice in the north, delivering a sombre line reading, "You have until fourteen weeks for a clinic abortion, twenty for a hospital."

He's holding a paper printout of the sea.

"Would you like this?" he asks. I take it anyway, fold it in half, a seam above an imaginary belly, and stick it in my wallet.

Elaine is in the waiting room, staring out the window. It would never occur to her to pick up a magazine in a place like this. She'd say something like, Why look at newsprint when there's a window right there? It's sad somehow, to catch Elaine quiet, by herself, vulnerable, aging. She turns and gives me a steady smile.

As I'm buttoning up my coat, the receptionist chirps, "Happy birthday. That'll be ten dollars for the printout."

I tell Elaine I need a little time and she says she'll meet me back on the island. I walk to the movie theatre. Before the movie starts, a preview for a terrible Adam Sandler movie I wrote about comes up: "*The Daily* calls it Delicious!" Did I say that, really? To what was I referring? Perhaps a meal someone ate on screen.

And then the film rolls and it's one of those lifestyle movies where everyone has good clothes and furniture and big, solvable problems. These kinds of movies used to comfort me. For as long as I can remember, the unreal has always made me feel more real, dramatic exaggerations showing up my own life as reasonable. But today, the film does nothing except bolster the sense of dread I've had since leaving the medical building. It offers me no solution. I hear the doctor's pitying voice in my head and there is no character like that in this movie, this stupid movie that knows nothing about my bad skin and my jelly belly and my photographs in my purse.

My father looks up from his hammering. "How was the doctor's appointment?" he says.

I ignore the question. "Can I borrow your hiking boots?"

He pauses. "These boots?"

I nod. He looks like he wants to ask me something more, but reads my hardened face – *This is not the time to ask questions* – and thinks better than to pry. As he unlaces the boots, I think that I could have found a pair in the house, but part of me likes making demands on him. Having him meet them is new.

I leave him in his stocking feet in the yard and make my way to the water.

The bones of the boathouse, covered in moss, have split in the salt air. Easily, I flip the canoe onto my shoulders, my head in the dark, eyes on the boots as I walk the dock. I always liked the portage, the hiding before the water.

And then I see, ahead of me, two small red running shoes sprinting back and forth in my path.

"Canooooing!" sings Franny Baumgarten.

I drop the canoe off the edge of the dock, where it smacks and bobs. I loop the rope through the mooring rings, surprised at how familiar this is, how much I haven't forgotten.

"Does Elaine know you're out here?"

Franny nods vigorously, still running back and forth, precariously close to the edge.

"Watch out!" I yell, trying to finish the knot.

"Can I come?" she asks.

"It's not a good time, Franny," I tell her, heading to the boathouse for the paddle.

"Later?" asks Franny. She shadows me back to the dock. I untie the canoe and climb into the stern, holding on to the dock with my paddle.

"Tomorrow?" she asks.

The boat slips in my hands, and I jolt backwards, tipping slightly, enough to feel uncertain again.

"The next day?" says Franny, and I want the silence I'm anticipating on the water. I want all of this to stop, and I shout at her: "No. Now get out of here!" Fierce, almost animal. She looks away, tears forming in her eyes.

"Franny —" I stop. She is already gone, disappearing into the woods, her small body slumped. I have never seen her walk slowly. I should run and gather her in my arms, tell her I'm ashamed of myself. But I don't. I am cowardly, and desperate for space. I watch her vanishing, and when she is gone, I push off into water as sidewalk grey as the sky.

At first, the paddle feels foreign, a thing that will give me calluses, break my pink skin. But quickly, my body remembers that the sensation of being in a canoe is one that makes you aware of scale. You ride the water like a fly on a buffalo.

I realize, my God, I know my north from south out here. I know that this nothing weather can turn to violent rain, or light up with sun, but it will not stay neutral for long. I know to keep to the shoreline because of the sky's uncertainty. I know rain.

The water yields as I move along the shore, out of the bay toward open water, my eyes marking my path by the tallest trees, like someone taught me once – who was it? My father.

The tide is so high that some rocks, landmarks, are covered by waves. But I keep going, the sky and the water darkening each other. And then, suddenly, the wind gets rowdy, rears itself against the boat. A few drops fall.

For several minutes, I let myself believe that this medium weather is going to hold. I listen to rain beading off my jacket. But then something is snuffed. The sky's crust goes dark.

"Fuck," I say, triggering the downpour. It's that fast. I am soaked to the skin. I didn't think to wear a life jacket. Wait, it's worse: I didn't think to wear a life jacket, and I am pregnant. This seems appalling now; what kind of mother wouldn't consider all that could go wrong?

I lean forward in the boat, paddle in and paddle out, my wrists pulled backwards from the force of the water. I'm aiming for the shore, to see if there's a break, some shelter where I can wait it out, but rocks keep bucking up from beneath, pushing me farther into the open ocean. The only way out is to go back. So I'll go back.

And now I have to turn around. I have to force my way through, stroking backwards, careening in the direction I've come. Each stroke moves the boat a few centimetres, and then the wind rights me back to where I started. I see only the immediate moment in front of me, the angry black water, bunching, unbunching, and I think, Get through that. Get through that one section of the world. And then there's another, and I get through that one too. I am almost righted. My wrists and shoulders feel aflame, and then it is done. Somehow I've turned around, and in doing so, the wind is behind me, propelling the boat forward. The space in front is like television static. I can't see through it, just shapes and colours, and the colour is brown, and the shape is a yellow blur flapping in the wind. As I get closer and closer, the yellow takes the shape of a person; my father in a raincoat, arms flapping, trying to signal the dock. Too late; I hit at top speed, a cracking noise. My father's hands, giant paws, clawing me from the boat, and the boat from the water.

I slip on the dock, one foot knocks the other. I fall forward onto my father to break my fall, to protect my maybe baby.

My father pulls the canoe onto the dock, turning it onto its side, revealing a huge mouthy gouge.

"I'm so sorry," I shout into the wind, and I start walking fast, away from the dock. Already I'm imagining Elaine's disappointment, my father's embarrassment at his flabby, urban daughter defeated by a little rain.

My father catches up to my side, grabs my shoulder roughly.

"You did well," he says.

"Are you high? I nearly drowned," I say, tears rising up in my throat, the hot, wet interior of the raincoat hood scratching my face.

"But you didn't," he says, blinking against the rain. "You're still great in a canoe." He squeezes my hand.

Still. Something for my memoir: She was great in a canoe once.

The rain thins out, lines instead of sheets, then breaks between the lines, ellipsis. My father gestures for me to walk ahead of him. He stays close behind right into the house where I open the door and collapse on a birch bench in Elaine's hallway. The bathtub runs off in the distance, the sounds of Elaine and Franny talking. I am exhausted, my body shivering, unable to open my mouth. My father sits next to me, silent. Eventually the bathtub shuts off and Franny can be heard splashing in the water.

I get hot in my jacket, feet entombed in wet wool inside my father's boots, but I can't bring myself to move. It's as if I don't want to end this raw, red feeling. Changing anything – unzipping or speaking – will take me out of the shock, and I need it right now.

But after a long time, my father crouches down in front of me. I have a strange, fleeting idea that he might rub my foot in prayer, like a pieta, but instead he unlaces his boots from my feet, one at a time. As it is happening, I know I am remembering it already. My father kneeling before me, busy and kind, his head bowed.

MY MOTHER HAD THE WHIRRING TONGUE; SHE LIVED close to the surface, moved waterbug fast, but my father dove down deep into himself. When he came back from the mountains, he couldn't answer questions for hours, just smiled and held up the fish he'd caught, and then set about cutting their heads into a bucket by the shed. My mother would wink at me, roll her eyes, and let him be.

What was it like for him, suddenly to be the sole parent of an eight-year-old girl? What must he have made of me, all over him, endless chatter about nothing, the running and jumping, pulling tree branches from seedlings, lighting fires in the schoolyard, calmly watching the flames flap around the edges of the garbage can? If he was unable to carry his own grief, where would he keep mine?

One day he looked at me and said, "We're leaving." Maybe he thought he could take me down deep with him, and we'd be quiet together; maybe, because he never noticed what I was like before, he assumed it was missing her that made me manic. He took me to the compound to calm me, but it felt like confinement, and only made me more frantic. The only place I sat still was at the movies.

I'm so tired of these stories and these questions that I tell myself and ask myself and answer myself on the loop I've been caught in for all these years. There's no comfort in it any more.

It's dark in the house except for the light in this room. I lie on the mattress staring at Elaine's weavings, warm in her long johns, a borrowed sweater. I rub my hands over my stomach, which is getting harder, toughening into something solid. I can't e-mail, or check my cellphone messages – can't push buttons, can't write – because my wrists are too battered from the storm, ropes of strained muscle protruding up my arm.

I hear a noise down the hall, like a pulp-movie spaceship landing. When I stand, my bruised bones shift and fall into one another.

A line of white light at the bottom of Franny's door. I knock. The spaceship sounds cease.

"It's me, Franny," I tell her.

"Okay, come in," she says. I'm afraid she'll be mad at me, but she's sitting in the centre of the guest bed with a flashlight and a comic book. Her blue pyjamas are covered in clouds. She is grinning.

"Did you hear the spaceship?"

"I did. Was that you making that sound?" She giggles and shakes her head.

"It's the comic book! It's realistic!" This cracks her up.

I sit down on the edge of the bed and look at the comic book. It's entirely in Japanese, but the pictures tell the story of four girls with stars on their foreheads flying through space and shopping malls, leaving explosions and fires in their wake. It is unclear what they are fighting for.

"Do they live on this spaceship?" I ask Franny. The spaceship looks like a compact.

"Mmhm." She turns the pages for me.

"Where would you go if you had a spaceship, Franny?" She thinks about this.

"I'd go canoeing in the ocean."

"But you have a spaceship. You could go anywhere."

She thinks again. "Boston."

I laugh. "What's in Boston?"

"I don't know. I've never been there. Boston," she says it again. "Boston, Boston, Boston. I wish that was my name."

Franny flips the pages, looking for something.

"Franny, I'm sorry about today," I say. She keeps looking at her book. I'm not clear enough. I add, "I shouldn't have yelled at you. You didn't deserve it."

Franny shrugs and says, "Okay. Where would you go in a spaceship?" It is that fast for her, forgiveness. What is in Franny that lets her drift through the world like this, so weightless? I don't think it's just youth. Theo is the same way. And Elaine. And all of these people have known tragedy, known loss, and all of them have put it somewhere for safe keeping, and moved forward. What is this grace I lack, and for this baby, could I learn it?

"I think I would go canoeing too," I say, and Franny nods.

"Ah-hah," she has found what she was looking for in the comic book and she shows me proudly. The last panel: a full page of blue black sky sprinkled with stars, stars of all sizes, all depths, and way up in the corner, the tiny ship hurtling through space with all the girls inside it.

ELAINE, FRANNY, AND I SIT AT THE BREAKFAST TABLE with our strange habits before us in bowls: Franny's Cheerios, no milk; Elaine with her muesli and figs; me with yogurt and bananas and the newspaper. *The Other Daily* doesn't have any news of Baby Baron today. Interest has faded that quickly, the scandal now an accepted fact.

A story on the business pages speculates that without the Olympics, the big box retailer has lost interest in developing Tent City. If the residents return, they will find the land detoxified and cleared of rubble. But so far, no settlers have shown up.

Elaine rises to make tea and gives me a kiss on the head. She knows I don't respond well to sentimental gestures.

My father appears. "Would you like to take that walk, Max?"

He is carrying a pink shoebox that says, *8 ½ flat. Mr. Rojo's Italian Leather* in rococo 1970 script. I know this box. It is the one possession my father protected from place to place. I get my jacket.

I follow him along a path that's overgrown from lack of use since they put in the road and cars started coming over. Everything is exaggerated, steroided. The salal is hip height, dotted with old rain, the swordfern curls and bends, tickles my shoulders.

We emerge from the wet onto a wide green field that looks across the water toward Horseshoe Bay, a short cliff-drop down to the water. I have been here before. I feel like one of those movies where the character steps out of his body and there's another one, and he keeps multiplying and multi-plying; I feel like there are a million of me, shadowy and celluloid, fanning across the greenery.

He has taken me to the compound. My dad is facing the barracks and the small cabins where the monks lived, and then us. The place is cleanly painted, carefully boarded up, windows patched with perfect white shutters that look tem-porary; in the summer, things will change. Near the old buildings are new bungalows built from logs. They're pretty and fairy tale next to the proletariat bunks we lived in. Ours look like they were built from crayon blueprints drawn by children whose imaginations hadn't kicked in yet: straight line, straight line, straight line, window.

"It's a summer camp now," my dad says. Of course: the tetherball pole in the middle of the field, the way the land has been cleared to discourage children from walking to the edge and falling onto the rocks.

"Do you know why I brought you here back then?" he asks me.

"Because I was lighting things on fire in Squamish?"

He frowns.

"Max, we came here because I thought it was the most beautiful place in the world, and because I didn't have a clue what to do with you. You were your mother's project."

"Jesus, project . . ." But this is true. He means that he could have been alone forever, that he is a man who should have been alone. His love for my mother made him try to overcome his nature.

"I know you were unhappy, and I'm sorry. I'm sorry I wasn't a better father to you." His voice cracks. I don't want to look at him because I'm afraid he'll be crying, and I don't want to comfort him. Now I know why I came here. This is the denouement, but it turns out I already know how it goes. Everything he is telling me, I have felt anyway my whole life. His answers aren't a release but a burden, and I don't want any of this, this nostalgia and heartache he uses to justify his vanishings, and goddamn it I don't want to make him feel better. I don't want to be the one who forgives and I'm shaking my head, no, no, no.

"Max," he says, and he says it loudly so I look at him. He's not crying. He's looking at me. His skin is dry, creping around his chin. "Max –" He puts down the box and places his hands on my shoulders, an arm's length away.

"Are we going to slow dance?" I say, and I'm the one who's crying.

"Max, I'm so sorry that she died," he says. This is the most he can give me. This is the sum of my father. It is almost enough. The air around us relaxes, a fist unclenched.

"Me too," I say, wiping my face on my sleeve.

We don't stand like that much longer. The wet ground is soaking through my runners and grass makes me nervous and suddenly I miss the city – I miss the surety of sidewalks – but we stay long enough to look out at the ocean and I count the boats obsessively, running the numbers across my teeth with my tongue.

We walk to Lower Lookout, a clearing closer to the water, two massive tiered rocks, one where the grown-ups would meditate and the other where the kids would take advantage of their closed eyes, making faces and giggling. The camp has planted a small cross on the big rock, and my father explains that they do a Sunday service here; the camp is Christian. I have to laugh. The prayer hall we gutted and turned into a school. The monks, the raisin nibblers, the endless declarations of progress, and all of it a great circle sailing.

The ground is slippery. On the edge of the rock, the mountains shake free the ocean and the city lies somewhere unseen through the fog. I take the box and empty my mother's ashes into the water, but a big gust of wind rises suddenly, pushing the plume in all directions, coating the rocks, the beach, my father's feet, my hands, and then – swear to God – the rain comes. It thumps bricks from the sky, and all turns to mud.

I WANT TO GIVE YOU THE DEATH SCENE BECAUSE YOU'VE been so patient, but then again the death scene was private; not even my father got to be there. Bright Sunday morning, my blinds were open, but I was looking up at the ceiling and counting footsteps, in and out, the descent of doctors and officials. I was wearing blue terry-cloth shorts and a green T-shirt that read, Ms. Behaving. One of my last baby teeth was on the cusp of falling out, hanging from a thread at the back of my mouth.

"Maxime, I'm going to the hospital," said my father from the doorway, my tired, tired father. He repeated himself: "Maxime, I'm going to the hospital now. You stay here with Mrs. Dalton."

No one ever said the words *she died.* Everyone assumed it was my father's job, but he must have forgotten. I knew anyway, I knew it from the silencing of the machines and some change in the rise and fall of the floors and windows, as if all the nervous panic that had settled in the house's belly was finally hissing free. I heard Mrs. Dalton crying in the kitchen and the front door shut and I went to my window. An ambulance pulled up quietly, no siren, and two young men in white uniforms pulled my mother's silhouette on a gurney, a white sheet shrouding her body. Across the street, a little boy bounced a blue rubber ball, a boy I'd never seen before, a blond boy with a curious face.

My father climbed in the back of the ambulance, and the doors shut. The wheels turned and pulled away and all that was left on the street was the boy with the ball, staring after the ambulance like he was watching television. A sharp taste of hatred rose up in my throat, and I tried to pry open my window to spit it out, but the window was glued shut from years of paint and it wouldn't open. I ran downstairs, past Mrs. Dalton, through the living room, and onto the porch.

I stumbled down the stairs and into the garden. The boy saw me, turned and kept bouncing, like he was setting some kind of world record. Today, of all days, he would bounce the ball forever. He bounced it when she was alive, and he bounced it now that she was dead.

I gathered rocks and larger pieces of gravel from the garden and I began to pitch them, one by one, at the boy with the ball. At first I missed, the pebbles scattered on the street, so I moved closer to the curb. The boy stopped his bouncing and stared. I ran onto the road, grabbing more gravel as I ran, pitching it as I got closer. The boy looked over his shoulder, puzzled, wondering if I was aiming at something he couldn't see, something he should be afraid of, and I kept coming, hailing him with stones until he was ducking and then whimpering and backing away, crouched and cowardly as I'd suspected and therefore, even more deserving, wailing under my hailstorm. There, I thought, do nothing, do nothing, do nothing, you blue ball bouncing fuck.

Mrs. Dalton grabbed me by the elbows and my rocks scattered over the street. She made all kinds of noises. Parents came out onto the street, a cascade of grown-ups murmuring and yelling things I couldn't understand. My ears were filled with the scream of the ambulance pulling away. I hadn't heard it when they'd taken her, but the sound was there suddenly, tearing at my skull. It was a signal, like something I'd read about happening to someone else.

FRANNY BAUMGARTEN IS ICING THE CAROB CARROT cake and she's got seaweed frosting smeared all over her face. She offers me a fingerful.

"You poor kid, you don't know how much that sucks yet, do you?"

"AND we have nutloaf!" she exclaims. I am getting the official island birthday treatment a day late because today is the day Franny's mom returns.

The back door swings open and Elaine is standing there with the kind of big-boned woman people describe as handsome, though her features are fine and pretty, like visitors to her body. Her eyes sweep the room until she sees her sticky daughter – hands up, a little guilty – and both their faces spark and smile and then there's that awkward moment for the unhugged when the room gets heated up by kisses and proclamations of love for someone else. Franny wraps around her mother's legs, beaming.

"I hope you don't mind my joining you for your birthday, Max," she says. "Your father said –"

Then my father darts in that open door, and he's still wearing his gardening gloves, but he leans in and gives this woman a long kiss on the lips that's more than friendly.

I raise an eyebrow and my father smiles.

I'm in my birthday suit, which is jeans and a T-shirt and lipstick, lipstick for the first time in days. Elaine's half-undone tapestry dangles above the computer.

E-mail:
There's something I need to tell you, but I'm not sure –

You can't e-mail this kind of thing, the circuits couldn't bear it.

Can you text message it over a cellphone? I type it in: PLZ CLL BG NWS. Maybe that's not the best method either. You should probably use vowels under these circumstances. Delete.

I pick up the phone and dial and hang up and breathe and pick up the phone and dial and hang up and pick up the phone and breathe and it rings rings rings right into his voice mail, and I leave one, as neutral as I can: "Hello, call me, can you? Yeah, uh, good. Okay bye." My voice cramped and Smurfy. No he won't know what's up at all.

Elaine loves a dinner party, and this is Mrs. Dalloway worthy, if Mrs. Dalloway was vegan. The dining-room table is set with towers of candles emerging from seashells and driftwood, fresh-cut forsythias float in glass-blown bowls, a pan flautist wails on the stereo. Baskets of freshly baked whole-grain bread and plates of cucumbers and tomatoes soaked in oil and herbs from the garden colour pottery plates. The candlelight catches the stained glass leaning against the walls.

"It's beautiful, Elaine," I tell her, and I mean it.

Franny Baumgarten is wearing a red dress with as much grace as if she had been wedged into a lead pipe for the evening. "Nice dress," I tell her as she pulls at the seams and snarls.

Dolores and my father carry trays of food to the table, their hips brushing against each other. Elaine brings out the nutloaf on a white platter, and we fall over our plates with hunger and I haven't tasted anything so sweet and weird in quite a long time; everyone says smell but I believe it's taste that pulls you backwards, and this chewy lumber taste reminds me of the compound smorgasbords with the piles of dishes that had been washed half-heartedly by children so that the food tasted always a little like peppermint soap.

Dolores is a serious person, but not in the way that Elaine is. She looks practical in her black button-down shirt, tucking Franny in at the table with one arm, a glass of wine in the other. She is a professor of classics who lived in San Francisco, Seattle, Vancouver, and then came here after her husband died. She travels for research quite often, and reluctantly, she says, and this makes me think of Theo. She asks me about movies, and the city, tells Franny to sit up straight and Franny loves this; does her best impression of an adult. My father looks at Dolores with awe. They have been dating for a month.

The doorbell rings. I look at Elaine, raising my eyebrows. She shrugs to say no one is expected. Franny scrambles down to the ground and comes running and jumping and Theo McArdle is behind her, glancing at the stained-glass hangings on the walls, confused. And how this must look to him: four faces peering up, cheeks filled with nutloaf. For a brief moment I'm filled with disbelief too, and embarrassment at the chaos, and all I want is a pot roast and white china and a father in a V-neck sweater.

But Franny is waving a sprig of tarragon like an orchestra conductor, and Elaine is already up and fussing, filling a new wineglass, my dad is clearing seashells to make a space for Theo. So this is what I have, and it's not that bad, really, because here's the thing I figure out instantly: He started coming to me before he got my message. He has been on his way for a long time.

I notice also that Theo McArdle, age thirty-three, is wearing a backpack. Theo McArdle doesn't own luggage either. I go to him, smiling.

THEO AND I ARE IN THE LITTLE HOUSE MY DAD HAS been building, knee to knee across from one another on two miniature benches. It is our first moment alone, and so it's the one I use to apologize for leaving him on the porch in Toronto. Theo looks distracted, and instead of accepting my apology, he says quickly, "I got the green light for England."

"Oh," I say, not a word, but a sound, the sound of a chest collapsing. We sit there quietly and I think of bobbies and the Queen's corgis and what this means for what I'm about to tell him.

"The thing is, I might not take it," Theo says.

"Might not," I repeat back to him.

"I came out here because I feel like you and I make sense together," he says, then shakes his head. "That's not it. Hang on." He runs his fingers over his face and looks at me, his knees pressing into mine. And then he lets loose a tangle of words whose order I will never remember, but in bits and pieces, they are seared into me, words like *you* and *extraordinary* and *us* and *effortless* and *love*. What he is telling me is that he is already fearless, but he wants us to be fearless together.

Then he fishes around in his pocket, pulls out a small black box. "Happy birthday." And my limbs go numb, because here it is, right? Here comes the long haul, the decisions are getting made and I'm drowning in a white taffeta dress and I'm carrying a baby around in some yuppie papoose and I'm not having sex or fun and I never go dancing – and I open the box and it's a pocket watch, antique with no strap.

"You don't have to use it, but just in case. You know." He shrugs.

I mean to say "Thank you" but instead I say, "I'm pregnant," and then I mean to say "What do you think?" but I say, "I'd like to have it." And then I add in a jokey voice: "It's yours, by the way. Hahaha."

And once something like that is said, it's just said, that's it. No going back, and you're just naked out there at the end of that long pier in the wind, the French Lieutenant's woman with fewer shawls.

There's a lot I don't know about Theo, but people have made dumber decisions based on less. I start talking: I tell him how I don't really know what family looks like and that I'm okay without the walk down the aisle, the ring, and I don't even know if we need to live together or be on the same continent if he has things to pursue, and I don't know if this baby will be accessorized with flippers and claws but I'm excited, I'm excited to learn something again and I'm feeling something at least I think I am and I'd like it if we could do it together but if he needs to go that's okay I don't expect —

Theo McArdle kisses me, like you're supposed to when you want to shut people up. How do we learn that kind of thing? We learn it from movies, of course.

"Give me the watch," he says.

Backfire, backfire. I give it to him. He takes my hands, opens the palms, and lays the watch inside. "Now it means something different," he says.

"What?" I ask. "And please don't say 'commitment watch' because I might have to leave you."

He clasps my hand around the watch. "I can't wait for all of this, Max," he says, and he's sort of giddy, goofy, hitting his head on the low ceiling. "I can't wait."

Theo McArdle is not what I expected, when I let myself expect. He's calm, like he always is, and he smiles and declares everything about this moment good, and everything about the next one better. He uses the word *love* generously, like it's not such a big deal. He can see it, he says; it's blue.

W E'RE FLYING BACK TO TORONTO AND ON THE SMALL television hanging from the ceiling is a news broadcast. The scene is a suburban office building with a stream of distraught professionals being escorted from its doors. One of them — and this is weird — is Marvin in his gigantic rave pants, and there's the Editor, almost serene, and Heather the Up-Talker, and Hard-Working Debbie wiping away her tears. *The Daily* has been sold to BFD Television. Mohsen is idling in the driveway waiting to take everyone back to the city.

We've all been fired, it turns out. I start laughing. But then I wonder how I'll be without the paper, and what I will do with this story I've been trying to tell for so long.

And yet I'm kind of glad it won't see the light of day because I'm tired of records. Everyone always says to write it down, get it out, set it free, but I doubt the usefulness of all this purging. It's overheating the airwaves. It's noisy.

I think I would like to give you something in a language that I haven't created yet. Maybe it would be edible, or soft to the touch. Even though I know it's impossible, I would like to tell an entirely new story for once, one that will never be published or talked about or forgotten.

ACKNOWLEDGEMENTS

Jennifer Lambert. Ellen Seligman. Jackie Kaiser. Heather Sangster. Kong Njo. Lawrence Hill. Gary and Cindy Onstad. Maryam Sanati. Jason Logan. Ethan Hawke. Kate Robson. Jude and Mia. And Julian, who knows.